HARRIET BEECHER STOWE (1811–1896) was born in Connecticut, the sixth child and third daughter of the Reverend Lyman Beecher. Beginning at a very early age, she was an avid reader and writer; when only twelve years old, she composed a precocious school essay titled "Can the Immortality of the Soul be Proved by the Light of Nature?" She worked with her sister Catharine, an educator, until marrying, in 1836, Professor Calvin Ellis Stowe, a teacher at her father's seminary. In 1852 *Uncle Tom's Cabin, or, Life Among the Lowly* was published, creating an immediate sensation. An extraordinary half-million copies were sold in its first five years, with subsequent translations into every language. Its anti-slavery sentiments certainly contributed to the national debate leading up to the Civil War, and Stowe became an abolitionist heroine. Yet, despite the popularity of *Uncle Tom* and continued success with other works such as *The Minister's Wooing* (1859), *The Pearl of Orr's Island* (1862), and *Oldtown Folks* (1869), financial security always eluded her. The mother of six children, she spent her last years living quietly with her daughters in Hartford.

JUDITH MARTIN writes the "Miss Manners" syndicated newspaper column, and is the author of two novels.

PINK AND WHITE TYRANNY

PINK AND WHITE TYRANNY

A SOCIETY NOVEL

by

Harriet Beecher Stowe

Introduction by Judith Martin

**PLUME AMERICAN WOMEN WRITERS
SERIES EDITOR: MICHELE SLUNG**

A PLUME BOOK

NEW AMERICAN LIBRARY

NEW YORK AND SCARBOROUGH, ONTARIO

NAL BOOKS ARE AVAILABLE AT QUANTITY DISCOUNTS WHEN USED TO PROMOTE PRODUCTS OR SERVICES. FOR INFORMATION PLEASE WRITE TO PREMIUM MARKETING DIVISION, NEW AMERICAN LIBRARY, 1633 BROADWAY, NEW YORK, NEW YORK 10019.

Grateful acknowledgment is made to the Stowe-Day Foundation, Hartford, Connecticut, for permission to use the quotations on pages vii and ix.

PLUME TRADEMARK REG. U.S. PAT. OFF. AND FOREIGN COUNTRIES
REGISTERED TRADEMARK—MARCA REGISTRADA
HECHO EN CHICAGO, U.S.A.

SIGNET, SIGNET CLASSIC, MENTOR, ONYX, PLUME, MERIDIAN and NAL BOOKS are published *in the United States* by NAL PENGUIN INC., 1633 Broadway, New York, New York 10019, *in Canada* by The New American Library of Canada Limited, 81 Mack Avenue, Scarborough, Ontario M1L 1M8

Library of Congress Cataloging-in-Publication Data

Stowe, Harriet Beecher, 1811–1896.
   Pink and white tyranny : a society novel / by Harriet Beecher Stowe; introduction by Judith Martin.

   p. cm.—(Plume American women writers)
Originally published: Boston: Roberts Brothers, 1871.
ISBN 0-452-26140-6
I. Title. II. Series.
PS2954.P45 1988
813'.3—dc19   86-12605
                                        CIP

First Plume Printing, October, 1988

1 2 3 4 5 6 7 8 9

PRINTED IN THE UNITED STATES OF AMERICA

Introduction

If President Lincoln amiably credited Harriet Beecher Stowe with starting the Civil War ("So you're the little lady who made this big war!" he is supposed to have remarked upon meeting the author of the inflammatory abolitionist novel, *Uncle Tom's Cabin, or Life Among the Lowly*), no one has accused Mrs. Stowe of being a little lady who fomented feminist revolution.

Rather, she extolled the special spirituality of Woman, encouraging and glorifying a wife's position as household saint. In this novel, "tyranny" is defined as the prevailing will of a woman who is uninterested in filling that function over a good, and therefore helpless, man who expects it of her.

"It will be in a quiet way an offset to a class of writings which I am sorry to see which represent men as in most cases oppressors and women as sufferers in domestic life,"* she wrote the editor of the magazine in which it was first serialized.

"Mrs. Stowe does justice to that sex which is not enough remembered in the discussion of the wrongs of woman," her Canadian publisher wrote to advertise the book. "For she describes, as no one else can describe, the tyranny under which a loyal and chivalrous gentleman suffers. This, the latest work of one through whose efforts the black slavery of centuries was broken, will render a service not less considerable, if it so awakens the conscience of men and women that

*From HBS letter to Edward Everett Hale, April 14, 1869.

vii

Pink and White Tyranny of women over men shall be impossible."

Ah, yes. Uncle Tom's mother speaks out on domestic injustice—to condemn her own sex.

Uncle Tom himself has notoriously failed the test of time. The loveable old slave whose sufferings inspired abolitionist fervor is not a model of black pride by modern standards. But he preferred beatings and death rather than betray his own people, and the author would probably be shocked to find that his affection for his owners made his name a by-word of obsequiousness toward one's oppressors.

No doubt she would also protest that her sympathy with out-manipulated husbands did not make her a traitor to her sex. In defending domesticity, she was far from demanding that all women confine themselves to that sphere.

"So much has been said of the higher sphere of woman, and so much has been done to find some better work for her that, insensibly, almost every body begins to feel that it is rather degrading for a woman in a good society to be much tied down to family affairs; especially since in these Woman's Rights Conventions there is so much dissatisfaction expressed at those who would confine her ideas to the kitchen and nursery," Mrs. Stowe and her sister, the educator Catharine E. Beecher, wrote in their household book, *American Woman's Home*.

Yet these Woman's Rights Conventions are a protest against many former absurb, unreasonable ideas—the mere physical and culinary idea of womanhood as connected only with puddings and shirt-buttons, the unjust and unequal burdens which the laws of harsher ages had cast upon the sex. Many of the women connected with these movements are as superior in every thing properly womanly as they are in exceptional talent and culture. There is no manner of doubt that the sphere of woman is properly to be enlarged. Every woman has rights as a human being which belong to no sex, and ought to be as freely conceded to her as if she were a man,— and first and foremost, the great right of doing any thing which God and nature evidently have fitted her to excel in. If she be made a natural orator, like Miss Dickinson, or an

astronomer, like Mrs. Somerville, or a singer, like Grisi, let
not the technical rules of womanhood be thrown in the way
of her free use of her powers.

Today, too, there are women, some with impeccable feminist credentials, who object that devaluing domesticity and
childrearing is not a legitimate part of the women's rights
movement. After outlining this book to her editor (whose
own wife she described as "neither a tyrant nor a martyr"*)
Mrs. Stowe informed him that "being *to some extents* a woman's rights woman, as I am *to some extents*, some thing of
almost every thing that goes—I shall have a right to say a
word or two on the other side."*

It is this "word or two"—actually a great deal more, both
explicit and implicit—that makes the book interesting today,
and not just an antique polemic about the nuisance of having a
frivolous woman around the house. In her fairness, the
author has delineated the pastel tyrant's own social griev-
ances, as well as the husband-victim's disappointment, going
beyond her stated intention of sympathizing with men who
have pretty wives to explore the social forces that made them
what they were.

No member of the masculine establishment, right up to
the Supreme Court, escapes blame. "Pretty girls, unless
they have wise mothers, are more educated by the opposite
sex than by their own," she writes.

Put them where you will, there is always some man busying
himself in their instruction; and the burden of masculine
teaching is generally about the same, and might be stereotyped
as follows: "You don't need to be or do anything. Your
business in life is to look pretty, and amuse us. You don't
need to study; you know all by nature that a woman need to
know. You are, by virtue of being a pretty woman, superior
to anything we can teach you; and we wouldn't, for the
world, have you anything but what you are." When Lillie
went to school, this was what her masters whispered in her
ear as they did her sums for her, and helped her through her

*From HBS letter to Edward Everett Hale, April 14, 1869

lessons and exercises, and looked into her eyes. This was what her young gentlemen friends, themselves delving in Latin and Greek and mathematics, told her, when they came to recreate from their severer studies in her smile. Men are held to account for talking sense. Pretty women are told that lively nonsense is their best sense. . . .

The life of a petted creature consists essentially in being deferred to, for being pretty and useless. A petted child runs a great risk if it is ever to outgrow childhood; but a pet woman is a perpetual child. The pet woman of society is everybody's toy. Everybody looks at her, admires her, praises and flatters her, stirs her up to play off her little airs and graces for their entertainment, and passes on. Men of profound sense encourage her to chatter nonsense for their amusement, just as we delight in the tottering steps and stammering mispronunications of a golden-haired child. When Lillie has been in Washington, she has had judges of the Supreme Court and secretaries of state delighted to have her give her opinions in their respective departments. Scholars and literary men flocked around her, to the neglect of many a more instructed woman, satisfied that she knew enough to blunder agreeably on every subject. . . . Lillie had numbered among her admirers many lights of the Church. She had flirted with bishops, priests and deacons. . . .

But if there is one subject Mrs. Stowe's Lillie understands only too well, it is the economic position of women. If masculine training made her selfish, it also alerted her that she must cash in her valuable assets quickly in order to secure the only job they will get her, that of being a wife. Thus she is as pathetic a creature as the hero-victim John Seymour, perhaps more so, as he entered the marriage merely to enhance an already comfortable life, whereas she knew she had no alternative.

Lillie's perilous situation before marriage is mirrored in that of her sister-in-law, Grace Seymour, portrayed as having all possible womanly virtues, which she has put at the disposal of her bachelor brother. But although Grace's saintliness is undestroyed by her being deposed in his household, the reader cannot fail to notice that her assets have left her isolated—"unable to think of anybody whom she could call from the approaching festivities of holiday life in the cities to share her snow Patmos with her"—until a suitable marriage proposal miraculously appears for her, too.

The question of job security in marriage is one that Mrs. Stowe amply recognizes. Grace puts it to her disillusioned brother that "if you stand by a business engagement with this faithfulness, how much more should you stand by that great engagement which concerns all other families and the stability of all society." In her own voice, the author argues, with righteous mixed-metaphors;

> Some people, who really at heart have the interest of women upon their minds, have been so short-sighted and reckless as to clamor for an easy dissolution of the marriage contract, as a means of righting their wrongs. Is is possible that they do not see that this is a liberty which, once granted, would always tell against the weaker sex? . . .
>
> What will become of women like Lillie, when the first gilding begins to wear off, if the man who has taken one of them shall be at liberty to cast her off and seek another? Have we not enough now of miserable, broken-winged butterflies, that sink down, down, down into the mud of the street? But are women reformers going to clamor for having every woman turned out helpless, when the man who has married her, and made her a mother, discovers that she has not the power to interest him, and to help his higher spiritual development?

With all her urging the weakness of women and the sacredness of the bond as arguments against divorce, the danger dramatized in the story is that "it is easy to see where the career of many women like Lillie would end."

Mrs. Stowe declared toward the end of the novel that she understood "well that there is not a woman among our readers who has the slightest patience with Lillie, and that the most of them are half out of patience with John for his enduring tenderness towards her." And then she defends John against anticipated charges of his being a muff and a spoon, describing him rather as a proper "protector of women" despite Lillie's unworthiness.

But as with Uncle Tom, Mrs. Stowe may have made a colossal error about future judgement of her characters. However impatient the female reader might be of Lillie's vanity, flashy taste, and trashy friends, surely she will sympathize with her plight. As the book opens, the calculating belle seems to be in even worse danger than her besotted admirer. Society, having long praised her qualifications for the career of marriage, is now openly sneering at her for not having secured a position. At the age of twenty-seven, she is perceived as shopworn.

The degradation of a woman's having to market herself was made more bluntly six years after *Pink and White Tyranny*, in Anthony Trollope's *The American Senator* where Arabella Trefoil, "one of the most unhappy young persons in England," is forever gearing herself for the unpleasant task of attracting men she doesn't admire, anticipating that, because one courtship after another comes to nothing, "there would be all the weary work to do again!"

> She had long known that it was her duty to marry, and especially her duty to marry well. Between her and her mother there had been no reticence on this subject . . . The daughter herself had been too honest for it. "As for caring about him, mamma," she had once said, speaking of a suitor, "of course I don't. He is nasty and odious in every way. But I have got to do the best I can, and what is the use of talking about such trash as that?"

Another weary Lily, in Edith Wharton's 1905 novel, *The House of Mirth*, explains to a man that in the economic position of a society woman, as opposed to his own, there is "the difference":

> A girl must [marry], a man may if he chooses . . . Your coat's a little shabby—but who cares? It doesn't keep people from asking you to dine. If I were shabby no one would have me: a woman is asked out as much for her clothes as for herself. The clothes are the background, the frame, if you like: they don't make success, but they are a part of it. Who wants a dingy woman? We are expected to be pretty and well-dressed

till we drop—and if we can't keep it up alone, we have to go into partnership.

The man's reply? "Ah, well, there must be plenty of capital on the lookout for such an investment. Perhaps you'll meet your fate to-night at the Trenors'."

Mrs. Stowe fondly excuses her hero, John Seymour, for making a poor investment because he was so overcome with the "manly sentiment" of love for a beautiful woman he hardly knows. It is nevertheless difficult to overlook the fact that he has not troubled to investigate the person clothed in the finery to which he loses his heart—nor the cost of having such finery laundered, as it turns out. He has positively spurned the idea of marrying a woman, such as anyone of his sister's friends, who is also pretty, but who frankly exhibits the qualities of sense, intellect, and nobility he expects in a wife.

Such attributes when visible kill his sense of romance:

The wife that John had imagined, his dream-wife, was not at all like his sister; though he loved his sister heartily, and thought her one of the best and noblest women that could possibly be. But his sister was all plain prose,—good, strong, earnest, respectable prose, it is true, but yet prose. He could read English history with her, talk accounts and business with her, discuss politics with her, and valued her opinions on all these topics as much as that of any man of his acquaintance. But with the visionary Mrs. John Seymour aforesaid he never seemed to be either reading history, or settling accounts, or talking politics; he was off with her in some sort of enchanted cloudland of happiness. . . .

Of course, it is exactly this inability to share his interests or worry about his accounts that Mrs. Stowe condemns in Mrs. John Seymour, and that John Seymour feels cheated that his wife lacks. But he wanted these qualities not only to be disguised, but to come unaccompanied by an independent will:

Somehow or other, he was persuaded, he should gradually bring his wife to all his own ways of thinking, and all his schemes and plans and opinions. This might, he thought, be difficult were she one of the pronounced, strong-minded sort, accustomed to thinking and judging for herself. Such a one, he could easily imagine, there might be a risk in encountering in the close intimacy of domestic life. Even in his dealings with his sister he was made aware of a force of character and a vigor of intellect that sometimes made the carrying of his own way over hers a matter of some difficulty. Were it not that Grace was the best of women, and her ways always the very best of ways, John was not so sure but that she might prove a little too masterful for him.

But this lovely bit of pink and white; this downy, gauzy, airy little elf; this creature, so slim and slender and unsubstantial—surely he need have no fear that he could not mould and control and manage her?

It is difficult, despite all the author's pleadings, to fail to take some satisfaction in the disillusionment of a man with such a fatuous folly. And after all, who has lost more, in the end: the woman who realizes only on her deathbed that she has frittered her life away, or the man who married her? Isn't it more of a tragedy to be a nit-wit than to marry one?

In her own preface, Harriet Beecher Stowe promises the reader a moral, unadorned by the conventional flourishes of novels. It seems to be that nobility of soul is more desirable in a wife than a dainty wardrobe, and one ought to choose well because marriage is sacred, no matter how unsuited the partners. But her story line suggests another lesson for those who, like John Seymour, would be good and noble husbands: Do not waste your time looking for a woman who has no will of her own.

—Judith Martin

PINK AND WHITE TYRANNY.

PINK AND WHITE TYRANNY.

A Society Novel.

BY

MRS. HARRIET BEECHER STOWE,

AUTHOR OF "UNCLE TOM'S CABIN," "THE MINISTER'S WOOING," ETC.

"Come, then, the colors and the ground prepare;
Dip in the rainbow, trick her off in air;
Choose a firm cloud before it fall, and in it
Catch, ere she change, the Cynthia of this minute."

POPE.

PREFACE.

MY DEAR READER, — This story is not to be a novel,
as the world understands the word; and we tell
you so beforehand, lest you be in ill-humor by not finding what you expected. For if you have been told that
your dinner is to be salmon and green pease, and made
up your mind to that bill of fare, and then, on coming
to the table, find that it is beefsteak and tomatoes,
you may be out of sorts; *not* because beefsteak and
tomatoes are not respectable viands, but because they
are not what you have made up your mind to enjoy.

Now, a novel, in our days, is a three-story affair, —
a complicated, complex, multiform composition, requiring no end of scenery and *dramatis personæ*, and plot
and plan, together with trap-doors, pit-falls, wonderful
escapes and thrilling dangers; and the scenes transport
one all over the earth, — to England, Italy, Switzerland,
Japan, and Kamtschatka. But this is a little common-

place history, all about one man and one woman, living straight along in one little prosaic town in New England. It is, moreover, a story with a moral; and for fear that you shouldn't find out exactly what the moral is, we shall adopt the plan of the painter who wrote under his pictures, "This is a bear," and "This is a turtle-dove." We shall tell you in the proper time succinctly just what the moral is, and send you off edified as if you had been hearing a sermon. So please to call this little sketch a parable, and wait for the exposition thereof.

CONTENTS.

PINK AND WHITE TYRANNY.

CHAPTER I.

FALLING IN LOVE.

LILLIE.

"WHO *is* that beautiful creature?" said John
Seymour, as a light, sylph-like form tripped

1

up the steps of the veranda of the hotel where he was lounging away his summer vacation.

"That! Why, don't you know, man? That is the celebrated, the divine Lillie Ellis, the most adroit 'fisher of men' that has been seen in our days."

"By George, but she's pretty, though!" said John, following with enchanted eyes the distant motions of the sylphide.

The vision that he saw was of a delicate little fairy form; a complexion of pearly white, with a cheek of the hue of a pink shell; a fair, sweet, infantine face surrounded by a fleecy radiance of soft golden hair. The vision appeared to float in some white gauzy robes; and, when she spoke or smiled, what an innocent, fresh, untouched, unspoiled look there was upon the face! John gazed, and thought of all sorts of poetical similes: of a "daisy just wet with morning dew;" of a "violet by a mossy stone;" in short, of all the things that poets have made and provided for the use of young gentlemen in the way of falling in love.

This John Seymour was about as good and honest a man as there is going in this world of ours. He was a generous, just, manly, religious young fellow. He was heir to a large, solid property; he was a well-read lawyer, established in a flourishing business; he was a man that all the world spoke well of, and had cause to speak well of. The only duty to society which John had left as yet unperformed was that of matrimony. Three and thirty years had passed; and, with every advantage for supporting a wife, with a charming home

all ready for a mistress, John, as yet, had not proposed
to be the defender and provider for any of the more
helpless portion of creation. The cause of this was, in
the first place, that John was very happy in the society
of a sister, a little older than himself, who managed his
house admirably, and was a charming companion to his
leisure hours; and, in the second place, that he had a
secret, bashful self-depreciation in regard to his power
of pleasing women, which made him ill at ease in their
society. Not that he did not mean to marry. He
certainly did. But the fair being that he was to marry
was a distant ideal, a certain undefined and cloudlike
creature; and, up to this time, he had been waiting to
meet her, without taking any definite steps towards
that end. To say the truth, John Seymour, like many
other outwardly solid, sober-minded, respectable citizens,
had deep within himself a little private bit of romance.
He could not utter it, he never talked it; he would
have blushed and stammered and stuttered wofully,
and made a very poor figure, in trying to tell any one
about it; but nevertheless it was there, a secluded
chamber of imagery, and the future Mrs. John Seymour formed its principal ornament.

The wife that John had imaged, his *dream*-wife, was
not at all like his sister; though he loved his sister
heartily, and thought her one of the best and noblest
women that could possibly be.

But his sister was all plain prose, — good, strong,
earnest, respectable prose, it is true, but yet prose. He
could read English history with her, talk accounts and

business with her, discuss politics with her, and valued her opinions on all these topics as much as that of any man of his acquaintance. But, with the visionary Mrs. John Seymour aforesaid, he never seemed to himself to be either reading history or settling accounts, or talking politics; he was off with her in some sort of enchanted cloudland of happiness, where she was all to him, and he to her, — a sort of rapture of protective love on one side, and of confiding devotion on the other, quite inexpressible, and that John would not have talked of for the world.

So when he saw this distant vision of airy gauzes, of pearly whiteness, of sea-shell pink, of infantine smiles, and waving, golden curls, he stood up with a shy desire to approach the wonderful creature, and yet with a sort of embarrassed feeling of being very awkward and clumsy. He felt, somehow, as if he were a great, coarse behemoth; his arms seemed to him awkward appendages; his hands suddenly appeared to him rough, and his fingers swelled and stumpy. When he thought of asking an introduction, he felt himself growing very hot, and blushing to the roots of his hair.

"Want to be introduced to her, Seymour?" said Carryl Ethridge. "I'll trot you up. I know her."

"No, thank you," said John, stiffly. In his heart, he felt an absurd anger at Carryl for the easy, assured way in which he spoke of the sacred creature who seemed to him something too divine to be lightly talked of. And then he saw Carryl marching up to her with his air of easy assurance. He saw the bewitching smile come over that fair, flowery face; he saw Carryl, with unabashed familiarity, take her fan out of her hand, look at it as if it were a mere common, earthly fan, toss it about, and pretend to fan himself with it.

"I didn't know he was such a puppy."

"I didn't know he was such a puppy!" said John to himself, as he stood in a sort of angry bashfulness, envying the man that was so familiar with that loveliness.

Ah! John, John! You wouldn't, for the world, have told to man or woman what a fool you were at that moment.

"What a fool I am!" was his mental commentary: "just as if it was any thing to me." And he turned, and walked to the other end of the veranda.

"I think you 've hooked another fish, Lillie," said Belle Trevors in the ear of the little divinity.

"Who ...?"

"Why! that Seymour there, at the end of the veranda. He is looking at you, do you know? He is rich, very rich, and of an old family. Didn't you see how he started and looked after you when you came up on the veranda?"

"Oh! I saw plain enough," said the divinity, with one of her unconscious, baby-like smiles.

"What are you ladies talking?" said Carryl Ethridge.

"Oh, secrets!" said Belle Trevors. "You are very presuming, sir, to inquire."

"Mr. Ethridge," said Lillie Ellis, "don't you think it would be nice to promenade?"

This was said with such a pretty coolness, such a quiet composure, as showed Miss Lillie to be quite mistress of the situation; there was, of course, no sort of design in it.

Ethridge offered his arm at once; and the two sauntered to the end of·the veranda, where John Seymour
was standing.

The blood rushed in hot currents over him, and he
could hear the beating of his heart: he felt somehow as
if the hour of his fate was coming. He had a wild
desire to retreat, and put it off. He looked over the
end of the veranda, with some vague idea of leaping it;
but alas! it was ten feet above ground, and a lover's leap
would have only ticketed him as out of his head. There
was nothing for it but to meet his destiny like a man.

Carryl came up with the lady on his arm; and as he
stood there for a moment, in the coolest, most indifferent
tone in the world, said, "Oh! by the by, Miss Ellis, let
me present my friend Mr. Seymour."

"Let me present my friend, Mr. Seymour."

The die was cast.

John's face burned like fire: he muttered something about "being happy to make Miss Ellis's acquaintance," looking all the time as if he would be glad to jump over the railing, or take wings and fly, to get rid of the happiness.

Miss Ellis was a belle by profession, and she understood her business perfectly. In nothing did she show herself master of her craft, more than in the adroitness with which she could soothe the bashful pangs of new votaries, and place them on an easy footing with her.

"Mr. Seymour," she said affably, "to tell the truth, I have been desirous of the honor of your acquaintance, ever since I saw you in the breakfast-room this morning."

"I am sure I am very much flattered," said John, his heart beating thick and fast. "May I ask why you honor me with such a wish?"

"Well, to tell the truth, because you strikingly resemble a very dear friend of mine," said Miss Ellis, with her sweet, unconscious simplicity of manner.

"I am still more flattered," said John, with a quicker beating of the heart; "only I fear that you may find me an unpleasant contrast."

"Oh! I think not," said Lillie, with another smile: "we shall soon be good friends, too, I trust."

"I trust so certainly," said John, earnestly.

Belle Trevors now joined the party; and the four were soon chatting together on the best footing of acquaintance. John was delighted to feel himself already on easy terms with the fair vision.

"You have not been here long?" said Lillie to John.

"No, I have only just arrived."

"And you were never here before?"

"No, Miss Ellis, I am entirely new to the place."

"I am an old *habituée* here," said Lillie, "and can recommend myself as authority on all points connected with it."

"Then," said John, "I hope you will take me under your tuition."

"Certainly, free of charge," she said, with another ravishing smile.

"You haven't seen the boiling spring yet?" she added.

"No, I haven't seen any thing yet."

"Well, then, if you'll give me your arm across the lawn, I'll show it to you."

All of this was done in the easiest, most matter-of-course manner in the world; and off they started, John in a flutter of flattered delight at the gracious acceptance accorded to him.

Ethridge and Belle Trevors looked after them with a nod of intelligence at each other.

"Hooked, by George!" said Ethridge.

"Well, it'll be a good thing for Lillie, won't it?"

"For her? Oh, yes, a capital thing *for her!*"

"Well, for *him* too."

"Well, I don't know. John is a pretty nice fellow; a very nice fellow, besides being rich, and all that; and Lillie is somewhat shop-worn by this time. Let me see: she must be seven and twenty."

"Oh, yes, she's all that!" said Belle, with ingenuous ardor. "Why, she was in society while I was a school-girl! Yes, dear Lillie is certainly twenty-seven, if not more; but she keeps her freshness wonderfully."

"Well, she looks fresh enough, I suppose, to a good, honest, artless fellow like John Seymour, who knows as little of the world as a milkmaid. John is a great, innocent, country steer, fed on clover and dew; and as honest and ignorant of all sorts of naughty, wicked things as his mother or sister. He takes Lillie in a sacred simplicity quite refreshing; but to me Lillie is played out. I know her like a book. I know all her smiles and wiles, advices and devices; and her system of tactics is an old story with me. I shan't interrupt any of her little games. Let her have her little field all to herself: it's time she was married, to be sure."

Meanwhile, John was being charmingly ciceroned by Lillie, and scarcely knew whether he was in the body or out. All that he felt, and felt with a sort of wonder, was that he seemed to be acceptable and pleasing in the eyes of this little fairy, and that she was leading him into wonderland.

They went not only to the boiling spring, but up and down so many wild, woodland paths that had been cut for the adornment of the Carmel Springs, and so well pleased were both parties, that it was supper-time before they reappeared on the lawn; and, when they did appear, Lillie was leaning confidentially on John's arm, with a wreath of woodbine in her hair that he had arranged there, wondering all the while at his own

"Lillie was leaning confidentially on John's arm."

wonderful boldness, and at the grace of the fair entertainer.

The returning couple were seen from the windows of Mrs. Chit, who sat on the lookout for useful information; and who forthwith ran to the apartments of Mrs. Chat, and told her to look out at them.

Billy This, who was smoking his cigar on the veranda, immediately ran and called Harry That to look at them, and laid a bet at once that Lillie had "hooked" Seymour.

"She'll have him, by George, she will!"

"Oh, pshaw! she is always hooking fellows, but you see she don't get married," said matter-of-fact Harry.

"It won't come to any thing, now, I'll bet. Everybody said she was engaged to Danforth, but it all ended in smoke."

Whether it would be an engagement, or would all end in smoke, was the talk of Carmel Springs for the next two weeks.

At the end of that time, the mind of Carmel Springs was relieved by the announcement that it was an engagement.

The important deciding announcement was first authentically made by Lillie to Belle Trevors, who had been invited into her room that night for the purpose.

"Well, Belle, it's all over. He spoke out to-night."

"He offered himself?"

"Certainly."

"And you took him?"

"Of course I did: I should be a fool not to."

"Oh, so I think, decidedly!" said Belle, kissing her friend in a rapture. "You dear creature! how nice! it's splendid!"

Lillie took the embrace with her usual sweet composure, and turned to her looking-glass, and began taking down her hair for the night. It will be perceived that this young lady was not overcome with emotion, but in a perfectly collected state of mind.

"He's a little bald, and getting rather stout," she said reflectively, "but he'll do."

"I never saw a creature so dead in love as he is," said Belle.

A quiet smile passed over the soft, peach-blow cheeks as Lillie answered, —

" Oh, dear, yes! He perfectly worships the ground I tread on."

"Lil, you fortunate creature, you! Positively it 's the best match that there has been about here this summer. He 's rich, of an old, respectable family; and then he has good principles, you know, and all that," said Belle.

"I think he 's nice myself," said Lillie, as she stood brushing out a golden tangle of curls. "Dear me!" she added, "how much better he is than that Danforth! Really, Danforth was a little too horrid: his teeth were dreadful. Do you know, I should have had something of a struggle to take him, though he was so terribly rich?

"I think he 's nice myself."

Then Danforth had been horridly dissipated, — you don't know, — Maria Sanford told me such shocking things about him, and she knows they are true. Now, I don't think John has ever been dissipated."

"Oh, no!" said Belle. "I heard all about him. He

joined the church when he was only twenty, and has been always spoken of as a perfect model. I only think you may find it a little slow, living in Springdale. He has a fine, large, old-fashioned house there, and his sister is a very nice woman; but they are a sort of respectable, retired set, — never go into fashionable company."

"Oh, I don't mind it!" said Lillie. "I shall have things my own way, I know. One isn't obliged to live in Springdale, nor with pokey old sisters, you know; and John will do just as I say, and live where I please."

She said this with her simple, soft air of perfect assurance, twisting her shower of bright, golden curls; with her gentle, childlike face, and soft, beseeching, blue eyes, and dimpling little mouth, looking back on her, out of the mirror. By these the little queen had always ruled from her cradle, and should she not rule now? Was it any wonder that John was half out of his wits with joy at thought of possessing *her?* Simply and honestly, she thought not. He was to be congratulated; though it wasn't a bad thing for her, either.

"Belle," said Lillie, after an interval of reflection, "I won't be married in white satin, — that I 'm resolved on. Now," she said, facing round with increasing earnestness, "there have been five weddings in our set, and all the girls have been married in just the same dress, — white satin and point lace, white satin and point lace, over and over, till I'm tired of it. *I'm* determined I 'll have something new."

"Well, I would, I'm sure," said Belle. "Say white tulle, for instance: you know you are so *petite* and fairy-like."

"No: I shall write out to Madame La Roche, and tell her she must get up something wholly original. I shall send for my whole *trousseau*. Papa will be glad enough to come down, since he gets me off his hands, and no more fuss about bills, you know. Do you know, Belle, that creature is just wild about me: he'd like to ransack all the jewellers' shops in New York for me. He's going up to-morrow, just to choose the engagement ring. He says he can't trust to an order; that he must go and choose one worthy of me."

"Oh! it's plain enough that that game is all in your hands, as to him, Lillie; but, Lil, what will your Cousin Harry say to all this?"

"Well, of course he won't like it; but I can't help it if he don't. Harry ought to know that it's all nonsense for him and me to think of marrying. He does know it."

"To tell the truth, I always thought, Lil, you were more in love with Harry than anybody you ever knew."

Lillie laughed a little, and then the prettiest sweet-pea flush deepened the pink of her cheeks.

"To say the truth, Belle, I could have been, if he had been in circumstances to marry. But, you see, I am one of those to whom the luxuries are essential. I never could rub and scrub and work; in fact, I had rather not live at all than live poor; and Harry is poor, and he always will be poor. It's a pity, too, poor fellow, for he's nice. Well, he is off in India! I know he will be tragical and gloomy, and all that," she said; and then the soft child-face smiled to itself in the glass, — such a pretty little innocent smile!

All this while, John sat up with his heart beating very fast, writing all about his engagement to his sister, and, up to this point, his nearest, dearest, most confidential friend. It is almost too bad to copy the letter of a shy man who finds himself in love for the first time in his life; but we venture to make an extract: —

"It is not her beauty merely that drew me to her, though she is the most beautiful human being I ever saw: it is the exquisite feminine softness and delicacy of her character, that sympathetic pliability by which she adapts herself to every varying feeling of the heart. You, my dear sister, are the noblest of women, and your place in my heart is still what it always was; but I feel that this dear little creature, while she fills a place no other has ever entered, will yet be a new bond to unite us. She will love us both; she will gradually come into all our ways and opinions, and be insensibly formed by us into a noble womanhood. Her extreme beauty, and the great admiration that has always followed her, have exposed her to many temptations, and caused most ungenerous things to be said of her.

"Hitherto she has lived only in the fashionable world; and her literary and domestic education, as she herself is sensible, has been somewhat neglected.

"But she longs to retire from all this; she is sick of fashionable folly, and will come to us to be all our own. Gradually the charming circle of cultivated families which form our society will elevate her taste, and form her mind.

"Love is woman's inspiration, and love will lead her to all that is noble and good. My dear sister, think not that any new ties are going to make you any less to me, or touch your place in my heart. I have already spoken of you to Lillie, and she longs to know you. You must be to her what you have always been to me, — guide, philosopher, and friend.

"I am sure I never felt better impulses, more humble, more thankful, more religious, than I do now. That the happiness of this soft, gentle, fragile creature is to be henceforth in my hands is to me a solemn and in-spiring thought. What man is worthy of a refined, delicate woman? I feel my unworthiness of her every hour; but, so help me God, I shall try to be all to her that a husband should; and you, my sister, I know, will help me to make happy the future which she so confidingly trusts to me.

"Believe me, dear sister, I never was so much your affectionate brother,

"JOHN SEYMOUR.

"P. S. — I forgot to tell you that Lillie remarkably resembles the ivory miniature of our dear sainted mother. She was very much affected when I told her of it. I think naturally Lillie has very much such a

2

character as our mother; though circumstances, in her case, have been unfavorable to the development of it."

Whether the charming vision was realized; whether the little sovereign now enthroned will be a just and clement one; what immunities and privileges she will allow to her slaves, — is yet to be seen in this story.

CHAPTER II.

WHAT SHE THINKS OF IT.

SPRINGDALE was one of those beautiful rural towns whose flourishing aspect is a striking exponent of the peculiarities of New-England life. The ride through it presents a refreshing picture of wide, cool, grassy streets, overhung with green arches of elm, with rows of large, handsome houses on either side, each standing back from the street in its own retired square of gardens, green turf, shady trees, and flowering shrubs. It was, so to speak, a little city of country-seats. It

"From John, good fellow."

spoke of wealth, thrift, leisure, cultivation, quiet, thoughtful habits, and moral tastes.

Some of these mansions were of ancestral reputation, and had been in the family whose name they bore for generations back; a circumstance sometimes occurring even in New-England towns where neither law nor custom unites to perpetuate property in certain family lines.

The Seymour house was a well-known, respected mansion for generations back. Old Judge Seymour, the grandfather, was the lineal descendant of Parson Seymour; the pastor who first came with the little colony of Springdale, when it was founded as a church in the wilderness, amid all the dangers of wild beasts and Indians.

This present Seymour mansion was founded on the spot where the house of the first minister was built by the active hands of his parishioners; and, from generation to generation, order, piety, education, and high respectability had been the tradition of the place.

The reader will come in with us, on this bright June morning, through the grassy front yard, which has only the usual New-England fault of being too densely shaded. The house we enter has a wide, cool hall running through its centre and out into a back garden, now all aglow with every beauty of June. The broad alleys of the garden showed bright stores of all sorts of good old-fashioned flowers, well tended and kept. Clumps of stately hollyhocks and scarlet peonies; roses of every hue, purple, blush, gold-color, and white, were showering down their leaves on the grassy turf; honeysuckles climbed and clambered over arbors;

and great, stately tufts of virgin-white lilies exalted their majestic heads in saintly magnificence. The garden was Miss Grace Seymour's delight and pride. Every root in it was fragrant with the invisible blossoms of memory, — memories of the mother who loved and planted and watched them before her, and the grandmother who had cared for them before that. The spirit of these charming old-fashioned gardens is the spirit of family love; and, if ever blessed souls from their better home feel drawn back to any thing on earth, we think it must be to their flower-garden.

Miss Grace had been up early, and now, with her garden hat on, and scissors in hand, was coming up the steps with her white apron full of roses, white lilies, meadow-sweets, and honeysuckle, for the parlor-vases, when the servant handed her a letter.

"From John," she said, "good fellow;" and then she laid it on the mantel-shelf of the parlor, while she busied herself in arranging her flowers.

"I must get these into water, or they will wilt," she said.

The large parlor was like many that you and I have seen in a certain respectable class of houses, — wide, cool, shady, and with a mellow *old* tone to every thing in its furniture and belongings. It was a parlor of the past, and not of to-day, yet exquisitely neat and well-kept. The Turkey carpet was faded: it had been part of the wedding furnishing of Grace's mother, years ago. The great, wide, motherly, chintz-covered sofa, which filled a recess commanding the window, was as different

as possible from any smart modern article of the name.
The heavy, claw-footed, mahogany chairs; the tall
clock that ticked in one corner; the footstools and
ottomans in faded embroidery, — all spoke of days
past. So did the portraits on the wall. One was of a
fair, rosy young girl, in a white gown, with powdered
hair dressed high over a cushion. It was the portrait
of Grace's mother. Another was that of a minister in
gown and bands, with black-silk gloved hands holding
up conspicuously a large Bible. This was the remote
ancestor, the minister. Then there was the picture of
John's father, placed lovingly where the eyes seemed
always to be following the slight, white-robed figure of
the young wife. The walls were papered with an old-
fashioned paper of a peculiar pattern, bought in France
seventy-five years before. The vases of India-china
that adorned the mantels, the framed engravings of
architecture and pictures in Rome, all were memorials of the taste of those long passed away. Yet the
room had a fresh, sweet, sociable air. The roses and
honeysuckles looked in at the windows; the table
covered with books and magazines, and the familiar
work-basket of Miss Grace, with its work, gave a sort
of impression of modern family household life. It
was a wide, open, hospitable, generous-minded room,
that seemed to breathe a fragrance of invitation and
general sociability; it was a room full of associations
and memories, and its daily arrangement and ornamentation made one of the pleasant tasks of Miss
Grace's life.

She spread down a newspaper on the large, square centre-table, and, emptying her apronful of flowers upon it, took her vases from the shelf, and with her scissors sat down to the task of clipping and arranging them.

Just then Letitia Ferguson came across the garden, and entered the back door after her, with a knot of choice roses in her hand, and a plate of seed-cakes covered with a hem-stitched napkin. The Fergusons and the Seymours occupied adjoining houses, and were on footing of the most perfect undress intimacy. They crossed each other's gardens, and came without knocking into each other's doors twenty times a day, *apropos* to any bit of chit-chat that they might have, a question to ask, a passage in a book to show, a household receipt that they had been trying. Letitia was the most intimate and confidential friend of Grace. In fact, the whole Ferguson family seemed like another portion of the Seymour family. There were two daughters, of whom Letitia was the eldest. Then came the younger Rose, a nice, charming, well-informed, good girl, always cheerful and chatty, and with a decent share of ability at talking lively nonsense. The brothers of the family, like the young men of New-England country towns generally, were off in the world seeking their fortunes. Old Judge Ferguson was a gentleman of the old school, — formal, stately, polite, always complimentary to ladies, and with a pleasant little budget of old-gentlemanly hobbies and prejudices, which it afforded him the greatest pleasure to air in the society of his

friends. Old Mrs. Ferguson was a pattern of mother-
liness, with her quaint, old-fashioned dress, her elaborate
caps, her daily and minute inquiries after the health of
all her acquaintances, and the tender pityingness of her
nature for every thing that lived and breathed in this
world of sin and sorrow.

Letitia and Grace, as two older sisters of families,
had a peculiar intimacy, and discussed every thing together, from the mode of clearing jelly up to the
profoundest problems of science and morals. They
were both charming, well-mannered, well-educated,
well-read women, and trusted each other to the utter-
most with every thought and feeling and purpose of
their hearts.

As we have said, Letitia Ferguson came in at the
back door without knocking, and, coming softly behind
Miss Grace, laid down her bunch of roses among the
flowers, and then set down her plate of seed-cakes.

Then she said, "I brought you some specimens of
my Souvenir de Malmaison bush, and my first trial of
your receipt."

"Oh, thanks!" said Miss Grace: "how charming those
roses are!   It was too bad to spoil your bush, though."

"No: it does it good to cut them; it will flower all
the more. But try one of those cakes, — are they
right?"

"Excellent! you have hit it exactly," said Grace;
"exactly the right proportion of seeds. I was hurry-
ing," she added, "to get these flowers in water, because
a letter from John is waiting to be read."

"A letter! How nice!" said Miss Letitia, looking towards the shelf. "John is as faithful in writing as if he were your lover."

"He is the best lover a woman can have," said Grace, as she busily sorted and arranged the flowers. "For my part, I ask nothing better than John."

"Let me arrange for you, while you read your letter," said Letitia, taking the flowers from her friend's hands.

Miss Grace took down the letter from the mantel-piece, opened, and began to read it. Miss Letitia, meanwhile, watched her face, as we often carelessly watch the face of a person reading a letter.

Miss Grace was not technically handsome, but she had an interesting, kindly, sincere face; and her friend saw gradually a dark cloud rising over it, as one watches a shadow on a field.

When she had finished the letter, with a sudden movement she laid her head forward on the table among the flowers, and covered her face with her hands. She seemed not to remember that any one was present.

Letitia came up to her, and, laying her hand gently on hers, said, "What is it, dear?"

Miss Grace lifted her head, and said in a husky voice, —

"Nothing, only it is so sudden! John is engaged!"

"Engaged! to whom?"

"To Lillie Ellis."

"John engaged to Lillie Ellis?" said Miss Ferguson, in a tone of shocked astonishment.

"She laid her head forward on the table."

"So he writes me. He is completely infatuated by her."

"How very sudden!" said Miss Letitia. "Who could have expected it? Lillie Ellis is so entirely out of the line of any of the women he has ever known."

"That's precisely what's the matter," said Miss Grace. "John knows nothing of any but good, noble women; and he thinks he sees all this in Lillie Ellis."

"There's nothing to her but her wonderful complexion," said Miss Ferguson, "and her pretty little coaxing ways; but she is the most utterly selfish, heartless little creature that ever breathed."

"Well, *she* is to be John's wife," said Miss Grace, sweeping the remainder of the flowers into her apron; "and so ends my life with John. I might have known it would come to this. I must make arrangements at once for another house and home. This house, so much, so dear to me, will be nothing to her; and yet she must be its mistress," she added, looking round on every thing in the room, and then bursting into tears.

Now, Miss Grace was not one of the crying sort, and so this emotion went to her friend's heart. Miss Letitia went up and put her arms round her.

"Come, Gracie," she said, "you must not take it so seriously. John is a noble, manly fellow. He loves you, and he will always be master of his own house."

"No, he won't,—no married man ever is," said Miss Grace, wiping her eyes, and sitting up very straight. "No man, that is a gentleman, is ever master in his own house. He has only such rights there as his wife chooses to give him; and this woman won't like me, I'm sure."

"Perhaps she will," said Letitia, in a faltering voice.

"No, she won't; because I have no faculty for lying, or playing the hypocrite in any way, and I shan't approve of her. These soft, slippery, pretty little fibbing women have always been my abomination."

"Oh, my *dear* Grace!" said Miss Ferguson, "do let us make the best of it."

"I *did* think," said Miss Grace, wiping her eyes, "that John had some sense. I wasn't such a fool, nor so selfish, as to want him always to live for me. I wanted him to marry; and if he had got engaged to your Rose, for instance... O Letitia! I always did so *hope* that he and Rose would like each other."

"We can't choose for our brothers," said Miss Letitia, "and, hard as it is, we must make up our minds to love those they bring to us. Who knows what good influences may do for poor Lillie Ellis? She never has had any yet. Her family are extremely common sort of people, without any culture or breeding, and only her wonderful beauty brought them into notice; and they have always used that as a sort of stock in trade."

"And John says, in this letter, that she reminds him of our mother," said Miss Grace; "and he thinks that naturally she was very much such a character. Just think of that, now!"

"He must be far gone," said Miss Ferguson; "but then, you see, she is distractingly pretty. She has just the most exquisitely pearly, pure, delicate, saint-like look, at times, that you ever saw; and then she knows exactly how she does look, and just how to use her looks; and John can't be blamed for believing in her. I, who know all about her, am sometimes taken in by her."

"Well," said Miss Grace, "Mrs. Lennox was at Newport last summer at the time that she was there, and she told me all about her. I think her an artful, unscrupulous, unprincipled woman, and her being made mistress of this house just breaks up our pleasant sociable life here. She has no literary tastes; she does not care for reading or study; she won't like our set here, and she will gradually drive them from the house. She won't like me, and she will want to alienate John from me,—so there is just the situation."

"You may read that letter," added Miss Grace, wiping her eyes, and tossing her brother's letter into Miss Letitia's lap. Miss Letitia took the letter and read it. "Good fellow!" she exclaimed warmly, "you see just what I say,—his heart is all with you."

"Oh, John's heart is all right enough!" said Miss Grace; "and I don't doubt his love. He's the best, noblest, most affectionate fellow in the world. I only think he reckons without his host, in thinking he can keep all our old relations unbroken, when he puts a new mistress into the house, and such a mistress."

"But if she really loves him"—

"Pshaw! she don't. That kind of woman can't love. They are like cats, that want to be stroked and caressed, and to be petted, and to lie soft and warm; and they will purr to any one that will pet them,—that's all. As for love that leads to any self-sacrifice, they don't begin to know any thing about it."

"Gracie dear," said Miss Ferguson, "this sort of thing will never do. If you meet your brother in this way, you will throw him off, and, maybe, make a fatal breach. Meet it like a good Christian, as you are. You know," she said gently, "where we have a right to carry our troubles, and of whom we should ask guidance."

"Oh, I do know, 'Titia!" said Miss Grace; "but I am letting myself be wicked just a little, you know, to relieve my mind. I ought to put myself to school to make the best of it; but it came on me so *very* suddenly. Yes," she added, "I am going to take a course of my Bible and Fénelon before I see John, —poor fellow."

"And try to have faith for her," said Miss Letitia.

"Well, I'll try to have faith," said Miss Grace; "but I do trust it will be some days before John comes down on me with his raptures, — men in love are such fools."

"But, dear me!" said Miss Letitia, as her head accidentally turned towards the window; "who is this riding up? Gracie, as sure as you live, it is John himself!"

"John himself!" repeated Miss Grace, becoming pale.

"Now do, dear, be careful," said Miss Letitia. "I'll just run out this back door and leave you alone;" and just as Miss Letitia's light heels were heard going down the back steps, John's heavy footsteps were coming up the front ones.

CHAPTER III.

THE SISTER.

GRACE SEYMOUR was a specimen of a class of whom we are happy to say New England possesses a great many.

She was a highly cultivated, intelligent, and refined woman, arrived at the full age of mature womanhood unmarried, and with no present thought or prospect of marriage. I presume all my readers, who are in a position to run over the society of our rural New-England towns, can recall to their minds hundreds of such. They are women too thoughtful, too conscientious, too delicate, to marry for any thing but a purely personal affection; and this affection, for various reasons, has not fallen in their way.

The tendency of life in these towns is to throw the young men of the place into distant fields of adventure and enterprise in the far Western and Southern States, leaving at their old homes a population in which the feminine element largely predominates. It is not, generally speaking, the most cultivated or the most attractive of the brethren who remain in the place where they were born. The ardent, the daring, the enterprising, are off to the ends of the earth; and the choice of the sisters who remain at home is, therefore, confined to a restricted list; and so it ends in these delightful rose-gardens of single women which abound in New England, — women who remain at home as housekeepers to aged parents, and charming persons in society; women over whose graces of conversation and manner the married men in their vicinity go off into raptures of eulogium, which generally end with, "Why hasn't that woman ever got married?"

It often happens to such women to expend on some brother that stock of hero-worship and devotion which it has not come in their way to give to a nearer friend. Alas! it is building on a sandy foundation; for, just as the union of hearts is complete, the chemical affinity which began in the cradle, and strengthens with every year of life, is dissolved by the introduction of that third element which makes of the brother a husband, while the new combination casts out the old, — sometimes with a disagreeable effervescence.

John and Grace Seymour were two only children of a very affectionate family; and they had grown up in the closest habits of intimacy. They had written to each other those long letters in which thoughtful people who live in retired situations delight; letters not of outward events, but of sentiments and opinions, the phases of the inner life. They had studied and pursued courses of reading together. They had together organized and carried on works of benevolence and charity.

The brother and sister had been left joint heirs of a large manufacturing property, employing hundreds of hands, in their vicinity; and the care and cultivation of these work-people, the education of their children, had been most conscientiously upon their minds. Half of every Sunday they devoted together to labors in the Sunday school of their manufacturing village; and the two worked so harmoniously together in the interests of their life, that Grace had never felt the want of any domestic ties or relations other than those that she had.

Our readers may perhaps, therefore, concede that, among the many claimants for their sympathy in this cross-grained world of ours, some few grains of it may properly be due to Grace.

Things are trials that try us: afflictions are what afflict us; and, under this showing, Grace was both tried and afflicted by the sudden engagement of her brother. When the whole groundwork on which one's daily life is built caves in, and falls into the cellar without one moment's warning, it is not in human nature to pick one's self up, and reconstruct and rearrange in a moment. So Grace thought, at any rate; but she made a hurried effort to dash back her tears, and gulp down a rising in her throat, anxious only not to be selfish, and not to disgust her brother in the outset with any personal egotism.

So she ran to the front door to meet him, and fell into his arms, trying so hard to seem congratulatory and affectionate that she broke out into sobbing.

"My dear Gracie," said John, embracing and kissing

her with that gushing fervor with which newly engaged gentlemen are apt to deluge every creature whom they meet, "you've got my letter. Well, were not you astonished?"

"O John, it was so sudden!" was all poor Grace could say. "And you know, John, since mother died, you and I have been all in all to each other."

"And so we shall be, Gracie. Why, yes, of course we shall," he said, stroking her hair, and playing with her trembling, thin, white hands. " Why, this only makes me love you the more now; and you will love my little Lillie: fact is, you can't help it. We shall both of us be happier for having her here."

"Well, you know, John, I never saw her," said Grace, deprecatingly, " and so you can't wonder."

"Oh, yes, of course! Don't wonder in the least. It comes rather sudden, — and then you haven't seen her. Look, here is her photograph!" said John, producing one from the most orthodox innermost region, directly over his heart. "Look there! isn't it beautiful?"

"It *is* a very sweet face," said Grace, exerting herself to be sympathetic, and thankful that she could say that much truthfully.

"I can't imagine," said John, "what ever made her like me. You know she has refused half the fellows in the country. I hadn't the remotest idea that she would have any thing to say to me; but you see there's no accounting for tastes;" and John plumed himself, as young gentlemen do who have carried off prizes.

"You see," he added, "it's odd, but she took a fancy

"It *is* a very sweet face."

to me the first time she saw me. Now, you know,
Gracie, I never found it easy to get along with ladies
at first; but Lillie has the most extraordinary way of
putting a fellow at his ease. Why, she made me feel
like an old friend the first hour."

"Indeed!"

"Look here," said John, triumphantly drawing out
his pocket-book, and producing thence a knot of rose-
colored satin ribbon. "Did you ever see such a lovely
color as this? It's so exquisite, you see! Well, she
always is wearing just such knots of ribbon, the most
lovely shades. Why, there isn't one woman in a thousand could wear the things she does. Every thing be-

comes her. Sometimes it's rose color, or lilac, or pale blue,—just the most trying things to others are what she can wear."

"Dear John, I hope you looked for something deeper than the complexion in a wife," said Grace, driven to moral reflections in spite of herself.

"Oh, of course!" said John: "she has such soft, gentle, winning ways; she is so sympathetic; she's just the wife to make home happy, to be a bond of union to us all. Now, in a wife, what we want is just that. Lillie's mind, for instance, hasn't been cultivated as yours and Letitia's. She isn't at all that sort of girl. She's just a dear, gentle, little confiding creature, that you'll delight in. You'll form her mind, and she'll look up to you. You know she's young yet."

"Young, John! Why, she's seven and twenty," said Grace, with astonishment.

"Oh, no, my dear Gracie! that is all a mistake. She told me herself she's only twenty. You see, the trouble is, she went into company injudiciously early, a mere baby, in fact; and that causes her to have the name of being older than she is. But, I do assure you, she's only twenty. She told me so herself."

"Oh, indeed!" said Grace, prudently choking back the contradiction which she longed to utter. "I know it seems a good many summers since I heard of her as a belle at Newport."

"Ah, yes, exactly! You see she went into company, as a young lady, when she was only thirteen. She told me all about it. Her parents were very injudicious, and they pushed her forward. She regrets it now. She knows that it wasn't the thing at all. She's very sensitive to the defects in her early education; but I made her understand that it was the *heart* more than the head that I cared for. I dare say, Gracie, she'll fall into all our little ways without really knowing; and you, in point of fact, will be mistress of the house as much as you ever were. Lillie is delicate, and never has had any care, and will be only too happy to depend on you. She's one of the gentle, dependent sort, you know."

To this statement, Grace did not reply. She only began nervously sweeping together the *débris* of leaves and flowers which encumbered the table, on which the newly arranged flower-vases were standing. Then she arranged the vases with great precision on the mantel-shelf. As she was doing it, so many memories rushed over her of that room and her mother, and the happy, peaceful family life that had hitherto been led there, that she quite broke down; and, sitting down in the chair, she covered her face, and went off in a good, hearty crying spell.

Poor John was inexpressibly shocked. He loved and revered his sister beyond any thing in the world; and it occurred to him, in a dim wise, that to be suddenly dispossessed and shut out in the cold, when one has hitherto been the first object of affection, is, to make the best of it, a real and sore trial.

But Grace soon recovered herself, and rose up smiling through her tears. "What a fool I am making of myself!" she said. "The fact is, John, I am only a little nervous. You mustn't mind it. You know," she said, laughing, "we old maids are like cats,—we find it hard to be put out of our old routine. I dare say we shall all of us be happier in the end for this, and I shall try to do all I can to make it so. Perhaps, John, I'd better take that little house of mine on Elm Street, and set up my tent in it, and take all the old furniture and old pictures, and old-time things. You'll be wanting to modernize and make over this house, you know, to suit a young wife."

"Nonsense, Gracie; no such thing!" said John. "Do you suppose I want to leave all the past associations of my life, and strip my home bare of all pleasant memorials, because I bring a little wife here? Why, the very idea of a wife is somebody to sympathize in your tastes; and Lillie will love and appreciate all these dear old things as you and I do. She has such a sympathetic heart! If you want to make me happy, Gracie, stay here, and let us live, as near as may be, as before."

"So we will, John," said Grace, so cheerfully that John considered the whole matter as settled, and rushed upstairs to write his daily letter to Lillie.

CHAPTER IV.

PREPARATION FOR MARRIAGE.

MISS LILLIE ELLIS was sitting upstairs in her
virgin bower, which was now converted into a
tumultuous, seething caldron of millinery and mantua-
making, such as usually precedes a wedding. To be sure,
orders had been forthwith despatched to Paris for the
bridal regimentals, and for a good part of the *trousseau ;*
but that did not seem in the least to stand in the way
of the time-honored confusion of sewing preparations
at home, which is supposed to waste the strength and
exhaust the health of every bride elect.

Whether young women, while disengaged, do not
have proper under-clothing, or whether they contem-
plate marriage as an awful gulf which swallows up all
future possibilities of replenishing a wardrobe, — certain it is that no sooner is a girl engaged to be married than there is a blind and distracting rush and
pressure and haste to make up for her immediately
a stock of articles, which, up to that hour, she has
managed to live very comfortably and respectably
without. It is astonishing to behold the number of

inexpressible things with French names which unmarried young ladies never think of wanting, but which there is a desperate push to supply, and have ranged in order, the moment the matrimonial state is in contemplation.

Therefore it was that the virgin bower of Lillie was knee-deep in a tangled mass of stuffs of various hues and description; that the sharp sound of tearing off breadths resounded there; that Miss Clippins and Miss Snippings and Miss Nippins were sewing there day and night; that a sewing-machine was busily rattling in mamma's room; and that there were all sorts of pinking and quilling, and braiding and hemming, and whipping and ruffling, and over-sewing and cat-stitching and hem-stitching, and other female mysteries, going on.

As for Lillie, she lay in a loose *negligé* on the bed, ready every five minutes to be called up to have something measured, or tried on, or fitted; and to be consulted whether there should be fifteen or sixteen tucks and then an insertion, or sixteen tucks and a series of puffs. Her labors wore upon her; and it was smilingly observed by Miss Clippins across to Miss Nippins, that Miss Lillie was beginning to show her "engagement bones." In the midst of these preoccupations, a letter was handed to her by the giggling chambermaid. It was a thick letter, directed in a bold honest hand. Miss ˙Lillie took it with a languid little yawn, finished the last sentences in a chapter of the novel she was reading, and then leisurely broke the seal and glanced it over. It was the one that the enraptured John had spent his morning in writing.

"Miss Ellis, now, if you 'll try on this jacket — oh! I beg your pardon," said Miss Clippins, observing the letter, "we can wait, *of course ;*" and then all three laughed as if something very pleasant was in their minds.

"No," said Lillie, giving the letter a toss; "it 'll *keep ;*" and she stood up to have a jaunty little blue jacket, with its pluffy bordering of swan's down, fitted upon her.

"It 's too bad, now, to take you from your letter," said Miss Clippins, with a sly nod.

"I 'm sure you take it philosophically," said Miss Nippins, with a giggle.

"Why shouldn't I?" said the divine Lillie. "I get one every day; and it 's all the old story. I 've heard it ever since I was born."

"Well, now, to be sure you have. Let 's see," said Miss Clippins, "this is the seventy-fourth or seventy-fifth offer, was it?"

"Oh, you must ask mamma! she keeps the lists: I 'm sure I don't trouble my head," said the little beauty; and she looked so natty and jaunty when she said it, just arching her queenly white neck, and making soft, downy dimples in her cheeks as she gave her fresh little childlike laugh; turning round and round before the looking-glass, and issuing her orders for the fitting of the jacket with a precision and real interest which showed that there *were* things in the world which didn't become old stories, even if one had been used to them ever since one was born.

Lillie never was caught napping when the point in question was the fit of her clothes.

When released from the little blue jacket, there was a rose-colored morning-dress to be tried on, and a grave discussion as to whether the honiton lace was to be set on plain or frilled.

So important was this case, that mamma was summoned from the sewing-machine to give her opinion. Mrs. Ellis was a fat, fair, rosy matron of most undisturbed conscience and digestion, whose main business in life had always been to see to her children's clothes. She had brought up Lillie with faithful and religious zeal; that is to say, she had always ruffled her underclothes with her own hands, and darned her stockings, sick or well; and also, as before intimated, kept a list of her offers, which she was ready in confidential moments to tell off to any of her acquaintance. The question of ruffled or plain honiton was of such vital importance, that the whole four took some time in considering it in its various points of view.

"Sarah Selfridge had hers ruffled," said Lillie.

"And the effect was perfectly sweet," said Miss Clippins.

"Perhaps, Lillie, you had better have it ruffled," said mamma.

"But three rows laid on plain has such a lovely effect," said Miss Nippins.

"Perhaps, then, she had better have three rows laid on plain," said mamma.

"Or she might have one row ruffled on the edge, with three rows laid on plain, with a satin fold," said Miss Clippins. "That's the way I fixed Miss Elliott's."

"That would be a nice way," said mamma. "Perhaps, Lillie, you'd better have it so."

"Oh! come now, all of you, just hush," said Lillie. "I know just how I want it done."

The words may sound a little rude and dictatorial; but Lillie had the advantage of always looking so pretty, and saying dictatorial things in such a sweet voice, that everybody was delighted with them; and she took the matter of arranging the trimming in hand with a clearness of head which showed that it was a subject to which she had given mature consideration. Mrs. Ellis shook her fat sides with a comfortable motherly chuckle.

"Lillie always did know exactly what she wanted: she's a smart little thing."

And, when all the trying on and arranging of folds and frills and pinks and bows was over, Lillie threw herself comfortably upon the bed, to finish her letter.

Shrewd Miss Clippins detected the yawn with which she laid down the missive.

"Seems to me your letters don't meet a very warm reception," she said.

"Well! every day, and such long ones!" Lillie answered, turning over the pages. "See there," she went on, opening a drawer, "What a heap of them! I can't see, for my part, what any one can want to write a letter every day to anybody for. John is such a goose about me."

"Shrewd Miss Clippins detected the yawn."

"He'll get over it after he's been married six months," said Miss Clippins, nodding her head with the air of a woman that has seen life.

"I'm sure I shan't care," said Lillie, with a toss of her pretty head. "It's *borous* any way."

Our readers may perhaps imagine, from the story thus far, that our little Lillie is by no means the person, in reality, that John supposes her to be, when he sits thinking of her with such devotion, and writing her such long, "borous" letters.

She is not. John is in love not with the actual Lillie Ellis, but with that ideal personage who looks like his mother's picture, and is the embodiment of all his mother's virtues. The feeling, as it exists in John's mind, is not only a most respectable, but in fact a truly divine one, and one that no mortal man ought to be ashamed of. The love that quickens all the nature, that makes a man twice manly, and makes him aspire to all that is high, pure, sweet, and religious, — is a feeling so sacred, that no unworthiness in its object can make it any less beautiful. More often than not it is spent on an utter vacancy. Men and women both pass through this divine initiation, — this sacred inspiration of our nature, — and find, when they have come into the innermost shrine, where the divinity ought to be, that there is no god or goddess there; nothing but the cold black ashes of commonplace vulgarity and selfishness. Both of them, when the grand discovery has been made, do well to fold their robes decently about them, and make the best of the matter. If they cannot love, they can at least be friendly. They can tolerate, as philosophers; pity, as Christians; and, finding just where and how the burden of an ill-assorted union galls the least, can then and there strap it on their backs, and walk on, not only without complaint, but sometimes in a cheerful and hilarious spirit.

Not a word of all this thinks our friend John, as he sits longing, aspiring, and pouring out his heart, day after day, in letters that interrupt Lillie in the all-important responsibility of getting her wardrobe fitted.

Shall we think this smooth little fair-skinned Lillie is a cold-hearted monster, because her heart does not beat faster at these letters which she does not understand,

and which strike her as unnecessarily prolix and prosy?
Why should John insist on telling her his feelings and
opinions on a vast variety of subjects that she does
not care a button for? She doesn't know any thing
about ritualism and anti-ritualism; and, what's more, she
doesn't care. She hates to hear so much about religion.
She thinks it's pokey. John may go to any church he
pleases, for all her. As to all that about his favorite
poems, she don't like poetry, — never could, — don't see
any sense in it; and John *will* be quoting ever so much
in his letters. Then, as to the love parts, — it may be
all quite new and exciting to John; but she has, as she
said, heard that story over and over again, till it strikes
her as quite a matter of course. Without doubt the
whole world is a desert where she is not: the thing has
been asserted, over and over, by so many gentlemen of
credible character for truth and veracity, that she is
forced to believe it; and she cannot see why John is
particularly to be pitied on this account. He is in no
more desperate state about her than the rest of them;
and secretly Lillie has as little pity for lovers' pangs as
a nice little white cat has for mice. They amuse her;
they are her appropriate recreation; and she pats and
plays with each mouse in succession, without any com-
prehension that it may be a serious thing for him.

When Lillie was a little girl, eight years old, she
used to sell her kisses through the slats of the fence for
papers of candy, and thus early acquired the idea that
her charms were a capital to be employed in trading for
the good things of life. She had the misfortune — and

a great one it is—to have been singularly beautiful
from the cradle, and so was praised and exclaimed over
and caressed as she walked through the streets. She
was sent for, far and near; borrowed to be looked at;
her picture taken by photographers. If one reflects how
many foolish and inconsiderate people there are in the
world, who have no scruple in making a pet and play-
thing·of a pretty child, one will see how this one unlucky lot of being beautiful in childhood spoiled Lillie's
chances of an average share of good sense and goodness. The only hope for such a case lies in the chance
of possessing judicious parents. Lillie had not these.
Her father was a shrewd grocer, and nothing more;
and her mother was a competent cook and seamstress.
While he traded in sugar and salt, and she made pickles
and embroided under-linen, the pretty Lillie was educated as pleased Heaven.

Pretty girls, unless they have wise mothers, are more
educated by the opposite sex than by their own. Put
them where you will, there is always some *man* busying himself in their instruction; and the burden of
masculine teaching is generally about the same, and
might be stereotyped as follows: "You don't need to
be or do any thing. Your business in life is to look
pretty, and amuse us. You don't need to study: you
know all by nature that a woman need to know. You
are, by virtue of being a pretty woman, superior to any
thing we can teach you; and we wouldn't, for the
world, have you any thing but what you are." When
Lillie went to school, this was what her masters

whispered in her ear as they did her sums for her, and helped her through her lessons and exercises, and looked into her eyes. This was what her young gentlemen friends, themselves delving in Latin and Greek and mathematics, told her, when they came to recreate from their severer studies in her smile. Men are held to account for talking sense. Pretty women are told that lively nonsense is their best sense. Now and then, an admirer bolder than the rest ventured to take Lillie's education more earnestly in hand, and recommended to her just a little reading, — enough to enable her to carry on conversation, and appear to know something of the ordinary topics discussed in society, — but informed her, by the by, that there was no sort of need of being either profound or accurate in these matters, as the mistakes of a pretty woman had a grace of their own.

At seventeen, Lillie graduated from Dr. Sibthorpe's school with a "finished education." She had, somehow or other, picked her way through various "ologies" and exercises supposed to be necessary for a well-informed young lady. She wrote a pretty hand, spoke French with a good accent, and could turn a sentimental note neatly; "and that, my dear," said Dr. Sibthorpe to his wife, "is all that a woman needs, who so evidently is intended for wife and mother as our little Lillie." Dr. Sibthorpe, in fact, had amused himself with a semi-paternal flirtation with his pupil during the whole course of her school exercises, and parted from her with tears in his eyes, greatly to her amusement; for

Lillie, after all, estimated his devotion at just about what it was worth. It amused her to see him make a fool of himself.

Of course, the next thing was — to be married; and Lillie's life now became a round of dressing, dancing, going to watering-places, travelling, and in other ways seeking the fulfilment of her destiny.

She had precisely the accessible, easy softness of manner that leads every man to believe that he may prove a favorite, and her run of offers became quite a source of amusement. Her arrival at watering-places was noted in initials in the papers; her dress on every public occasion was described; and, as acknowledged queen of love and beauty, she had everywhere her little court of men and women flatterers. The women flatterers around a belle are as much a part of the *cortége* as the men. They repeat the compliments they hear, and burn incense in the virgin's bower at hours when the profaner sex may not enter.

The life of a petted creature consists essentially in being deferred to, for being pretty and useless. A petted child runs a great risk, if it is ever to outgrow childhood; but a pet woman is a perpetual child. The pet woman of society is everybody's toy. Everybody looks at her, admires her, praises and flatters her, stirs her up to play off her little airs and graces for their entertainment; and passes on. Men of profound sense encourage her to chatter nonsense for their amusement, just as we delight in the tottering steps and stammering mispronunciations of a golden-haired child. When

4

Lillie has been in Washington, she has had judges of
the supreme court and secretaries of state delighted to
have her give her opinions in their respective departments.   Scholars and literary men flocked around her,
to the neglect of many a more instructed woman,
satisfied that she knew enough to blunder agreeably on
every subject.

Nor is there any thing in the Christian civilization
of our present century that condemns the kind of life
we are describing, as in any respect unwomanly or un-
becoming.   Something very like it is in a measure
considered as the appointed rule of attractive young
girls till they are married.

Lillie had numbered among her admirers many lights
of the Church.   She had flirted with bishops, priests,
and deacons, — who, none of them, would, for the
world, have been so ungallant as to quote to her such
dreadful professional passages as, " She that liveth in
pleasure is dead while she liveth."

In fact, the clergy, when off duty, are no safer guides
of attractive young women than other mortal men;
and Lillie had so often seen their spiritual attentions
degenerate into downright, temporal love-making, that
she held them in as small reverence as the rest of their
sex.   Only one dreadful John the Baptist of her acquaintance, one of the camel's-hair-girdle and locust-
and-wild-honey species, once encountering Lillie at
Saratoga, and observing the ways and manners of the
court which she kept there, took it upon him to give
her a spiritual admonition.

"Miss Lillie," he said, "I see no chance for the salvation of your soul, unless it should please God to send the small-pox upon you. I think I shall pray for that."

"Oh, horrors! don't! I'd rather never be saved," Lillie answered with a fervent sincerity.

The story was repeated afterwards as an amusing *bon mot*, and a specimen of the barbarity to which religious fanaticism may lead; and yet we question whether John the Baptist had not the right of it.

For it must at once appear, that, had the small-pox made the above-mentioned change in Lillie's complexion at sixteen, the entire course of her life would have taken another turn. The whole world then would have united in letting her know that she must live to some useful purpose, or be nobody and nothing. Schoolmasters would have scolded her if she idled over her lessons; and her breaking down in arithmetic, and mistakes in history, would no longer have been regarded as interesting. Clergymen, consulted on her spiritual state, would have told her freely that she was a miserable sinner, who, except she repented, must likewise perish. In short, all those bitter and wholesome truths, which strengthen and invigorate the virtues of plain people, might possibly have led her a long way on towards saintship.

As it was, little Lillie was confessedly no saint; and yet, if much of a sinner, society has as much to answer for as she. She was the daughter and flower of the Christian civilization of the nineteenth century, and the kind of woman, that, on the whole, men of quite distinguished sense have been fond of choosing for wives, and will go on seeking to the end of the chapter.

Did she love John? Well, she was quite pleased to be loved by him, and she liked the prospect of being his wife. She was sure he would always let her have her own way, and that he had a plenty of worldly means to do it with.

Lillie, if not very clever in a literary or scientific point of view, was no fool. She had, in fact, under all her softness of manner, a great deal of that real hard grit which shrewd, worldly people call common sense. She saw through all the illusions of fancy and feeling, right to the tough material core of things. However soft and tender and sentimental her habits of speech and action were in her professional capacity of a charming woman, still the fair Lillie, had she been a man, would have been respected in the business world, as one that had cut her eye-teeth, and knew on which side her bread was buttered.

A husband, she knew very well, was the man who undertook to be responsible for his wife's bills: he was the giver, bringer, and maintainer of all sorts of solid and appreciable comforts.

Lillie's bills had hitherto been sore places in the domestic history of her family. The career of a fashionable belle is not to be supported without something of an outlay; and that innocence of arithmetical combinations, over which she was wont to laugh bewitchingly among her adorers, sometimes led to results quite astounding to the prosaic, hard-working papa, who stood financially responsible for all her finery.

Mamma had often been called in to calm the tumult of his feelings on such semi-annual developments; and she did it by pointing out to him that this heavy present expense was an investment by which Lillie was, in the end, to make her own fortune and that of her family.

When Lillie contemplated the marriage-service with a view to going through it with John, there was one clause that stood out in consoling distinctness, — "*With all my worldly goods I thee endow.*"

As to the other clause, which contains the dreadful word "OBEY," about which our modern women have such fearful apprehensions, Lillie was ready to swallow it without even a grimace.

"Obey John!" Her face wore a pretty air of droll assurance at the thought. It was too funny.

"My dear," said Belle Trevors, who was one of Lillie's incense-burners and a bridesmaid elect, "*have* you the least idea how rich he is?"

"He is well enough off to do about any thing I want," said Lillie.

"Well, you know he owns the whole village of Spindlewood, with all those great factories, besides law business," said Belle. "But then they live in a dreadfully slow, pokey way down there in Springdale. They haven't the remotest idea how to use money."

"I can show him how to use it," said Lillie.

"He and his sister keep a nice sort of old-fashioned

place there, and jog about in an old countrified carriage, picking up poor children and visiting schools. She is a *very* superior woman, that sister."

"I don't like superior women," said Lillie.

"But you must like her, you know. John is perfectly devoted to her, and I suppose she is to be a fixture in the establishment."

"We shall see about that," said Lillie. "One thing at a time. I don't mean he shall live at Springdale. It 's horridly pokey to live in those little country towns. He must have a house in New York."

"And a place at Newport for the summer," said Belle Trevors.

"Yes," said Lillie, "a cottage in Newport does very well in the season; and then a country place well fitted up to invite company to in the other months of summer."

"Delightful," said Belle, "*if* you can make him do it."

"See if I don't," said Lillie.

"You dear, funny creature, you, — how you do always ride on the top of the wave!" said Belle.

"It 's what I was born for," said Lillie. "By the by, Belle, I got a letter from Harry last night."

"Poor fellow, had he heard" —

"Why, of course not. I didn't want he should till it 's all over. It 's best, you know."

"He is such a good fellow, and so devoted, — it does seem a pity."

"Devoted! well, I should rather think he was," said

Lillie. "I believe he would cut off his right hand for me, any day. But I never gave him any encouragement. I've always told him I could be to him only as a sister, you know."

"You ought not to write to him," said Belle.

"What can I do? He is perfectly desperate if I don't, and still persists that he means to marry me some day, spite of my screams."

"Well, he'll have to stop making love to you after you're married."

"Oh, pshaw! I don't believe that old-fashioned talk. Lovers make a variety in life. I don't see why a married woman is to give up all the fun of having admirers. Of course, one isn't going to do any thing wrong, you know; but one doesn't want to settle down into Darby and Joan at once. Why, some of the young married women, the most stunning belles at Newport last year, got a great deal more attention after they were married than they did before. You see the fellows like it, because they are so sure not to be drawn in."

"I think it's too bad on us girls, though," said Belle. "You ought to leave us our turn."

"Oh! I'll turn over any of them to you, Belle," said Lillie. "There's Harry, to begin with. What do you say to him?"

"Thank you, I don't think I shall take up with second-hand articles," said Belle, with some spirit.

But here the entrance of the chamber-maid, with a fresh dress from the dressmaker's, resolved the conversation into a discussion so very minute and technical that it cannot be recorded in our pages.

CHAPTER V.

WEDDING, AND WEDDING-TRIP.

WELL, and so they were married, with all the newest modern forms, ceremonies, and accessories.

Every possible thing was done to reflect lustre on the occasion. There were eight bridesmaids, and every one of them fair as the moon; and eight groomsmen, with white-satin ribbons and white rosebuds in their button-holes; and there was a bishop, assisted by a priest, to give the solemn benedictions of the church; and there was a marriage-bell of tuberoses and lilies, of enormous size, swinging over the heads of the pair at the altar; and there were voluntaries on the organ, and chantings, and what not, all solemn and impressive as possible. In the midst of all this, the fair Lillie promised, "forsaking all others, to keep only unto him, so long as they both should live," — "to love, honor, and obey, until death did them part."

During the whole agitating scene, Lillie kept up her presence of mind, and was perfectly aware of what she was about; so that a very fresh, original, and crisp style of trimming, that had been invented in Paris

specially for her wedding toilet, received no detriment
from the least unguarded movement. We much regret
that it is contrary to our literary principles to write
half, or one third, in French; because the wedding-
dress, by far the most important object on this occasion, and certainly one that most engrossed the thoughts
of the bride, was one entirely indescribable in English.
Just as there is no word in the Hottentot vocabulary
for "holiness," or "purity," so there are no words in
our savage English to describe a lady's dress; and,
therefore, our fair friends must be recommended, on
this point, to exercise their imagination in connection
with the study of the finest French plates, and they
may get some idea of Lillie in her wedding robe and
train.

Then there was the wedding banquet, where everybody ate quantities of the most fashionable, indigestible
horrors, with praiseworthy courage and enthusiasm; for
what is to become of "*paté de fois gras*" if we don't
eat it? What is to become of us if we do is entirely a
secondary question.

On the whole, there was not one jot nor tittle of the
most exorbitant requirements of fashion that was not
fulfilled on this occasion. The house was a crush of
wilting flowers, and smelt of tuberoses enough to give
one a vertigo for a month. A band of music brayed
and clashed every minute of the time; and a jam of
people, in elegant dresses, shrieked to each other above
the din, and several of Lillie's former admirers got tipsy
in the supper-room. In short, nothing could be finer;

and it was agreed, on all hands, that it was "stunning."
Accounts of it, and of all the bride's dresses, presents,
and even wardrobe, went into the daily papers; and
thus was the charming Lillie Ellis made into Mrs. John
Seymour.

Then followed the approved wedding journey, the
programme of which had been drawn up by Lillie herself, with *carte blanche* from John, and included every
place where a bride's new toilets could be seen in
the most select fashionable circles. They went to
Niagara and Trenton, they went to Newport and Saratoga, to the White Mountains and Montreal; and Mrs.
John Seymour was a meteor of fashionable wonder
and delight at all these places. Her dresses and her
diamonds, her hats and her bonnets, were all wonderful
to behold. The stir and excitement that she had
created as simple Miss Ellis was nothing to the stir
and excitement about Mrs. John Seymour. It was the
mere grub compared with the full-blown butterfly, —
the bud compared with the rose. Wherever she appeared, her old admirers flocked in her train. The
unmarried girls were, so to speak, nowhere. Marriage
was a new lease of power and splendor, and she revelled
in it like a humming-bird in the sunshine.

And was John equally happy? Well, to say the
truth, John's head was a little turned by the possession
of this curious and manifold creature, that fluttered
and flapped her wings about the eyes and ears of his
understanding, and appeared before him every day in
some new device of the toilet, fair and fresh; smiling

and bewitching, kissing and coaxing, laughing and crying, and in all ways bewildering him, the once sober-
minded John, till he scarce knew whether he stood on
his head or his heels. He knew that this sort of rattling, scatter-brained life must come to an end some
time. He knew there was a sober, serious life-work
for him; something that must try his mind and soul
and strength, and that would, by and by, leave him
neither time nor strength to be the mere wandering
attaché of a gay bird, whose string he held in hand,
and who now seemed to pull him hither and thither at
her will.

John thought of all these things at intervals; and
then, when he thought of the quiet, sober, respectable
life at Springdale, of the good old staple families, with
their steady ways, — of the girls in his neighborhood
with their reading societies, their sewing-circles for the
poor, their book-clubs and art-unions for practice in
various accomplishments, — he thought, with appre-
hension, that there appeared not a spark of interest in
his charmer's mind for any thing in this direction. She
never had read any thing, — knew nothing on all those
subjects about which the women and young girls in his
circle were interested; while, in Springdale, there were
none of the excitements which made her interested in
life. He could not help perceiving that Lillie's five
hundred particular friends were mostly of the other sex,
and wondering whether he alone, when the matter
should be reduced to that, could make up to her for all
her retinue of slaves.

Like most good boys who grow into good men, John had unlimited faith in women. Whatever little defects and flaws they might have, still at heart he supposed they were all of the same substratum as his mother and sister. The moment a woman was married, he imagined that all the lovely domestic graces would spring up in her, no matter what might have been her previous disadvantages, merely because she was a woman. He had no doubt of the usual orthodox oak-and-ivy theory in relation to man and woman; and that his wife, when he got one, would be the clinging ivy that would bend her flexible tendrils in the way his strong will and wisdom directed. He had never, perhaps, seen, in southern regions, a fine tree completely smothered and killed in the embraces of a gay, flaunting parasite; and so received no warning from vegetable analogies.

Somehow or other, he was persuaded, he should gradually bring his wife to all his own ways of thinking, and all his schemes and plans and opinions. This might, he thought, be difficult, were she one of the pronounced, strong-minded sort, accustomed to thinking and judging for herself. Such a one, he could easily imagine, there might be a risk in encountering in the close intimacy of domestic life. Even in his dealings with his sister, he was made aware of a force of character and a vigor of intellect that sometimes made the carrying of his own way over hers a matter of some difficulty. Were it not that Grace was the best of women, and her ways always the very best of ways,

John was not so sure but that she might prove a little too masterful for him.

But this lovely bit of pink and white; this downy, gauzy, airy little elf; this creature, so slim and slender and unsubstantial, — surely he need have no fear that he could not mould and control and manage her? Oh, no! He imagined her melting, like a moon-beam, into all manner of sweet compliances, becoming an image and reflection of his own better self; and repeated to himself the lines of Wordsworth, —

> "I saw her, on a nearer view,
>   A spirit, yet a woman too, —
>   Her household motions light and free,
>   And steps of virgin liberty.
>   A creature not too bright or good
>   For human nature's daily food,
>   For transient pleasures, simple wiles,
>   Praise, blame, love, kisses, tears, and smiles."

John fancied he saw his little Lillie subdued into a pattern wife, weaned from fashionable follies, eagerly seeking mental improvement under his guidance, and joining him and Grace in all sorts of edifying works and ways.

The reader may see, from the conversations we have detailed, that nothing was farther from Lillie's intentions than any such conformity.

The intentions of the married pair, in fact, ran exactly contrary to one another. John meant to bring Lillie to a sober, rational, useful family life; and Lillie meant to run a career of fashionable display, and make John pay for it.

Neither, at present, stated their purposes precisely to the other, because they were "honey-mooning." John, as yet, was the enraptured lover; and Lillie was his pink and white sultana, — his absolute mistress, her word was law, and his will was hers. How the case was ever to be reversed, so as to suit the terms of the marriage service, John did not precisely inquire.

But, when husband and wife start in life with exactly opposing intentions, which, think you, is likely to conquer, — the man, or the woman? That is a very nice question, and deserves further consideration.

CHAPTER VI.

HONEY-MOON, AND AFTER.

WE left Mr. and Mrs. John Seymour honey-moon-ing. The honey-moon, dear ladies, is supposed to be the period of male subjection. The young queen is enthroned; and the first of her slaves walks obediently in her train, carries her fan, her parasol, runs of her errands, packs her trunk, writes her letters, buys her any thing she cries for, and is ready to do the impossible for her, on every suitable occasion.

A great strong man sometimes feels awkwardly, when thus led captive; but the greatest, strongest, and most boastful, often go most obediently under woman-rule; for which, see Shakspeare, concerning Cleopatra and Julius Cæsar and Mark Antony.

But then all kingdoms, and all sway, and all authority must come to an end. Nothing lasts, you see. The plain prose of life must have its turn, after the poetry and honey-moons—stretch them out to their utmost limit—have their terminus.

So, at the end of six weeks, John and Lillie, somewhat dusty and travel-worn, were received by Grace into the old family-mansion at Springdale.

Grace had read her Bible and Fénelon to such purpose, that she had accepted her cross with open arms.

Dear reader, Grace was not a severe, angular, old-maid sister, ready to snarl at the advent of a young beauty; but an elegant and accomplished woman, with a wide culture, a trained and disciplined mind, a charming taste, and polished manners; and, above all, a thorough self-understanding and discipline. Though past thirty, she still had admirers and lovers; yet, till now, her brother, insensibly to herself, had blocked up the doorway of her heart; and the perfectness of the fraternal friendship had prevented the wish and the longing by which some fortunate man might have found and given happiness.

Grace had resolved she would love her new sister; that she would look upon all her past faults and errors with eyes of indulgence; that she would put out of her head every story she ever had heard against her, and unite with her brother to make her lot a happy one.

"John is so good a man," she said to Miss Letitia Ferguson, "that I am sure Lillie cannot but become a good woman."

So Grace adorned the wedding with her presence, in an elegant Parisian dress, ordered for the occasion, and presented the young bride with a set of pearl and amethyst that were perfectly bewitching, and kisses and notes of affection had been exchanged between them; and during various intervals, and for weeks past, Grace had been pleasantly employed in preparing the family-mansion to receive the new mistress.

John's bachelor apartments had been new furnished, and furbished, and made into a perfect bower of roses.

The rest of the house, after the usual household process of purification, had been rearranged, as John and his sister had always kept it since their mother's death in the way that she loved to see it. There was something quaint and sweet and antique about it, that suited Grace. Its unfashionable difference from the smart, flippant, stereotyped rooms of to-day had a charm in her eyes.

Lillie, however, surveyed the scene, the first night that she took possession, with a quiet determination to re-modernize on the very earliest opportunity. What would Mrs. Frippit and Mrs. Nippit say to such rooms, she thought. But then there was time enough to attend to that. Not a shade of these internal reflections was visible in her manner. She said, "Oh, how sweet! How perfectly charming! How splendid!" in all proper places; and John was delighted.

She also fell into the arms of Grace, and kissed her with effusion; and John saw the sisterly union, which he had anticipated, auspiciously commencing.

The only trouble in Grace's mind was from a terrible sort of clairvoyance that seems to beset very sincere people, and makes them sensitive to the presence of any thing unreal or untrue. Fair and soft and caressing as the new sister was, and determined as Grace was to believe in her, and trust her, and like her, — she found an invisible, chilly barrier between her heart and Lillie. She scolded herself, and, in the effort to confide,

5

became unnaturally demonstrative, and said and did
more than was her wont to show affection; and yet,
to her own mortification, she found herself, after all,
seeming to herself to be hypocritical, and professing
more than she felt.

As to the fair Lillie, who, as we have remarked, was
no fool, she took the measure of her new sister with
that instinctive knowledge of character which is the
essence of womanhood. Lillie was not in love with
John, because that was an experience she was not capable of. But she had married him, and now considered
him as her property, her subject, — *hers,* with an inten-
sity of ownership that should shut out all former pro-
prietors.

We have heard much talk, of late, concerning the
husband's ownership of the wife. But, dear ladies, is that
any more pronounced a fact than every wife's ownership
of her husband? — an ownership so intense and pervading that it may be said to be the controlling nerve of
womanhood. Let any one touch your right to the first
place in your husband's regard, and see!

Well, then, Lillie saw at a glance just what Grace
was, and what her influence with her brother must be;
and also that, in order to live the life she meditated,
John must act under her sway, and not under his
sister's; and so the resolve had gone forth, in her
mind, that Grace's dominion in the family should come
to an end, and that she would, as sole empress, reconstruct the state. But, of course, she was too wise to
say a word about it.

"Dear me!" she said, the next morning, when Grace proposed showing her through the house and delivering up the keys, "I'm sure I don't see why you want to show things to me. I'm nothing of a housekeeper, you know: all I know is what I want, and I've always had what I wanted, you know; but, you see, I haven't the least idea how it's to be done. Why, at home I've been everybody's baby. Mamma laughs at the idea of my knowing any thing. So, Grace dear, you must just be prime minister; and I'll be the good-for-nothing Queen, and just sign the papers, and all that, you know."

Grace found, the first week, that to be housekeeper to a young duchess, in an American village and with American servants, was no sinecure.

The young mistress, the next week, tumbled into the wash an amount of muslin and lace and French puffing and fluting sufficient to employ two artists for two or three days, and by which honest Bridget, as she stood at her family wash-tub, was sorely perplexed.

But, in America, no woman ever dies for want of speaking her mind; and the lower orders have their turn in teaching the catechism to their superiors, which they do with an effectiveness that does credit to democracy.

"And would ye be plased to step here, Miss Saymour," said Bridget to Grace, in a voice of suppressed emotion, and pointing oratorically, with her soapy right arm, to a snow-wreath of French finery and puffing on the floor. "What *I* asks, Miss Grace, is, *Who* is to do all this? I'm sure it would take me and Katy a week, workin' day and night, let alone the cookin' and the silver

"*Who* is to do all this?"

and the beds, and all them. It's a pity, now, somebody shouldn't spake to that young crather; fur she's nothin' but a baby, and likely don't know any thing, as ladies mostly don't, about what's right and proper." Bridget's Christian charity and condescension in this last sentence was some mitigation of the crisis; but still Grace was appalled. We all of us, my dear sisters, have stood appalled at the tribunal of good Bridgets rising in their majesty and declaring their ultimatum.

Bridget was a treasure in the town of Springdale, where servants were scarce and poor ; and, what was more, she was a treasure that knew her own worth. Grace knew very well how she had been beset with applications and offers of higher wages to draw her to various hotels and boarding-houses in the vicinity, but had preferred the comparative dignity and tranquillity of a private gentleman's family.

But the family had been small, orderly, and systematic, and Grace the most considerate of housekeepers. Still it was not to be denied, that, though an indulgent and considerate mistress, Bridget was, in fact, mistress of the Seymour mansion, and that her mind and will concerning the washing must be made known to the young queen.

It was a sore trial to speak to Lillie; but it would be sorer to be left at once desolate in the kitchen department, and exposed to the marauding inroads of unskilled Hibernians.

In the most delicate way, Grace made Lillie acquainted with the domestic crisis; as, in old times, a prime minister might have carried to one of the Charleses the remonstrance and protest of the House of Commons.

"Oh! I'm sure I don't know how it's to be done," said Lillie, gayly. "Mamma always got my things done *somehow*. They always *were* done, and always must be : you just tell her so. I think it's always best to be decided with servants. Face 'em down in the beginning."

"But you see, Lillie dear, it's almost impossible to *get* servants at all in Springdale; and such servants as ours everybody says are an exception. If we talk to Bridget in that way, she'll just go off and leave us; and then what shall we do?"

"What in the world does John want to live in such a place for?" said Lillie, peevishly. "There are plenty of servants to be got in New York; and that's the only place fit to live in. Well, it's no affair of mine! Tell John he married me, and must take care of me. He must settle it some way: I shan't trouble my head about it."

The idea of living in New York, and uprooting the old time-honored establishment in Springdale, struck Grace as a sort of sacrilege; yet she could not help feeling, with a kind of fear, that the young mistress had power to do it.

"Don't, darling, talk so, for pity's sake," she said. "I will go to John, and we will arrange it somehow."

A long consultation with faithful John, in the evening, revealed to him the perplexing nature of the material processes necessary to get up his fair puff of thistle-down in all that wonderful whiteness and fancifulness of costume which had so entranced him.

Lillie cried, and said she never had any trouble before about "getting her things done." She was sure mamma or Trixie or somebody did them, or got them done, — she never knew how or when. With many tears and sobs, she protested her ardent desire to realize the Scriptural idea of the fowls of the air and the lilies of the field, which were fed and clothed, "like Solomon in all his glory," without ever giving a moment's care to the matter.

John kissed and embraced, and wiped away her tears, and declared she should have every thing just as she desired it, if it took the half of his kingdom.

After consoling his fair one, he burst into Grace's room in the evening, just at the hour when they used to have their old brotherly and sisterly confidential talks.

"You see, Grace,—poor Lillie, dear little thing,—you don't know how distressed she is; and, Grace, we must find somebody to do up all her fol-de-rols and fiz-gigs for her, you know. You see, she's been *used* to this kind of thing; can't do without it."

"Well, I'll try to-morrow, John," said Grace, patiently. "There is Mrs. Atkins,—she is a very nice woman."

"Oh, exactly! just the thing," said John. "Yes, we'll get her to take all Lillie's things every week. That settles it."

"Do you know, John, at the prices that Mrs. Atkins asks, you will have to pay more than for all your family service together? What we have this week would be twenty dollars, at the least computation; and it is worth it too,—the work of getting up is so elaborate."

John opened his eyes, and looked grave. Like all stable New-England families, the Seymours, while they practised the broadest liberality, had instincts of great sobriety in expense. Needless profusion shocked them as out of taste; and a quiet and decent reticence in matters of self-indulgence was habitual with them.

Such a price for the fine linen of his little angel rather staggered him; but he gulped it down.

"Well, well, Gracie," he said, "cost what it may, she must have it as she likes it. The little creature, you see, has never been accustomed to calculate or reflect in these matters; and it is trial enough to come down to our stupid way of living, — so different, you know, from the gay life she has been leading."

Miss Seymour's saintship was somewhat rudely tested by this remark. That anybody should think it a sacrifice to be John's wife, and a trial to accept the homestead at Springdale, with all its tranquillity and comforts, — that John, under her influence, should speak of the Springdale life as *stupid*, — was a little drop too much in her cup. A bright streak appeared in either cheek, as she said, —

"Well, John, I never knew you found Springdale stupid before. I'm sure, we *have* been happy here," — and her voice quavered.

"Pshaw, Gracie! you know what I mean. I don't mean that *I* find it stupid. I don't like the kind of rattle-brained life we've been leading this six weeks. But, then, it just suits Lillie; and it's so sweet and patient of her to come here and give it all up, and say not a word of regret; and then, you see, I shall be just up to my ears in business now, and can't give up all my time to her, as I have. There's ever so much law business coming on, and all the factory matters at Spindlewood; and I can see that Lillie will have rather a hard time of it. You must devote yourself to her,

Gracie, like a dear, good soul, as you always were, and try to get her interested in our kind of life. Of course, all our set will call, and that will be something; and then — there will be some invitations out."

"Oh, yes, John! we'll manage it," said Grace, who had by this time swallowed her anger, and shouldered her cross once more with a womanly perseverance. "Oh, yes! the Fergusons, and the Wilcoxes, and the Lennoxes, will all call; and we shall have picnics, and lawn teas, and musicals, and parties."

"Yes, yes, I see," said John. "Gracie, *isn't* she a dear little thing? Didn't she look cunning in that white wrapper this morning? How do women do those things, I wonder?" said John. "Don't you think her manners are lovely?"

"They are very sweet, and she is charmingly pretty," said Grace; "and I love her dearly."

"And so affectionate! Don't you think so?" continued John. "She's a person that you can do any thing with through her heart. She's all heart, and very little head. I ought not to say that, either. I think she has fair natural abilities, had they ever been cultivated."

"My dear John," said Grace, "you forget what time it is. Good-night!"

CHAPTER VII.

WILL SHE LIKE IT?

"JOHN," said Grace, "when are you going out again to our Sunday school at Spindlewood? They are all asking after you. Do you know it is now two months since they have seen you?"

"I know it," said John. "I am going to-morrow. You see, Gracie, I couldn't well before."

"Oh! I have told them all about it, and I have kept things up; but then there are so many who want to see *you*, and so many things that you alone could settle and manage."

"Oh, yes! I'll go to-morrow," said John. "And, after this, I shall be steady at it. I wonder if we could get Lillie to go," said he, doubtfully.

Grace did not answer. Lillie was a subject on which it was always embarrassing to her to be appealed to. She was so afraid of appearing jealous or unappreciative; and her opinions were so different from those of her brother, that it was rather difficult to say any thing.

"Do you think she would like it, Grace?"

"Indeed, John, you must know better than I. If

anybody could make her take an interest in it, it would be you."

Before his marriage, John had always had the idea that pretty, affectionate little women were religious and self-denying at heart, as matters of course. No matter through what labyrinths of fashionable follies and dissipation they had been wandering, still a talent for saintship was lying dormant in their natures, which it needed only the touch of love to develop. The wings of the angel were always concealed under the fashionable attire of the belle, and would unfold themselves when the hour came. A nearer acquaintance with Lillie, he was forced to confess, had not, so far, confirmed this idea. Though hers was a face so fair and pure that, when he first knew her, it suggested ideas of prayer, and communion with angels, yet he could not disguise from himself that, in all near acquaintance with her, she had proved to be most remarkably "of the earth, earthy." She was alive and fervent about fashionable gossip, — of who is who, and what does what; she was alive to equipages, to dress, to sight-seeing, to dancing, to any thing of which the whole stimulus and excitement was earthly and physical. At times, too, he remembered that she had talked a sort of pensive sentimentalism, of a slightly religious nature; but the least idea of a moral purpose in life — of self-denial, and devotion to something higher than immediate self-gratification — seemed never to have entered her head. What is more, John had found his attempts to introduce such topics with her always unsuccessful.

Lillie either gaped in his face, and asked him what time
it was; or playfully pulled his whiskers, and asked him
why he didn't take to the ministry; or adroitly turned
the conversation with kissing and compliments.

Sunday morning came, shining down gloriously
through the dewy elm-arches of Springdale. The green
turf on either side of the wide streets was mottled and
flecked with vivid flashes and glimmers of emerald, like
the sheen of a changeable silk, as here and there long
arrows of sunlight darted down through the leaves
and touched the ground.

The gardens between the great shady houses that
flanked the street were full of tall white and crimson
phloxes in all the majesty of their summer bloom, and
the air was filled with fragrance; and Lillie, after a
two hours' toilet, came forth from her chamber fresh
and lovely as the bride in the Canticles. "Thou art all
fair, my love; there is no spot in thee." She was kill-
ingly dressed in the rural-simplicity style. All her robes
and sashes were of purest white; and a knot of field-
daisies and grasses, with French dew-drops on them,
twinkled in an infinitesimal bonnet on her little head,
and her hair was all *créped* into a filmy golden aureole
round her face. In short, dear reader, she was a perfectly got-up angel, and wanted only some tulle clouds
and an opening heaven to have gone up at once, as
similar angels do from the Parisian stage.

"You like me, don't you?" she said, as she saw the
delight in John's eyes.

John was tempted to lay hold of his plaything.

"Don't, now,—you'll crumple me," she said, fighting him off with a dainty parasol. "Positively you shan't touch me till after church."

John laid the little white hand on his arm with pride, and looked down at her over his shoulder all the way to church. He felt proud of her. They would look at her, and see how pretty she was, he thought. And so they did. Lillie had been used to admiration in church. It was one of her fields of triumph. She had received compliments on her toilet even from young clergymen, who, in the course of their preaching and praying, found leisure to observe the beauties of nature and grace in their congregation. She had been quite used to knowing of young men who got good seats in church simply for the purpose of seeing her; consequently, going to church had not the moral advantages for her that it has for people who go simply to pray and be instructed. John saw the turning of heads, and the little movements and whispers of admiration; and his heart was glad within him. The thought of her mingled with prayer and hymn; even when he closed his eyes, and bowed his head, she was there.

Perhaps this was not exactly as it should be; yet let us hope the angels look tenderly down on the sins of too much love. John felt as if he would be glad of a chance to die for her; and, when he thought of her in his prayers, it was because he loved her better than himself.

As to Lillie, there was an extraordinary sympathy of sentiment between them at that moment. John was thinking only of her; and she was thinking only of herself, as was her usual habit, — herself, the one object of her life, the one idol of her love.

Not that she knew, in so many words, that she, the little, frail bit of dust and ashes that she was, was her own idol, and that she appeared before her Maker, in those solemn walls, to draw to herself the homage and the attention that was due to God alone; but yet it was true that, for years and years, Lillie's unconfessed yet only motive for appearing in church had been the display of herself, and the winning of admiration.

But is she so much worse than others? — than the clergyman who uses the pulpit and the sacred office to show off his talents? — than the singers who sing God's praises to show their voices, — who intone the agonies of their Redeemer, or the glories of the *Te Deum*, confident on the comments of the newspaper press on their performance the next week? No: Lillie may be a little sinner, but not above others in this matter.

"Lillie," said John to her after dinner, assuming a careless, matter-of-course air, "would you like to drive with me over to Spindlewood, and see my Sunday school?"

"*Your* Sunday school, John? Why, bless me! do *you* teach Sunday school?"

"Certainly I do. Grace and I have a school of two hundred children and young people belonging to our factories. I am superintendent."

"I never did hear of any thing so odd!" said Lillie. "What in the world can you want to take all that trouble for, — go basking over there in the hot sun, and be shut up with a room full of those ill-smelling factory-people? Why, I'm sure it can't be your duty! I wouldn't do it for the wo ld. Nothing would tempt me. Why, gracious, John, you might catch small-pox or something!"

"Pooh! Lillie, child, you don't know any thing about them. They are just as cleanly and respectable as any-body."

"Oh, well! they may be. But these Irish and Germans and Swedes and Danes, and all that low class, do smell so, — you needn't tell me, now! — that working-class smell is a thing that can't be disguised."

"But, Lillie, these are our people. They are the laborers from whose toils our wealth comes; and we owe them something."

"Well! you pay them something, don't you?"

"I mean morally. We owe our efforts to instruct their children, and to elevate and guide them. Lillie, I feel that it is wrong for us to use wealth merely as a means of self-gratification. We ought to labor for those who labor for us. We ought to deny ourselves, and make some sacrifices of ease for their good."

"You dear old preachy creature!" said Lillie. "How good you must be! But, really, I haven't the smallest vocation to be a missionary, — not the smallest. I can't think of any thing that would induce me to take a long, hot ride in the sun, and to sit in that stived-up room with those common creatures."

John looked grave. "Lillie," he said, "you shouldn't

speak of any of your fellow-beings in that heartless way."

"Well now, if you are going to scold me, I'm sure I don't want to go. I'm sur`, if everybody that stays at home, and has comfortable times, Sunday., instead of going out on missions, is heartless, there are a good many heartless people in the world."

"I beg your pardon, my darling. I didn't mean, dear, that *you* were heartless, but that what you said *sounded* so. I knew you didn't really mean it. I didn't ask you, dear, to go to *work*, — only to be company for me."

"And I ask you to stay at home, and be company for *me*. I'm sure it is lonesome enough here, and you are off on business almost all your days; and you might stay with me Sundays. You could hire some poor, pious young man to do all the work over there. There are plenty of them, dear knows, that it would be a real charity to help, and that could preach and pray better than you can, I know. I don't think a man that is busy all the week ought to work Sundays. It is breaking the Sabbath."

"But, Lillie, I am *interested* in my Sunday school. I know all my people, and they know me; and no one else in the world could do for them what I could."

"Well, I should think you might be interested in *me:* nobody else can do for me what you can, and I want you to stay with me. That's just the way with you men: you don't care any thing about us after you get us."

" Now, Lillie, darling, you know that isn't so."

" It's just so.   You care more for your old missionary work, now, than you do for me.   I'm sure I never knew that I'd married a home-missionary."

" Darling, please, now, don't laugh at me, and try to make me selfish and worldly. You have such power over me, you ought to be my inspiration."

" I'll be your common-sense, John. When you get on stilts, and run benevolence into the ground, I'll pull you down. Now, I know it must be bad for a man, that has as much as you do to occupy his mind all the week, to go out and work Sundays; and it's foolish, when you could perfectly well hire somebody else to do it, and stay at home, and have a good time."

" But, Lillie, I *need* it myself."

" Need it, — what for?   I can't imagine."

" To keep me from becoming a mere selfish, worldly man, and living for mere material good and pleasure."

" You dear old Don Quixote! Well, you are altogether in the clouds above me.   I can't understand a word of all that."

" Well, good-by, darling," said John, kissing her, and hastening out of the room, to cut short the interview.

Milton has described the peculiar influence of woman over man, in lowering his moral tone, and bringing him down to what he considered the peculiarly womanly level. "You women," he said to his wife, when she tried to induce him to seek favors at court by some concession of principle, — " you women never care for

6

any thing but to be fine, and to ride in your coaches."
In Father Adam's description of the original Eve, he
says, —

> "All higher knowledge in her presence falls
> Degraded; wisdom, in discourse with her,
> Loses, discountenanced, and like folly shows."

Something like this effect was always produced on
John's mind when he tried to settle questions relating
to his higher nature with Lillie.   He seemed, somehow,
always to get the worst of it.   All her womanly graces
and fascinations, so powerful over his senses and imagination, arrayed themselves formidably against him,
and for the time seemed to strike him dumb.   What
he believed, and believed with enthusiasm, when he
was alone, or with Grace, seemed to drizzle away, and
be belittled, when he undertook to convince her of it.
Lest John should be called a muff and a spoon for this
peculiarity, we cite once more the high authority aforesaid, where Milton makes poor Adam tell the angel, —

> "Yet when I approach
> Her loveliness, so absolute she seems
> And in herself complete, so well to know
> Her own, that what she wills to do or say
> Seems wisest, virtuousest, discreetest, best."

John went out from Lillie's presence rather humbled
and over-crowed.   When the woman that a man loves
laughs at his moral enthusiasms, it is like a black frost
on the delicate tips of budding trees.   It is up-hill work,
as we all know, to battle with indolence and selfishness,
and self-seeking and hard-hearted worldliness.   Then
the highest and holiest part of our nature has a bash-

fulness of its own. It is a heavenly stranger, and
easily shamed. A nimble-tongued, skilful woman can
so easily show the ridiculous side of what seemed
heroism; and what is called common-sense, so generally, is only some neatly put phase of selfishness. Poor
John needed the angel at his elbow, to give him the
caution which he is represented as giving to Father
Adam: —

> " What transports thee so ?
> An outside ? — fair, no doubt, and worthy well
> Thy cherishing, thy honor, and thy love,
> Not thy subjection.   Weigh her with thyself,
> Then value.   Oft-times nothing profits more
> Than self-esteem, grounded on just and right
> Well managed : of that skill the more thou knowest,
> The more she will acknowledge thee her head,
> And to realities yield all her shows."

But John had no angel at his elbow. He was a
fellow with a great heart, — good as gold, — with upward aspirations, but with slow speech; and, when not
sympathized with, he became confused and incoherent,
and even dumb. So his only way with his little pink
and white empress was immediate and precipitate flight.

Lillie ran to the window when he was gone, and saw
him and Grace get into the carriage together; and then
she saw them drive to the old Ferguson House, and
Rose Ferguson came out and got in with them. "Well,"
she said to herself, " he shan't do that many times
more, — I'm resolved."

No, she did not say it. It would be well for us all
if we *did* put into words, plain and explicit, many in-

stinctive resolves and purposes that arise in our hearts,
and which, for want of being so expressed, influence us
undetected and unchallenged. If we would say out
boldly, "I don't care for right or wrong, or good or evil,
or anybody's rights or anybody's happiness, or the
general good, or God himself, — all I care for, or feel
the least interest in, is to have a good time myself,
and I mean to do it, come what may," — we should be
only expressing a feeling which often lies in the dark
back-room of the human heart; and saying it might
alarm us from the drugged sleep of life. It might
rouse us to shake off the slow, creeping paralysis of
selfishness and sin before it is for ever too late.

But Lillie was a creature who had lost the power
of self-knowledge. She was, my dear sir, what you
suppose the true woman to be, — a bundle of blind
instincts; and among these the strongest was that of
property in her husband, and power over him. She had
lived in her power over men; it was her field of ambition.
She knew them thoroughly. Women are called ivy;
and the ivy has a hundred little fingers in every inch of
its length, that strike at every flaw and crack and weak
place in the strong wall they mean to overgrow; and
so had Lillie. She saw, at a glance, that the sober,
thoughtful, Christian life of Springdale was wholly opposed to the life she wanted to lead, and in which John
was to be her instrument. She saw that, if such
women as Grace and Rose had power with him, she
should not have; and her husband should be hers alone.
He should do her will, and be her subject, — so she

thought, smiling at herself as she looked in the looking-glass, and then curled herself peacefully and languidly down in the corner of the sofa, and drew forth the French novel that was her usual Sunday companion.

Lillie liked French novels. There was an atmosphere of things in them that suited her. The young married women had lovers and admirers; and there was the constant stimulus of being courted and adored, under the safe protection of a good-natured "*mari.*"

In France, the flirting is all done after marriage, and the young girl looks forward to it as her introduction to a career of conquest. In America, so great is our democratic liberality, that we think of uniting the two systems. We are getting on in that way fast. A knowledge of French is beginning to be considered as the pearl of great price, to gain which, all else must be sold. The girls must go to the French theatre, and be stared at by French *débauchées*, who laugh at them while they pretend they understand what, thank Heaven, they cannot. Then we are to have series of French novels, carefully translated, and puffed and praised even by the religious press, written by the corps of French female reformers, which will show them exactly how the naughty French women manage their cards; so that, by and by, we shall have the latest phase of eclecticism, — the union of American and French manners. The girl will flirt till twenty *à l'Américaine*, and then marry and flirt till forty *à la Française*. This was about Lillie's plan of life. Could she hope to carry it out in Springdale?

CHAPTER VIII.

SPINDLEWOOD.

IT seemed a little like old times to Grace, to be once more going with Rose and John over the pretty romantic road to Spindlewood.

John did not reflect upon how little she now saw of him, and how much of a trial the separation was; but he noticed how bright and almost gay she was, when they were by themselves once more. He was gay too. In the congenial atmosphere of sympathy, his confidence in himself, and his own right in the little controversy that had occurred, returned. Not that he said a word of it; he did not do so, and would not have done so for the world. Grace and Rose were full of anecdotes of this, that, and the other of their scholars; and all the particulars of some of their new movements were discussed. The people had, of their own accord, raised a subscription for a library, which was to be presented to John that day, with a request that he would select the books.

"Gracie, that must be your work," said John; "you know I shall have an important case next week."

"Oh, yes! Rose and I will settle it," said Grace. "Rose, we'll get the catalogues from all the book-stores, and mark the things."

"We'll want books for the children just beginning to read; and then books for the young men in John's Bible-class, and all the way between," said Rose. "It will be quite a work to select."

"And then to bargain with the book-stores, and make the money go 'far as possible,'" said Grace.

"And then there'll be the covering of the books," said Rose. "I'll tell you. I think I'll manage to have a lawn tea at our house; and the girls shall all come early, and get the books covered,—that'll be charming."

"I think Lillie would like that," put in John.

"I should be so glad!" said Rose. "What a lovely little thing she is! I hope she'll like it. I wanted to get up something pretty for her. I think, at this time of the year, lawn teas are a little variety."

"Oh, she'll like it of course!" said John, with some sinking of heart about the Sunday-school books.

There were so many pressing to shake hands with John, and congratulate him, so many histories to tell, so many cases presented for consultation, that it was quite late before they got away; and tea had been waiting for them more than an hour when they returned.

Lillie looked pensive, and had that indescribable air of patient martyrdom which some women know how to make so very effective. Lillie had good general knowledge of the science of martyrdom, — a little spice and flavor of it had been gently infused at times into her demeanor ever since she had been at Springdale. She could do the uncomplaining sufferer with the happiest effect. She contrived to insinuate at times how she didn't complain, — how dull and slow she found her life, and yet how she endeavored to be cheerful.

"I know," she said to John when they were by themselves, "that you and Grace both think I'm a horrid creature."

"Why, no, dearest; indeed we don't."

"But you do, though; oh, I feel it! The fact is, John, I haven't a particle of constitution; and, if I should try to go on as Grace does, it would kill me in a month. Ma never would let me try to do any thing; and, if I did, I was sure to break all down under it: but, if you say so, I'll try to go into this school."

"Oh, no, Lillie! I don't want you to go in. I know, darling, you could not stand any fatigue. I only wanted you to take an interest, — just to go and see them for my sake."

"Well, John, if you must go, and must keep it up, I must try to go. I'll go with you next Sunday. It will make my head ache perhaps; but no matter, if you wish it. You don't think badly of me, do you?" she said coaxingly, playing with his whiskers.

"No, darling, not the least."

"I suppose it would be a great deal better for you if you had married a strong, energetic woman, like your sister. I do admire her so; but it discourages me."

"Darling, I'd a thousand times rather have you what you are," said John; for—

> "What she wills to do,
> Seems wisest, virtuousest, discreetest, best."

"O John! come, you ought to be sincere."

"Sincere, Lillie! I am sincere."

"You really would rather have poor, poor little me than a woman like Gracie,—a great, strong, energetic woman?" And Lillie laid her soft cheek down on his arm in pensive humility.

"Yes, a thousand million times," said John in his enthusiasm, catching her in his arms and kissing her. "I wouldn't for the world have you any thing but the darling little Lillie you are. I love your faults more than the virtues of other women. You are a thousand times better than I am. I am a great, coarse blockhead, compared to you. I hope I didn't hurt your feelings this noon; you know, Lillie, I'm hasty, and apt to be inconsiderate. I don't really know that I ought to let you go over next Sunday."

"O John, you are so good! Certainly if you go I ought to; and I shall try my best." Then John told her all about the books and the lawn tea, and Lillie listened approvingly.

So they had a lawn tea at the Fergusons that week, where Lillie was the cynosure of all eyes. Mr. Mathews, the new young clergyman of Springdale, was there. Mr. Mathews had been credited as one of the admirers of Rose Ferguson; but on this occasion he promenaded and talked with Lillie, and Lillie alone, with an exclusive devotion.

"What a lovely young creature your new sister is!" he said to Grace. "She seems to have so much religious sensibility."

"I say, Lillie," said John, "Mathews seemed to be smitten with you. I had a notion of interfering."

"Did you ever see any thing like it, John? I couldn't shake the creature off. I was so thankful when you came up and took me. He's Rose's admirer, and he hardly spoke a word to her. I think it's shameful."

The next Sunday, Lillie rode over to Spindlewood with John and Rose and Mr. Mathews.

Never had the picturesque of religion received more lustre than from her presence. John was delighted to see how they all gazed at her and wondered. Lillie looked like a first-rate French picture of the youthful Madonna, — white, pure, and patient. The day was hot, and the hall crowded ; and John noticed, what he never did before, the close smell and confined air, and it made him uneasy. When we are feeling with the nerves of some one else, we notice every roughness and inconvenience. John thought he had never seen his school appear so little to advantage. Yet Lillie was an image of patient endurance, trying to be pleased ; and John thought her, as she sat and did nothing, more of a saint than Rose and Grace, who were laboriously sorting books, and gathering around them large classes of factory boys, to whom they talked with an exhausting devotedness.

When all was over, Lillie sat back on the carriage-cushions, and smelled at her gold vinaigrette.

"You are all worn out, dear," said John, tenderly.

"It's no matter," she said faintly.

"O Lillie darling! *does* your head ache?"

"A little, — you know it was close in there. I'm very sensitive to such things. I don't think they affect others as they do me," said Lillie, with the voice of a dying zephyr.

"Lillie, *it is not your duty to go*," said John; "if you are not made ill by this, I never will take you again; you are too precious to be risked."

"How can you say so, John? I'm a poor little creature, — no use to anybody."

Hereupon John told her that her only use in life was to be lovely and to be loved, — that a thing of beauty was a joy forever, &c., &c. But Lillie was too much exhausted, on her return, to appear at the tea-table. She took to her bed at once with sick headache, to the poignant remorse of John. "You see how it is, Gracie," he said. "Poor dear little thing, she is willing enough, but there's nothing of her. We mustn't allow her to exert herself; her feelings always carry her away."

The next Sunday, John sat at home with Lillie, who found herself too unwell to go to church, and was in a state of such low spirits as to require constant soothing to keep her quiet.

"It is fortunate that I have you and Rose to trust the school with," said John; "you see, it's my first duty to take care of Lillie."

CHAPTER IX.

A CRISIS.

ONE of the shrewdest and most subtle modern French writers has given his views of woman-kind in the following passage : —

"There are few women who have not found themselves, at least once in their lives, in regard to some incontestable fact, faced down by precise, keen, searching inquiry, — one of those questions pitilessly put by their husbands, the very idea of which gives a slight chill, and the first word of which enters the heart like a stroke of a dagger. Hence comes the maxim, *Every woman lies* — obliging lies — venial lies — sublime lies — horrible lies — but always the obligation of lying.

"This obligation once admitted, must it not be a necessity to know how to lie well? In France, the women lie admirably. Our customs instruct them so well in imposture. And woman is so naïvely impertinent, so pretty, so graceful, so true, in her lying! They so well understand its usefulness in social life for avoiding those violent shocks which would destroy happiness, — it is like the cotton in which they pack their jewelry.

"Lying is to them the very foundation of language,

and truth is only the exception; they speak it, as they are virtuous, from caprice or for a purpose. According to their character, some women laugh when they lie, and some cry; some become grave, and others get angry. Having begun life by pretending perfect insensibility to that homage which flatters them most, they often finish by lying even to themselves. Who has not admired their apparent superiority and calm, at the moment when they were trembling for the mysterious treasures of their love? Who has not studied their ease and facility, their presence of mind in the midst of the most critical embarrassments of social life? There is nothing awkward about it; their deception flows as softly as the snow falls from heaven.

"Yet there are men that have the presumption to expect to get the better of the Parisian woman!—of the woman who possesses thirty-seven thousand ways of saying 'No,' and incommensurable variations in saying 'Yes.'"

This is a Frenchman's view of life in a country where women are trained more systematically for the mere purposes of attraction than in any other country, and where the pursuit of admiration and the excitement of winning lovers are represented by its authors as constituting the main staple of woman's existence. France, unfortunately, is becoming the great society-teacher of the world. What with French theatres, French operas, French novels, and the universal rush of American women for travel, France is becoming so powerful on

American fashionable society, that the things said of
the Parisian woman begin in some cases to apply to
some women in America.

Lillie was as precisely the woman here described as
if she had been born and bred in Paris. She had all
the thirty-seven thousand ways of saying "No," and
the incommensurable variations in saying "Yes," as completely as the best French teaching could have given it.
She possessed, and had used, all that graceful facility,
in the story of herself that she had told John in the
days of courtship. Her power over him was based on
a dangerous foundation of unreality. Hence, during
the first few weeks of her wedded life, came a critical
scene, in which she was brought in collision with one
of those "pitiless questions" our author speaks of.

Her wedding-presents, manifold and brilliant, had
remained at home, in the charge of her mother, during the wedding-journey. One bright day, a few weeks
after her arrival in Springdale, the boxes containing
the treasures were landed there; and John, with all
enthusiasm, busied himself with the work of unpacking
these boxes, and drawing forth the treasures.

Now, it so happened that Lillie's maternal grandfather, a nice, pious old gentleman, had taken the
occasion to make her the edifying and suggestive
present of a large, elegantly bound family Bible.

The binding was unexceptionable; and Lillie assigned
it a proper place of honor among her wedding-gear.
Alas! she had not looked into it, nor seen what
dangers to her power were lodged between its leaves.

But John, who was curious in the matter of books, sat quietly down in a corner to examine it; and on the middle page, under the head "Family Record," he found, in a large, bold hand, the date of the birth of "Lillie Ellis" in figures of the most uncompromising

"He found the date of the birth of 'Lillie Ellis.'"

plainness; and thence, with one flash of his well-trained arithmetical sense, came the perception that, instead of being twenty years old, she was in fact twenty-seven, — and that of course she had lied to him.

It was a horrid and a hard word for an American young man to have suggested in relation to his wife, If we may believe the French romancer, a Frenchman would simply have smiled in amusement on detecting this petty feminine *ruse* of his beloved.　But American men are in the habit of expecting the truth from respectable women as a matter of course; and the want of it in the smallest degree strikes them as shocking. Only an Englishman or an American can understand the dreadful pain of that discovery to John.

The Anglo-Saxon race have, so to speak, a worship of truth; and they hate and abhor lying with an energy which leaves no power of tolerance.

The Celtic races have a certain sympathy with deception.　They have a certain appreciation of the value of lying as a fine art, which has never been more skilfully shown than in the passage from De Balzac we have quoted.　The woman who is described by him as lying so sweetly and skilfully is represented as one of those women "qui ont je ne sais quoi de saint et de sacré, qui inspirent tant de respect que l'amour,"—"a woman who has an indescribable something of holiness and purity which inspires respect as well as love."　It was no detraction from the character of Jesus, according to the estimate of Renan, to represent him as consenting to a benevolent fraud, and seeming to work miracles when he did not work them, by way of increasing his good influence over the multitude.

But John was the offspring of a generation of men for hundreds of years, who would any of them have gone to the stake rather than have told the smallest untruth; and for him who had been watched and guarded and catechised against this sin from his cradle, till he was as true and pure as a crystal rock, to have his faith shattered in the woman he loved, was a terrible thing.

As he read the fatal figures, a mist swam before his eyes, — a sort of faintness came over him. It seemed for a moment as if his very life was sinking down through his boots into the carpet. He threw down the book hastily, and, turning, stepped through an open window into the garden, and walked quickly off.

"Where in the world is John going?" said Lillie, running to the door, and calling after him in imperative tones.

"John, John, come back. I haven't done with you yet;" but John never turned his head.

"How very odd! what in the world is the matter with him?" she said to herself.

John was gone all the afternoon. He took a long, long walk, all by himself, and thought the matter over. He remembered that fresh, childlike, almost infantine face, that looked up into his with such a bewitching air of frankness and candor, as she professed to be telling all about herself and her history; and now which or what of it was true? It seemed as if he loathed her; and yet he couldn't help loving her, while he despised himself for doing it.

When he came home to supper, he was silent and morose. Lillie came running to meet him; but he threw her off, saying he was tired. She was frightened; she had never seen him look like that.

"John, what is the matter with you?" said Grace at

the tea-table. "You are upsetting every thing, and
don't drink your tea."

"Nothing — only — I have some troublesome business
to settle," he said, getting up to go out again. "You
needn't wait for me; I shall be out late."

"What can be the matter?"

Lillie, indeed, had not the remotest idea. Yet she
remembered his jumping up suddenly, and throwing
down the Bible; and mechanically she went to it, and
opened it. She turned it over; and the record met
her eye.

"Provoking!" she said. "Stupid old creature! must
needs go and put that out in full." Lillie took a paper-
folder, and cut the leaf out quite neatly; then folded
and burned it.

She knew now what was the matter. John was
angry at her; but she couldn't help wondering that he
should be so angry. If he had laughed at her, teased
her, taxed her with the trick, she would have understood what to do. But this terrible gloom, this awful
commotion of the elements, frightened her.

She went to her room, saying that she had a headache, and would go to bed. But she did not. She
took her French novel, and read till she heard him
coming; and then she threw down her book, and began
to cry. He came into the room, and saw her leaning
like a little white snow-wreath over the table, sobbing
as if her heart would break. To do her justice,
Lillie's sobs were not affected. She was lonesome and
thoroughly frightened; and, when she heard him com-

ing, her nerves gave out. John's heart yearned towards her. His short-lived anger had burned out; and he was perfectly longing for a reconciliation. He felt as if he must have her to love, no matter what she was. He came up to her, and stroked her hair. "O Lillie!" he said, "why couldn't you have told me the truth? What made you deceive me?"

"I was afraid you wouldn't like me if I did," said Lillie, in her sobs.

"O Lillie! I should have liked you, no matter how old you were,—only you should have told me *the truth.*"

"I know it—I know it—oh, it *was* wrong of me!" and Lillie sobbed, and seemed in danger of falling into convulsions; and John's heart gave out. He gathered her in his arms. "I can't help loving you; and I can't live without you," he said, "be you what you may!"

Lillie's little heart beat with triumph under all her sobs: she had got him, and should hold him yet.

"There can be no confidence between husband and wife, Lillie," said John, gravely, "unless we are perfectly true with each other. Promise me, dear, that you will never deceive me again."

Lillie promised with ready fervor. "O John!" she said, "I never should have done so wrong if I had only come under your influence earlier. The fact is, I have been under the worst influences all my life. I never had anybody like you to guide me."

John may of course be excused for feeling that his flattering little penitent was more to him than ever; and as to Lillie, she gave a sigh of relief. *That* was over, "anyway;" and she had him not only safe, but more completely hers than before.

A generous man is entirely unnerved by a frank confession. If Lillie had said one word in defence, if she had raised the slightest shadow of an argument, John would have roused up all his moral principle to oppose her; but this poor little white water-sprite, dissolving in a rain of penitent tears, quite washed away all his anger and all his heroism.

The next morning, Lillie, all fresh in a ravishing toilet, with field-daisies in her hair, was in a condition to laugh gently at John for his emotion of yesterday. She triumphed softly, not too obviously, in her power. He couldn't do without her, — do what she might, — that was plain.

"Now, John," she said, "don't you think we poor women are judged rather hardly? Men, you know, tell all sorts of lies to carry on their great politics and their ambition, and nobody thinks it so dreadful of *them.*"

"I *do* — I should," interposed John.

"Oh, well! *you* — you are an exception. It is not one man in a hundred that is so good as you are. Now, we women have only one poor little ambition, — to be pretty, to please you men; and, as soon as you know we are getting old, you don't like us. And can you think it's so very shocking if we don't come square up to the dreadful truth about our age? Youth and beauty is all there is to us, you know."

"O Lillie! don't say so," said John, who felt the necessity of being instructive, and of improving the occasion to elevate the moral tone of his little elf. "Goodness lasts, my dear, when beauty fades."

"Oh, nonsense! Now, John, don't talk humbug. I'd like to see *you* following goodness when beauty is gone. I've known lots of plain old maids that were perfect saints and angels; and yet men crowded and jostled by them to get the pretty sinners. I dare say now," she added, with a bewitching look over her shoulder at him, "you'd rather have me than Miss Almira Carraway, — hadn't you, now?"

And Lillie put her white arm round his neck, and her downy cheek to his, and said archly, "Come, now, confess."

Then John told her that she was a bad, naughty girl; and she laughed; and, on the whole, the pair were more hilarious and loving than usual.

But yet, when John was away at his office, he thought of it again, and found there was still a sore spot in his heart.

She had cheated him once; would she cheat him again? And she could cheat so prettily, so serenely, and with such a candid face, it was a dangerous talent.

No: she wasn't like his mother, he thought with a sigh. The "je ne sais quoi de saint et de sacré," which had so captivated his imagination, did not cover the saintly and sacred nature; it was a mere outward purity of complexion and outline. And then Grace, — she must not be left to find out what he knew about

Lillie. He had told Grace that she was only twenty,—
told it on her authority; and now must he become an
accomplice? If called on to speak of his wife's age,
must he accommodate the truth to her story, or must
he palter and evade? Here was another brick laid on
the wall of separation between his sister and himself.
It was rising daily. Here was another subject on which
he could never speak frankly with Grace; for he must
defend Lillie,— every impulse of his heart rushed to
protect her.

But it is a terrible truth, and one that it will not hurt
any of us to bear in mind, that our judgments of our
friends are involuntary.

We may long with all our hearts to confide; we may
be fascinated, entangled, and wish to be blinded; but
blind we cannot be. The friend that has lied to us
once, we may long to believe; but we cannot. Nay,
more; it is the worse for us, if, in our desire to hold the
dear deceiver in our hearts, we begin to chip and ham-
mer on the great foundations of right and honor, and
to say within ourselves, "After all, why be so particular?" Then, when we have searched about for all the
reasons and apologies and extenuations for wrong-doing,
are we sure that in our human weakness we shall not
be pulling down the moral barriers in ourselves? The
habit of excusing evil, and finding apologies, and wish-
ing to stand with one who stands on a lower moral
plane, is not a wholesome one for the soul.

As fate would have it, the very next day after this
little scene, who should walk into the parlor where

Lillie, John, and Grace were sitting, but that terror of American democracy, the census-taker. Armed with the whole power of the republic, this official steps with elegant ease into the most sacred privacies of the family. Flutterings and denials are in vain. Bridget and Katy and Anne, no less than Seraphina and Isabella, must give up the critical secrets of their lives.

John took the paper into the kitchen. Honest old Bridget gave in her age with effrontery as "twinty-five." Anne giggled and flounced, and declared on her word she didn't know, — they could put it down as they liked. "But, Anne, you *must* tell, or you may be sent to jail, you know."

Anne giggled still harder, and tossed her head: "Then it's to jail I'll have to go; for I don't know."

"Dear me," said Lillie, with an air of edifying candor, "what a fuss they make! Set down my age 'twenty-seven,' John," she added.

Grace started, and looked at John; he met her eye, and blushed to the roots of his hair.

"Why, what's the matter?" said Lillie, "are you embarrassed at telling your age?"

"Oh, nothing!" said John, writing down the numbers hastily; and then, finding a sudden occasion to give directions in the garden, he darted out. "It's so silly to be ashamed of our age!" said Lillie, as the census-taker withdrew.

"Of course," said Grace; and she had the humanity never to allude to the subject with her brother.

CHAPTER X.

CHANGES.

SCENE.—*A chamber at the Seymour House. Lillie discovered weeping. John rushing in with empressement.*

"LILLIE, you *shall* tell me what ails you."

"Nothing ails me, John."

"Yes, there does; you were crying when I came in."

"Oh, well, that's nothing!"

"Oh, but it *is* a great deal! What is the matter? I can see that you are not happy."

"Oh, pshaw, John! I am as happy as I ought to be, I dare say; there isn't much the matter with me, only a little blue, and I don't feel quite strong."

"You don't feel strong! I've noticed it, Lillie."

"Well, you see, John, the fact is, that I never have got through this month without going to the sea-side. Mamma always took me. The doctors told her that my constitution was such that I couldn't get along without it; but I dare say I shall do well enough in time, you know."

"But, Lillie," said John, "if you do need sea-air, you must go. I can't leave my business; that's the trouble."

"Oh, no, John! don't think of it. I ought to make an effort to get along. You see, it's very foolish in me, but places affect my spirits so. It's perfectly absurd how I am affected."

"Well, Lillie, I hope this place doesn't affect you unpleasantly," said John.

"It's a nice, darling place, John, and it's very silly in me; but it is a fact that this house somehow has a depressing effect on my spirits. You know it's not like the houses I've been used to. It has a sort of old look; and I can't help feeling that it puts me in mind of those who are dead and gone; and then I think I shall be dead and gone too, some day, and it makes me cry so. Isn't it silly of me, John?"

"Poor little pussy!" said John.

"You see, John, our rooms are lovely; but they are n't modern and cheerful, like those I've been accustomed to. They make me feel pensive and sad all the time; but I'm trying to get over it."

"Why, Lillie!" said John, "would you like the rooms refurnished? It can easily be done if you wish it."

"Oh, no, no, dear! You are too good; and I'm sure the rooms are lovely, and it would hurt Gracie's feelings to change them. No: I must try and get over it. I know just how silly it is, and I shall try to overcome it. If I had only more strength, I believe I could."

"Well, darling, you must go to the sea-side. I shall have you sent right off to Newport. Gracie can go with you."

"Oh, no, John! not for the world. Gracie must stay,

and keep house for you. She's such a help to you, that it would be a shame to take her away. But I think mamma would go with me, — if you could take me there, and engage my rooms and all that, why, mamma could stay with me, you know. To be sure, it would be a trial not to have you there; but then if I could get up my strength, you know," —

"Exactly, certainly; and, Lillie, how would you like the parlors arranged if you had your own way?"

"Oh, John! don't think of it."

"But I just want to know for curiosity. Now, how would you have them if you could?"

"Well, then, John, don't you think it would be lovely to have them frescoed? Did you ever see the Folingsbees' rooms in New York? They were so lovely! — one was all in blue, and the other in crimson, opening into each other; with carved furniture, and those *marquetrie* tables, and all sorts of little French things. They had such a gay and cheerful look."

"Now, Lillie, if you want our rooms like that, you shall have them."

"O John, you are too good! I couldn't ask such a sacrifice."

"Oh, pshaw! it isn't a sacrifice. I don't doubt I shall like them better myself. Your taste is perfect, Lillie; and, now I think of it, I wonder that I thought of bringing you here without consulting you in every particular. A woman ought to be queen in her own house, I am sure."

"But, Gracie! Now, John, I know she has associations with all the things in this house, and it would be cruel to her," said Lillie, with a sigh.

"Pshaw! Gracie is a good, sensible girl, and ready to make any rational change. I suppose we have been living rather behind the times, and are somewhat rusty, that's a fact; but Gracie will enjoy new things as much as anybody, I dare say."

"Well, John, since you are set on it, there's Charlie Ferrola, one of my particular friends; he's an architect, and does all about arranging rooms and houses and furniture. He did the Folingsbees', and the Hortons', and the Jeromes', and no end of real nobby people's houses; and made them perfectly lovely. People say that one wouldn't know that they weren't in Paris, in houses that he does."

Now, our John was by nature a good solid chip of the old Anglo-Saxon block; and, if there was any thing that he had no special affinity for, it was for French things. He had small opinion of French morals, and French ways in general; but then at this moment he saw his Lillie, whom, but half an hour before, he found all pale and tear-drenched, now radiant and joyous, sleek as a humming-bird, with the light in her eyes, and the rattle on the tip of her tongue; and he felt so delighted to see her bright and gay and joyous, that he would have turned his house into the Jardin Mabille, if that were possible.

Lillie had the prettiest little caressing tricks and graces imaginable; and she perched herself on his knee, and laughed and chatted so gayly, and pulled his

whiskers so saucily, and then, springing up, began array-
ing herself in such an astonishing daintiness of device,
and fluttering before him with such a variety of well-
assorted plumage, that John was quite taken off his feet.

"She perched herself on his knee."

He did not care so much whether what she willed to
do were, "Wisest, virtuousest, discreetest, best," as feel
that what she wished to do must be done at any rate.

"Why, darling!" he said in his rapture; "why
didn't you tell me all this before? Here you have
been growing sad and blue, and losing your vivacity
and spirits, and never told me why!"

"I thought it was my duty, John, to try to bear it," said Lillie, with the sweet look of a virgin saint. "I thought perhaps I should get used to things in time; and I think it is a wife's duty to accommodate herself to her husband's circumstances."

"No, it's a husband's duty to accommodate himself to his wife's wishes," said John. "What's that fellow's address? I'll write to him about doing our house, forthwith."

"But, John, do pray tell Gracie that it's *your* wish. I don't want her to think that it's I that am doing this. Now, pray do think whether you really want it yourself. You see it must be so natural for you to like the old things! They must have associations, and I wouldn't for the world, now, be the one to change them; and, after all, how silly it was of me to feel blue!"

"Don't say any more, Lillie. Let me see,—next week," he said, taking out his pocket-book, and looking over his memoranda,—"next week I'll take you down to Newport; and you write to-day to your mother to meet you there, and be your guest. I'll write and engage the rooms at once."

"I don't know what I shall do without you, John."

"Oh, well, I couldn't stay possibly! But I may run down now and then, for a night, you know."

"Well, we must make that do," said Lillie, with a pensive sigh.

Thus two very important moves on Miss Lillie's checker-board of life were skilfully made. The house

was to be refitted, and the Newport precedent established.

Now, dear friends, don't think Lillie a pirate, or a
conspirator, or a wolf-in-sheep's-clothing, or any thing
else but what she was, — a pretty little, selfish woman;
undeveloped in her conscience and affections, and strong
in her instincts and perceptions; in a blind way using
what means were most in her line to carry her purposes.
Lillie had always found her prettiness, her littleness,
her helplessness, and her tears so very useful in carrying her points in life that she resorted to them as
her lawful stock in trade. Neither were her blues
entirely shamming. There comes a time after marriage, when a husband, if he be any thing of a man,
has something else to do than make direct love to
his wife. He cannot be on duty at all hours to fan her,
and shawl her, and admire her. His love must express
itself through other channels. He must be a full man
for her sake; and, as a man, must go forth to a whole
world óf interests that takes him from her. Now
what in this case shall a woman do, whose only life lies
in petting and adoration and display?

Springdale had no *beau monde*, no fashionable circle,
no Bois de Boulogne, and no beaux, to make amends
for a husband's engrossments. Grace was sisterly and
kind; but what on earth had they in common to
talk about? Lillie's wardrobe was in all the freshness
of bridal exuberance, and there was nothing more to be
got, and so, for the moment, no stimulus in this line.
But then where to wear all these fine French dresses?

Lillie had been called on, and invited once to little social evening parties, through the whole round of old, respectable families that lived under the elm-arches of Springdale; and she had found it rather stupid. There was not a man to make an admirer of, except the young minister, who, after the first afternoon of seeing her, returned to his devotion to Rose Ferguson.

You know, ladies, Æsop has a pretty little fable as follows: A young man fell desperately in love with a cat, and prayed to Jupiter to change her to a woman for his sake. Jupiter was so obliging as to grant his prayer; and, behold, a soft, satin-skinned, purring, graceful woman was given into his arms.

But the legend goes on to say that, while he was delighting in her charms, she heard the sound of *mice* behind the wainscot, and left him forthwith to rush after her congenial prey.

Lillie had heard afar the sound of *mice* at Newport, and she longed to be after them once more. Had she not a prestige now as a rich young married lady? Had she not jewels and gems to show? Had she not any number of mouse-traps, in the way of ravishing toilets? She thought it all over, till she was sick with longing, and was sure that nothing but the sea-air could do her any good; and so she fell to crying, and kissing her faithful John, till she gained her end, like a veritable little cat as she was.

CHAPTER XI.

NEWPORT; OR, THE PARADISE OF NOTHING TO DO.

BEHOLD, now, our Lillie at the height of her
heart's desire, installed in fashionable apartments
at Newport, under the placid chaperonship of dear
mamma, who never saw the least harm in any earthly
thing her Lillie chose to do.

All the dash and flash and furbelow of upper-tendom
were there; and Lillie now felt the full power and glory
of being a rich, pretty, young married woman, with
oceans of money to spend, and nothing on earth to do
but follow the fancies of the passing hour.

This was Lillie's highest ideal of happiness; and
didn't she enjoy it?

Wasn't it something to flame forth in wondrous
toilets in the eyes of Belle Trevors and Margy Sillo-
way and Lottie Cavers, who were *not* married; and
before the Simpkinses and the Tomkinses and the
Jenkinses, who, last year, had said hateful things about
her, and intimated that she had gone off in her looks,
and was on the way to be an old maid?

And wasn't it a triumph when all her old beaux
came flocking round her, and her parlors became a

daily resort and lounging-place for all the idle swains, both of her former acquaintance and of the new-comers, who drifted with the tide of fashion? Never had she been so much the rage; never had she been declared so "stunning." The effect of all this good fortune on her health was immediate. We all know how the spirits affect the bodily welfare; and hence, my dear gentlemen, we desire it to be solemnly impressed on you, that there is nothing so good for a woman's health as to give her her own way.

Lillie now, from this simple cause, received enormous accessions of vigor. While at home with plain, sober John, trying to walk in the quiet paths of domesticity, how did her spirits droop! If you only could have had a vision of her brain and spinal system, you would have seen how there was no nervous fluid there, and how all the fine little cords and fibres that string the muscles were wilting like flowers out of water; but now she could bathe the longest and the strongest of any one, could ride on the beach half the day, and dance the German into the small hours of the night, with a degree of vigor which showed conclusively what a fine thing for her the Newport air was. Her dancing-list was always over-crowded with applicants; bouquets were showered on her; and the most superb "turn-outs," with their masters for charioteers, were at her daily disposal.

All this made talk. The world doesn't forgive success; and the ancients informed us that even the gods were envious of happy people. It is astonishing to see

8

the quantity of very proper and rational moral reflection that is excited in the breast of society, by any sort of success in life. How it shows them the vanity of earthly enjoyments, the impropriety of setting one's heart on it! How does a successful married flirt impress all her friends with the gross impropriety of having one's head set on gentlemen's attentions!

"I must say," said Belle Trevors, "that dear Lillie does astonish me. Now, I shouldn't want to have that dissipated Danforth lounging in my rooms every day, as he does in Lillie's: and then taking her out driving day after day; for my part, I don't think it's respectable."

"Why don't you speak to her?" said Lottie Cavers.

"Oh, my dear! she wouldn't mind *me*. Lillie always was the most imprudent creature; and, if she goes on so, she'll certainly get awfully talked about. That Danforth is a horrid creature; I know all about him."

As Miss Belle had herself been driving with the "horrid creature" only the week before Lillie came, it must be confessed that her opportunities for observation were of an authentic kind.

Lillie, as queen in her own parlor, was all grace and indulgence. Hers was now to be the sisterly *rôle*, or, as she laughingly styled it, the maternal. With a ravishing morning-dress, and with a killing little cap of about three inches in extent on her head, she enacted the young matron, and gave full permission to Tom, Dick, and Harry to make themselves at home in her room, and smoke their cigars there in peace. She "adored the smell;" in fact, she accepted the present of a fancy box of cigarettes from Danforth with graciousness, and would sometimes smoke one purely for good company. She also encouraged her followers to

"And would sometimes smoke one purely for good company."

unveil the tender secrets of their souls confidentially to her, and offered gracious mediations on their behalf with any of the flitting Newport fair ones. When they, as in duty bound, said that they saw nobody whom they cared about now she was married, that she was the only woman on earth for them, — she rapped their knuckles briskly with her fan, and bid them mind their manners. All this mode of proceeding gave her an immense success.

But, as we said before, all this was talked about; and ladies in their letters, chronicling the events of the passing hour, sent the tidings up and down the country; and so Miss Letitia Ferguson got a letter from Mrs. Wilcox with full pictures and comments; and she brought the same to Grace Seymour.

"I dare say," said Letitia, "these things have been exaggerated; they always are: still it does seem desirable that your brother should go there, and be with her."

"He can't go and be with her," said Grace, "without neglecting his business, already too much neglected. Then the house is all in confusion under the hands of painters; and there is that young artist up there, — a very elegant gentleman, — giving orders to right and left, every one of which involves further confusion and deeper expense; for my part, I see no end to it. Poor John has got 'the Old Man of the Sea' on his back in the shape of this woman; and I expect she'll be the ruin of him yet. I can't want to break up his illusion about her; because, what good will it do? He has married her, and must live with her; and, for Heaven's sake, let the illusion last while it can! I'm going to draw off, and leave them to each other; there's no other way."

"You are, Gracie?"

"Yes; you see John came to me, all stammering and embarrassment, about this making over of the old place; but I put him at ease at once. 'The most natural thing in the world, John,' said I. 'Of course

Lillie has her taste; and it's her right to have the
house arranged to suit it.' And then I proposed to
take all the old family things, and furnish the house
that I own on Elm Street, and live there, and let John
and Lillie keep house by themselves. You see there is
no helping the thing. Married people must be left
to themselves; nobody can help them. They must
make their own discoveries, fight their own battles,
sink or swim, together; and I have determined that
not by the winking of an eye will I interfere between
them."

"Well, but do you think John wants you to go?"

"He feels badly about it; and yet I have convinced
him that it's best. Poor fellow! all these changes
are not a bit to his taste. He liked the old place as
it was, and the old ways; but John is so unselfish. He
has got it in his head that Lillie is very sensitive
and peculiar, and that her spirits require all these
changes, as well as Newport air."

"Well," said Letitia, "if a man begins to say A in
that line, he must say B."

"Of course," said Grace; "and also C and D, and
so on, down to X, Y, Z. A woman, armed with sick-
headaches, nervousness, debility, presentiments, fears,
horrors, and all sorts of imaginary and real diseases,
has an eternal armory of weapons of subjugation.
What can a man do? Can he tell her that she is lying
and shamming? Half the time she isn't; she can actually work herself into about any physical state she
chooses. The fortnight before Lillie went to Newport,

she really looked pale, and ate next to nothing; and
she managed admirably to seem to be trying to keep
up, and not to complain, — yet you see how she can go
on at Newport."

"It seems a pity John couldn't understand her."

"My dear, I wouldn't have him for the world. Whenever he does, he will despise her; and then he will be
wretched. For John is no.hypocrite, any more than I
am. No, I earnestly pray that his soap-bubble may not
break."

"Well, then," said Letitia, "at least, he might go
down to Newport for a day or two; and his presence
there might set some things right: it might at least
check reports. You might just suggest to him that
unfriendly things were being said."

"Well, I'll see what I can do," said Grace.

So, by a little feminine tact in suggestion, Grace despatched her brother to spend a day or two in Newport.

His coming and presence interrupted the lounging
hours in Lillie's room; the introduction to "my husband" shortened the interviews. John was courteous
and affable; but he neither smoked nor drank, and
there was a mutual repulsion between him and many
of Lillie's *habitués*.

"I say, Dan," said Bill Sanders to Danforth, as they
were smoking on one end of the veranda, "you are
driven out of your lodgings since Seymour came."

"No more than the rest of you," said Danforth.

"I don't know about that, Dan. I think *you* might

have been taken for master of those premises. Look here now, Dan, why didn't you *take* little Lill yourself? Everybody thought you were going to last year."

"Didn't want her; knew too much," said Danforth. "Didn't want to keep her; she's too cursedly extravagant. It's jolly to have this sort of concern on hand; but I'd rather Seymour'd pay her bills than I."

"Who thought you were so practical, Dan?"

"Practical! that I am; I'm an old bird. Take my advice, boys, now: keep shy of the girls, and flirt with the married ones,— then you don't get roped in."

"I say, boys," said Tom Nichols, "isn't she a case, now? What a head she has! I bet she can smoke equal to any of us."

"Yes; I keep her in cigarettes," said Danforth; "she's got a box of them somewhere under her ruffles now."

"What if Seymour should find them?" said Tom.

"Seymour? pooh! he's a muff and a prig. I bet you he won't find her out; she's the jolliest little humbugger there is going. She'd cheat a fellow out of the sight of his eyes. It's perfectly wonderful."

"How came Seymour to marry her?"

"He? Why, he's a pious youth, green as grass itself; and I suppose she talked religion to him. Did you ever hear her talk religion?"

A roar of laughter followed this, out of which Danforth went on. "By George, boys, she gave me a prayer-book once! I've got it yet."

"Well, if that isn't the best thing I ever heard!" said Nichols.

"It was at the time she was laying siege to me, you see. She undertook the part of guardian angel, and used to talk lots of sentiment. The girls get lots of that out of George Sand's novels about the *holiness* of doing just as you've a mind to, and all that," said Danforth.

"By George, Dan, you oughtn't to laugh. She may have more good in her than you think."

"Oh, humbug! don't I know her?"

"Well, at any rate she's a wonderful creature to hold her looks. By George! how she *does* hold out! You'd say, now, she wasn't more than twenty."

"Yes; she understands getting herself up," said Danforth, "and touches up her cheeks a bit now and then."

"She don't paint, though?"

"Don't paint! *Don't* she? I'd like to know if she don't; but she does it like an artist, like an old master, in fact."

"Or like a young mistress," said Tom, and then laughed at his own wit.

Now, it so happened that John was sitting at an open window above, and heard occasional snatches of this conversation quite sufficient to impress him disagreeably. He had not heard enough to know exactly what had been said, but enough to feel that a set of coarse, low-minded men were making quite free with the name and reputation of his Lillie; and he was indignant.

"She is so pretty, so frank, and so impulsive," he said. "Such women are always misconstrued. I'm resolved to caution her."

"Lillie," he said, "who is this Danforth?"

"Charlie Danforth — oh! he's a millionnaire that I refused. He was wild about me, — is now, for that matter. He perfectly haunts my rooms, and is always teasing me to ride with him."

"Well, Lillie, if I were you, I wouldn't have any thing to do with him."

"John, I don't mean to, any more than I can help. I try to keep him off all I can; but one doesn't want to be rude, you know."

"My darling," said John, "you little know the wickedness of the world, and the cruel things that men will allow themselves to say of women who are meaning no harm. You can't be too careful, Lillie."

"Oh! I am careful. Mamma is here, you know, all the while; and I never receive except she is present."

John sat abstractedly fingering the various objects on the table; then he opened a drawer in the same mechanical manner.

"Why, Lillie! what's this? what in the world are these?"

"O John! sure enough! well, there is something I was going to ask you about. Danforth used always to be sending me things, you know, before we were married, — flowers and confectionery, and one thing or other; and, since I have been here now, he has done the same, and I really didn't know what to do about it. You know I didn't want to quarrel with him, or get his ill-will; he's a high-spirited fellow, and a man one doesn't want for an enemy; so I have just passed it over easy as I could."

"But, Lillie, a box of cigarettes! — of course, they can be of no use to you."

"Of course: they are only a sort of curiosity that he imports from Spain with his cigars."

"I've a great mind to send them back to him myself," said John.

"Oh, don't, John! why, how it would look! as if you were angry, or thought he meant something wrong. No; I'll contrive a way to give 'em back without offending him. I am up to all such little ways."

"Come, now," she added, "don't let's be cross just the little time you have to stay with me. I do wish our house were not all torn up, so that I could go home with you, and leave Newport and all its bothers behind."

"Well, Lillie, you could go, and stay with me at Gracie's," said John, brightening at this proposition.

"Dear Gracie, — so she has got a house all to herself; how I shall miss her! but, really, John, I think she will be happier. Since you would insist on revolutionizing our house, you know " —

"But, Lillie, it was to please you."

"Oh, I know it! but you know I begged you not to. Well, John, I don't think I should like to go in and settle down on Grace; perhaps, as I am here, and the sea-air and bathing strengthens me so, we may as well put it through. I will come home as soon as the house is done."

"But perhaps you would want to go with me to New York to select the furniture?"

"Oh, the artist does all that! Charlie Ferrola will give his orders to Simon & Sauls, and they will do every thing up complete. It's the way they all do — saves lots of trouble."

John went home, after three days spent in Newport, feeling that Lillie was somehow an injured fair one, and that the envious world bore down always on beauty and prosperity.

But incidentally he heard and overheard much that made him uneasy. He heard her admired as a "bully" girl, a "fast one;" he heard of her smoking, he overheard something about "painting."

The time was that John thought Lillie an embryo angel, — an angel a little bewildered and gone astray, and with wings a trifle the worse for the world's wear, — but essentially an angel of the same nature with his own revered mother.

Gradually the mercury had been falling in the tube of his estimation. He had given up the angel; and now to himself he called her "a silly little pussy," but he did it with a smile. It was such a neat, white, graceful pussy; and all his own pussy too, and purred and rubbed its little head on no coat-sleeve but his, — of that he was certain. Only a bit silly. She would still *fib* a little, John feared, especially when he looked back to the chapter about her age, — and then, perhaps, about the cigarettes.

Well, she might, perhaps, in a wild, excited hour, have smoked *one or two*, just for fun, and the thing had been exaggerated. She had promised fairly to return those cigarettes, — he dared not say to himself that he feared she would not. He kept saying to himself that she would. It was necessary to say this often to make himself believe it.

As to painting — well, John didn't like to ask her, because, what if she shouldn't tell him the truth? And, if she did paint, was it so great a sin, poor little thing? he would watch, and bring her out of it. After all, when the house was all finished and arranged, and he got her back from Newport, there would be a long, quiet, domestic winter at Springdale; and they would get up their reading-circles, and he would set her to improving her mind, and gradually the vision of this empty, fashionable life would die out of her horizon, and she would come into his ways of thinking and doing.

But, after all, John managed to be proud of her. When he read in the columns of "The Herald" the account of the Splandangerous ball in Newport, and of the entrancingly beautiful Mrs. J. S., who appeared in a radiant dress of silvery gauze made *à la nuage*, &c., &c., John was rather pleased than otherwise. Lillie danced till daylight, — it showed that she must be getting back her strength, — and she was voted the belle of the scene. Who wouldn't take the comfort that is to be got in any thing? John owned this fashionable meteor, — why shouldn't he rejoice in it?

Two years ago, had anybody told him that one day he should have a wife that told fibs, and painted, and smoked cigarettes, and danced all night at Newport, and yet that he should love her, and be proud of her, he would have said, Is thy servant a dog? He was then a considerate, thoughtful John, serious and careful in his life-plans; and the wife that was to be his companion was something celestial. But so it is. By degrees, we accommodate ourselves to the actual and existing. To all intents and purposes, for us it is the inevitable.

CHAPTER XII.

HOME À LA POMPADOUR.

WELL, Lillie came back at last; and John conducted her over the transformed Seymour mansion, where literally old things had passed away, and all things become new.

There was not a relic of the past. The house was furbished and resplendent — it was gilded — it was frescoed — it was à la Pompadour, and à la Louis Quinze and Louis Quatorze, and à la every thing Frenchy and pretty, and gay and glistening. For, though the parlors at first were the only apartments contemplated in this *renaissance*, yet it came to pass that the parlors, when all tricked out, cast such invidious reflections on the chambers that the chambers felt themselves old and rubbishy, and prayed and stretched out hands of imploration to have something done for *them!*

So the spare chamber was first included in the glorification programme; but, when the spare chamber was once made into a Pompadour pavilion, it so flouted and despised the other old-fashioned Yankee chambers, that they were ready to die with envy; and, in short, there was no way to produce a sense of artistic unity, peace, and quietness, but to do the whole thing over, which was done triumphantly.

The French Emperor, Louis Napoleon, who was a shrewd sort of a man in his day and way, used to talk a great deal about the "logic of events;" which language, being interpreted, my dear gentlemen, means a good deal in domestic life. It means, for instance, that when you drive the first nail, or tear down the first board, in the way of alteration of an old house, you will have to make over every room and corner in it, and pay as much again for it as if you built a new one.

John was able to sympathize with Lillie in her childish delight in the new house, because he *loved* her, and was able to put himself and his own wishes out of the question for her sake; but, when all the bills connected with this change came in, he had emotions with which Lillie could not sympathize: first, because she knew nothing about figures, and was resolved never to know any thing; and, like all people who know nothing about them, she cared nothing; — and, second, because she did *not* love John.

Now, the truth is, Lillie would have been quite astonished to have been told this. She, and many other women, suppose that they love their husbands, when, unfortunately, they have not the beginning of an idea what love is. Let me explain it to you, my dear lady. Loving to be admired by a man, loving to be petted by him, loving to be caressed by him, and loving to be praised by him, is not loving a man. All these may be when a woman has no power of loving at all, — they may all be simply because she loves herself, and loves to be flattered, praised, caressed, coaxed; as a cat likes to be coaxed and stroked, and fed with cream, and have a warm corner.

But all this *is not love.* It may exist, to be sure, where there *is* love; it generally does. But it may also exist where there is no love. Love, my dear ladies, is *self-sacrifice;* it is a life out of self and in another. Its very essence is the preferring of the comfort, the ease, the wishes of another to one's own, *for the* love we bear them. Love is giving, and not receiving. Love is not a sheet of blotting-paper or a sponge, sucking in every thing to itself; it is an out-springing fountain, giving from itself. Love's motto has been dropped in this world as a chance gem of great price by the loveliest, the fairest, the purest, the strongest of Lovers that ever trod this mortal earth, of whom it is recorded that He said, "It is more blessed to give than to receive." Now, in love, there are ten receivers to one giver. There are ten persons in this world who like to be loved and love love, where there is one who knows *how to love.* That, O my dear ladies, is a nobler attainment than all your French and music and dancing. You may lose the very power of it by smothering it under a load of early self-indulgence. By living just as you are all wanting to live, — living to be petted, to be flattered, to be admired, to be praised, to have your own way, and to do only that which is easy and agreeable,—you may lose the power of self-denial and self-sacrifice; you may lose the power of loving nobly and worthily, and become a mere sheet of blotting-paper all your life.

You will please to observe that, in all the married life of these two, as thus far told, all the accommodations, compliances, changes, have been made by John for Lillie.

He has been, step by step, giving up to her his ideal of life, and trying, as far as so different a nature can, to accommodate his to hers; and she accepts all this as her right and due.

She sees no particular cause of gratitude in it,—it is what she expected when she married. Her own specialty, the thing which she has always cultivated, is to get that sort of power over man, by which she can carry her own points and purposes, and make him flexible to her will; nor does a suspicion of the utter worthlessness and selfishness of such a life ever darken the horizon of her thoughts.

John's bills were graver than he expected. It is true he was rich; but riches is a relative term. As related to the style of living hitherto practised in his establishment, John's income was princely, and left a large balance to be devoted to works of general benevolence; but he perceived that, in this year, that balance would be all absorbed; and this troubled him.

Then, again, his establishment being now given up by his sister must be reorganized, with Lillie at its head; and Lillie declared in the outset that she could not, and would not, take any trouble about any thing.

"John would have to get servants; and the servants would have to see to things:" she "was resolved, for one thing, that she wasn't going to be a slave to house-keeping."

By great pains and importunity, and an offer of high wages, Grace and John retained Bridget in the establishment, and secured from New York a seamstress and a waitress, and other members to make out a domestic staff.

This sisterhood were from the isle of Erin, and not an unfavorable specimen of that important portion of our domestic life. They were quick-witted, well-versed in a certain degree of household and domestic skill, guided in well-doing more by impulsive good feeling than by any very enlightened principle. The dominant idea with them all appeared to be, that they were living in the house of a millionnaire, where money flowed through the establishment in a golden stream, out of which all might drink freely and rejoicingly, with no questions asked. Mrs. Lillie concerned herself only with results, and paid no attention to ways and means. She wanted a dainty and generous table to be spread for her, at all proper hours, with every pleasing and agreeable variety; to which she should come as she would to the table of a boarding-house, without troubling her head where any thing came from or went to. Bridget, having been for some years under the training and surveillance of Grace Seymour, was more than usually competent as cook and provider; but Bridget had abundance of the Irish astuteness, which led her to feel the genius of circumstances, and to shape her course accordingly.

With Grace, she had been accurate, saving, and economical; for Miss Grace was so. Bridget had felt, under her sway, the beauty of that economy which saves because saving is in itself so fitting and so respectable; and because, in this way, a power for a wise generosity is accumulated. She was sympathetic with the ruling spirit of the establishment.

But, under the new mistress, Bridget declined in virtue. The announcement that the mistress of a family isn't going to give herself any trouble, nor bother her head with care about any thing, is one the influence of which is felt downward in every department. Why should Bridget give herself any trouble to save and economize for a mistress who took none for herself? She had worked hard all her life, why not take it easy? And it was so much easier to send daily a basket of cold victuals to her cousin on Vine Street than to contrive ways of making the most of things, that Bridget felt perfectly justified in doing it. If, once in a while, a little tea and a paper of sugar found their way into the same basket, who would ever miss it?

The seamstress was an elegant lady. She kept all Lillie's dresses and laces and wardrobe, and had something ready for her to put on when she changed her toilet every day. If this very fine lady wore her

mistress's skirts and sashes, and laces and jewelry, on
the sly, to evening parties among the upper servant
circles of Springdale, who was to know it? Mrs. John
Seymour knew nothing about where her things were,
nor what was their condition, and never wanted to
trouble herself to inquire.

It may therefore be inferred that when John began
to settle up accounts, and look into financial matters,
they seemed to him not to be going exactly in the
most promising way.

He thought he would give Lillie a little practical
insight into his business, — show her exactly what his
income was, and make some estimates of his expenses,
just that she might have some little idea how things
were going.

So John, with great care, prepared a nice little
account-book, prefaced by a table of figures, showing
the income of the Spindlewood property, and the income
of his law business, and his income from other sources.
Against this, he placed the necessary out-goes of his
business, and showed what balance might be left. Then
he showed what had hitherto been spent for various
benevolent purposes connected with the schools and
his establishments at Spindlewood. He showed what
had been the bills for the refitting of the house, and
what were now the running current expenses of the
family.

He hoped that he had made all these so plain and
simple, that Lillie might easily be made to understand
them, and that thus some clear financial boundaries

might appear in her mind. Then he seized a favorable hour, and produced his book.

"Lillie," he said, "I want to make you understand a little about our expenditures and income."

"Oh, dreadful, John! don't, pray! I never had any head for things of that kind."

"But, Lillie, *please* let me show you," persisted John. "I've made it just as simple as can be."

"I never had the least head for figures."

"O John! now—I just—can't—there now! Don't bring that book now; it'll just make me low-spirited and cross. I never had the least head for figures;

mamma always said so; and if there *is* any thing
that seems to me perfectly dreadful, it is accounts. I
don't think it's any of a woman's business—it's all
man's work, and men have got to see to it. Now,
please don't," she added, coming to him coaxingly,
and putting her arm round his neck.

"But, you see, Lillie," John persevered, in a pleading
tone,—"you see, all these alterations that have been
made in the house have involved very serious expenses;
and then, too, we are living at a very different rate
of expense from what we ever lived before"—

"There it is, John! Now, you oughtn't to reproach
me with it; for you know it was your own idea. I didn't
want the alterations made; but you would insist on it.
I didn't think it was best; but you would have them."

"But, Lillie, it was all because you wanted them."

"Well, I dare say; but I shouldn't have wanted
them if I thought it was going to bring in all this
bother and trouble, and make me have to look over old
accounts, and all such things. I'd rather never have
had any thing!" And here Lillie began to cry.

"Come, now, my darling, do be a sensible woman,
and not act like a baby."

"There, John! it's just as I knew it would be; I
always said you wanted a different sort of a woman for
a wife. Now, you knew when you took me that I
wasn't in the least strong-minded or sensible, but a
poor little helpless thing; and you are beginning to
get tired of me already. You wish you had married a
woman like Grace, I know you do."

"Lillie, how silly! Please do listen, now. You have no idea how simple and easy what I want to explain to you is."

"Well, John, I can't to-night, anyhow, because I have a headache. Just this talk has got my head to thumping so,—it's really dreadful! and I'm so low-spirited! I do wish you had a wife that would suit you better." And forthwith Mrs. Lillie dissolved in tears; and John stroked her head, and petted her, and called her a nice little pussy, and begged her pardon for being so rough with her, and, in short, acted like a fool generally.

"If that woman was *my* wife now," I fancy I hear some youth with a promising moustache remark, "I'd make her behave!"

Well, sir, supposing she was your wife, what are you going to do about it?

What are you going to do when accounts give your wife a sick headache, so that she cannot possibly attend to them? Are you going to enact the Blue Beard, and rage and storm, and threaten to cut her head off? What good would that do? Cutting off a wrong little head would not turn it into a right one. An ancient proverb significantly remarks, "You can't have more of a cat than her skin,"—and no amount of fuming and storming can make any thing more of a woman than she is. *Such* as your wife is, sir, you must take her, and make the best of it. Perhaps you want your own way. Don't you wish you could get it?

But didn't she promise to obey? Didn't she? Of

course. Then why is it that I must be all the while yielding points, and she never? Well, sir, that is for you to settle. The marriage service gives you authority; so does the law of the land. John could lock up Mrs. Lillie till she learned her lessons; he could do any of twenty other things that no gentleman would ever think of doing, and the law would support him in it. But, because John is a gentleman, and not Paddy from Cork, he strokes his wife's head, and submits.

We understand that our brethren, the Methodists, have recently decided to leave the word "obey" out of the marriage-service. Our friends are, as all the world knows, a most wise and prudent denomination, and guided by a very practical sense in their arrangements. If they have left the word "obey" out, it is because they have concluded that it does no good to put it in, — a decision that John's experience would go a long way to justify.

CHAPTER XIII.

JOHN'S BIRTHDAY.

"MY dear Lillie," quoth John one morning, "next week Wednesday is my birthday."

"Is it? How charming! What shall we do?"

"Well, Lillie, it has always been our custom — Grace's and mine — to give a grand *fête* here to all our work-people. We invite them all over *en masse*, and have the house and grounds all open, and devote ourselves to giving them a good time."

Lillie's countenance fell.

"Now, really, John, how trying! what shall we do? You don't really propose to bring all those low, dirty, little factory children in Spindlewood through our elegant new house? Just look at that satin furniture, and think what it will be when a whole parcel of freckled, tow-headed, snubby-nosed children have eaten bread and butter and doughnuts over it! Now, John, there is reason in all things; *this* house is not made for a missionary asylum."

John, thus admonished, looked at his house, and was fain to admit that there was the usual amount of that

good, selfish, hard grit — called common sense — in
Lillie's remarks.

Rooms have their atmosphere, their necessities, their
artistic proprieties. Apartments *à la* Louis Quatorze
represent the ideas and the sympathies of a period
when the rich lived by themselves in luxury, and the
poor were trodden down in the gutter; when there was
only aristocratic contempt and domination on one side,
and servility and smothered curses on the other. With
the change of the apartments to the style of that past
era, seemed to come its maxims and morals, as artisti-
cally indicated for its completeness. So John walked
up and down in his Louis Quinze *salon*, and into his
Pompadour *boudoir*, and out again into the Louis
Quatorze dining-rooms, and reflected. He had had
many reflections in those apartments before. Of all ill-
adapted and unsuitable pieces of furniture in them, he
had always felt himself the most unsuitable and ill-
adapted. He had never felt at home in them. He
never felt like lolling at ease on any of those elegant
sofas, as of old he used to cast himself into the motherly
arms of the great chintz one that filled the recess. His
Lillie, with her smart paraphernalia of hoops and puffs
and ruffles and pinkings and bows, seemed a perfectly
natural and indigenous production there; but he himself seemed always to be out of place. His Lillie might
have been any of Balzac's charming duchesses, with
their "thirty-seven thousand ways of saying 'Yes;'"
but, as to himself, he must have been taken for her
steward or gardener, who had accidentally strayed in,

and was fraying her satin surroundings with rough coats and heavy boots. There was not, in fact, in all the reorganized house, a place where he felt *himself* to be at all the proper thing; nowhere where he could lounge, and read his newspaper, without a feeling of impropriety; nowhere that he could indulge in any of the slight Hottentot-isms wherein unrenewed male nature delights, — without a feeling of rebuke.

John had not philosophized on the causes of this. He knew, in a general and unconfessed way, that he was not comfortable in his new arrangements; but he supposed it was his own fault. He had fallen into rusty, old-fashioned, bachelor ways; and, like other things that are not agreeable to the natural man, he supposed his trim, resplendent, genteel house was good for him, and that he ought to like it, and by grace should attain to liking it, if he only tried long enough.

Only he took long rests every day while he went to Grace's, on Elm Street, and stretched himself on the old sofa, and sat in his mother's old arm-chair, and told Grace how very elegant their house was, and how much taste the architect had shown, and how much Lillie was delighted with it.

But this silent walk of John's, up and down his brilliant apartments, opened his eyes to another troublesome prospect. He was a Christian man, with a high aim and ideal in life. He believed in the Sermon on the Mount, and other radical preaching of that nature; and he was a very honest man, and hated humbug in every shape. Nothing seemed meaner to him than to profess a sham. But it began in a cloudy way to appear to him that there is a manner of arranging one's houses that makes it difficult — yes, well-nigh impossible — to act out in them any of the brotherhood principles of those discourses.

There are houses where the self-respecting poor, or the honest laboring man and woman, cannot be made to enter or to feel at home. They are made for the selfish luxury of the privileged few. Then John reflected, uneasily, that this change in his house had absorbed that whole balance which usually remained on his accounts to be devoted to benevolent purposes, and with which this year he had proposed to erect a reading-room for his work-people.

"Lillie," said John, as he walked uneasily up and down, "I wish you would try to help me in this thing. I always have done it, — my father and mother did it before me, — and I don't want all of a sudden to depart from it. It may seem a little thing, but it does a great deal of good. It produces kind feeling; it refines and educates and softens them."

"Oh, well, John! if you say so, I must, I suppose," said Lillie, with a sigh. "I can have the carpets and furniture all covered, I suppose; it'll be no end of trouble, but I'll try. But I must say, I think all this kind of petting of the working-classes does no sort of good; it only makes them uppish and exacting: you never get any gratitude for it."

"But you know, dearie, what is said about doing good, 'hoping for nothing again,'" said John.

"Now, John, please don't preach, of all things. Haven't I told you that I'll try my best? I am going to,—I'll work with all my strength,—you know that isn't much,—but I shall exert myself to the utmost if you say so."

"My dear, I don't want you to injure yourself!"

"Oh! I don't mind," said Lillie, with the air of a martyr. "The servants, I suppose, will make a fuss about it; and I shouldn't wonder if it was the means of sending them every one off in a body, and leaving me without any help in the house, just as the Follingsbees and the Simpkinses are coming to visit us."

"I didn't know that you had invited the Follingsbees and Simpkinses," said John.

"Didn't I tell you? I meant to," said Mrs. Lillie, innocently.

"I don't like those Follingsbees, Lillie. He is a man I have no respect for; he is one of those shoddy upstarts, not at all our sort of folks. I'm sorry you asked him."

"But his wife is my particular friend," said Lillie, "and they were very polite to mamma and me at Newport; and we really owe them some attention."

"Well, Lillie, since you have asked them, I will be polite to them; and I will try and do every thing to save you care in this entertainment. I'll speak to Bridget myself; she knows our ways, and has been used to managing."

And so, as John was greatly beloved by Bridget, and as all the domestic staff had the true Irish fealty to the

man of the house, and would run themselves off their
feet in his service any day, — it came to pass that the
fête was holden, as of yore, in the grounds. Grace was
there and helped, and so were Letitia and Rose Ferguson; and all passed off better than could be expected.
But John did not enjoy it. He felt all the while that
he was dragging Lillie as a thousand-pound weight
after him; and he inly resolved that, once out of that
day's festival, he would never try to have it again.

Lillie went to bed with sick headache, and lay two
days after it, during which she cried and lamented in-
cessantly. She "knew she was not the wife for John;"
she "always told him he wouldn't be satisfied with her,
and now she saw he wasn't; but she had tried her very
best, and now it was cruel to think she should not succeed any better."

"My dearest child," said John, who, to say the truth,
was beginning to find this thing less charming than it
used to be, "I *am* satisfied. I am much obliged to
you. I'm sure you have done all that could be asked."

"Well, I'm sure I hope those folks of yours were
pleased," quoth Lillie, as she lay looking like a martyr,
with a cloth wet in ice-water bound round her head.
"They ought to be; they have left grease-spots all over
the sofa in my boudoir, from one end to the other; and
cake and raisins have been trodden into the carpets;
and the turf around the oval is all cut up; and they
have broken my little Diana; and such a din as there
was! — oh, me! it makes my head ache to think of it."

"Never mind, Lillie, I'll see to it, and set it all right."

"No, you can't. One of the children broke that
model of the Leaning Tower too. I found it. You
can't teach such children to let things alone. Oh, dear
me! my head!"

"Oh, me! it makes my head ache to think of it."

"There, there, pussy! only don't worry," said John,
in soothing tones.

"Don't think me horrid, *please* don't," said Lillie, pit-
eously. "I did try to have things go right; didn't I?"

"Certainly you did, dearie; so don't worry. I'll get
all the spots taken out, and all the things mended, and
make every thing right."

So John called Rosa, on his way downstairs. "Show me the sofa that they spoiled," said he.

"Sofa?" said Rosa.

"Yes; I understand the children greased the sofa in Mrs. Seymour's boudoir."

"Oh, dear, no! nothing of the sort; I've been putting every thing to rights in all the rooms, and they look beautifully."

"Didn't they break something?"

"Oh, no, nothing! The little things were good as could be."

"That Leaning Tower, and that little Diana," suggested John.

"Oh, dear me, no! I broke those a month ago, and showed them to Mrs. Seymour, and promised to mend them. Oh! she knows all about that."

"Ah!" said John, "I didn't know that. Well, Rosa, put every thing up nicely, and divide this money among the girls for extra trouble," he added, slipping a bill into her hand.

"I'm sure there's no trouble," said Rosa. "We all enjoyed it; and I believe everybody did; only I'm sorry it was too much for Mrs. Seymour; she is very delicate."

"Yes, she is," said John, as he turned away, drawing a long, slow sigh.

That long, slow sigh had become a frequent and unconscious occurrence with him of late. When our ideals are sick unto death; when they are slowly dying and

passing away from us, we sigh thus. John said to himself softly,—no matter what; but he felt the pang of
knowing again what he had known so often of late,
that his Lillie's word was not golden. What she said
would not bear close examination. Therefore, why
examine?

"Evidently, she is determined that this thing shall
not go on," said John. " Well, I shall never try again;
it's of no use;" and John went up to his sister's, and
threw himself down upon the old chintz sofa as if it had
been his mother's bosom. His sister sat there, sewing.
The sun came twinkling through a rustic frame-work of
ivy which it had been the pride of her heart to arrange
the week before. All the old family pictures and heir-
looms, and sketches and pencillings, were arranged in
the most charming way, so that her rooms seemed a
reproduction of the old home.

"Hang it all!" said John, with a great flounce as he
turned over on the sofa. "I'm not up to par this
morning."

Now, Grace had that perfect intuitive knowledge of
just what the matter was with her brother, that women always have who have grown up in intimacy with
a man. These fine female eyes see farther between the
rough cracks and ridges of the oak bark of manhood
than men themselves. Nothing would have been easier,
had Grace been a jealous *exigeante* woman, than to have
passed a fine probe of sisterly inquiry into the weak
places where the ties between John and Lillie were
growing slack, and untied and loosened them more and

more. She could have done it so tenderly, so conscientiously, so pityingly, — encouraging John to talk and to complain, and taking part with him, — till there should come to be two parties in the family, the brother and sister against the wife.

How strong the temptation was, those may feel who reflect that this one subject caused an almost total eclipse of the life-long habit of confidence which had existed between Grace and her brother, and that her brother was her life and her world.

But Grace was one of those women formed under the kindly severe discipline of Puritan New England, to act not from blind impulse or instinct, but from high principle. The habit of self-examination and self-inspection, for which the religious teaching of New England has been peculiar, produced a race of women who rose superior to those mere feminine caprices and impulses which often hurry very generous and kindly-natured persons into ungenerous and dishonorable conduct. Grace had been trained, by a father and mother whose marriage union was an ideal of mutual love, honor, and respect, to feel that marriage was the holiest and most awful of obligations. To her, the idea of a husband or a wife betraying each other's weaknesses or faults by complaints to a third party seemed something sacrilegious; and she used all her womanly tact and skill to prevent any conversation that might lead to such a result.

"Lillie is entirely knocked up by the affair yesterday; she had a terrible headache this morning," said John.

"Poor child! She is a delicate little thing," said Grace.

"She couldn't have had any labor," continued John, "for I saw to every thing and provided every thing myself; and Bridget and Rosa and all the girls entered into it with real spirit, and Lillie did the best she could, poor girl! but I could see all the time she was worrying about her new fizgigs and folderols in the house. Hang it! I wish they were all in the Red Sea!" burst out John, glad to find something to vent himself upon. "If I had known that making the house over was going to be such a restraint on a fellow, I would never have done it."

"Oh, well! never mind that now," said Grace. "Your house will get rubbed down by and by, and the new gloss taken off; and so will your wife, and you will all be cosey and easy as an old shoe. Young mistresses, you see, have nerves all over their house at first. They tremble at every dent in their furniture, and wink when you come near it, as if you were going to hit it a blow; but that wears off in time, and they they learn to take it easy."

John looked relieved; but after a minute broke out again:—

"I say, Gracie, Lillie has gone and invited the Simpkinses and the Follingsbees here this fall. Just think of it!"

"Well, I suppose you expect your wife to have the right of inviting her company," said Grace.

"But, you know, Gracie, they are not at all our sort

of folks," said John. "None of our set would ever think of visiting them, and it 'll seem so odd to see them here. Follingsbee is a vulgar sharper, who has made his money out of our country by dishonest contracts during the war. I don't know much about his wife. Lillie says she is her intimate friend."

"Oh, well, John! we must get over it in the quietest way possible. It wouldn't be handsome not to make the agreeable to your wife's company; and if you don't like the quality of it, why, you are a good deal nearer to her than any one else can be, — you can gradually detach her from them."

"Then you think I ought to put a good face on their coming?" said John, with a sigh of relief.

"Oh, certainly! of course. What else can you do? It's one of the things to be expected with a young wife."

"And do you think the Wilcoxes and the Fergusons and the rest of our set will be civil?"

"Why, of course they will," said Grace. "Rose and Letitia will, certainly; and the others will follow suit. After all, John, perhaps we old families, as we call ourselves, are a little bit pharisaical and self-righteous, and too apt to thank God that we are not as other men are. It 'll do us good to be obliged to come a little out of our crinkles."

"It isn't any old family feeling about Follingsbee," said John. "But I feel that that man deserves to be in State's prison much more than many a poor dog that is there now."

"And that may be true of many another, even in the selectest circles of good society," said Grace; "but we are not called on to play Providence, nor pronounce judgments. The common courtesies of life do not commit us one way or the other. The Lord himself does not express his opinion of the wicked, but allows all an equal share in his kindliness."

"Well, Gracie, you are right; and I'll constrain myself to do the thing handsomely," said John.

"The thing with you men," said Grace, "is, that you want your wives to see with your eyes, all in a minute, what has got to come with years and intimacy, and the gradual growing closer and closer together. The husband and wife, of themselves, drop many friendships and associations that at first were mutually distasteful, simply because their tastes have grown insensibly to be the same."

John hoped it would be so with himself and Lillie; for he was still very much in love with her; and it comforted him to have Grace speak so cheerfully, as if it were possible.

"You think Lillie will grow into our ways by and by?"—he said inquiringly.

"Well, if we have patience, and give her time. You know, John, that you knew when you took her that she had not been brought up in our ways of living and thinking. Lillie comes from an entirely different set of people from any we are accustomed to; but a man must face all the consequences of his marriage honestly and honorably."

"I know it," said John, with a sigh. "I say, Gracie, do you think the Fergusons like Lillie? I want her to be intimate with them."

"Well, I think they admire her," said Grace, evasively, "and feel disposed to be as intimate as she will let them."

"Because," said John, "Rose Ferguson is such a splendid girl; she is so strong, and so generous, and so perfectly true and reliable, — it would be the joy of my heart if Lillie would choose her for a friend."

"Then, pray don't tell her so," said Grace, earnestly; "and don't praise her to Lillie, — and, above all things, never hold her up as a pattern, unless you want your wife to hate her."

John opened his eyes very wide.

"So!" said he, slowly, "I never thought of that. You think she would be jealous?" and John smiled, as men do at the idea that their wives may be jealous, not disliking it on the whole.

"I know *I* shouldn't be in much charity with a woman my husband proposed to me as a model; that is to say, supposing I had one," said Grace.

"That reminds me," said John, suddenly rising up from the sofa. "Do you know, Gracie, that Colonel Sydenham has come back from his cruise?"

"I had heard of it," said Grace, quietly. "Now, John, don't interrupt me. I'm just going to turn this corner, and must count, — 'one, two, three, four, five, six,'" —

John looked at his sister. "How handsome she looks when her cheeks have that color!" he thought. "I wonder if there ever was any thing in that affair between them."

CHAPTER XIV.

A GREAT MORAL CONFLICT.

"NOW, John dear, I have something very particular that I want you to promise me," said Mrs. Lillie, a day or two after the scenes last recorded. Our Lillie had recovered her spirits, and got over her headache, and had come down and done her best to be delightful; and when a very pretty woman, who has all her life studied the art of pleasing, does that, she generally succeeds.

John thought to himself he "didn't care *what* she was, he loved her;" and that she certainly was the prettiest, most bewitching little creature on earth. He flung his sighs and his doubts and fears to the wind, and suffered himself to be coaxed, and cajoled, and led captive, in the most amiable manner possible.

His fair one had a point to carry,—a point that instinct told her was to be managed with great adroitness.

"Well," said John, over his newspaper, "what is this something so very particular?"

"First, sir, put down that paper, and listen to me," said Mrs. Lillie, coming up and seating herself on his knee, and sweeping down the offending paper with an air of authority.

"Yes 'm," said John, submissively. "Let's see, — how was that in the marriage service? I promised to obey, didn't I?"

"Of course you did; that service is always interpreted by contraries, — ever since Eve made Adam mind her in the beginning," said Mrs. Lillie, laughing.

"And got things into a pretty mess in that way," said John; "but come, now, what is it?"

"Well, John, you know the Follingsbees are coming next week?"

"I know it," said John, looking amiable and conciliatory.

"Well, dear, there are some things about our establishment that are not just as I should feel pleased to receive them to."

"Ah!" said John; "why, Lillie, I thought we were fine as a fiddle, from the top of the house to the bottom."

"Oh! it's not the house; the house is splendid. I shouldn't be in the least ashamed to show it to anybody; but about the table arrangements."

"Now, really, Lillie, what can one have more than real old china and heavy silver plate? I rather pique myself on that; I think it has quite a good, rich, solid old air."

"Well, John, to say the truth, why do we never have any wine? I don't care for it, — I never drink it; but the decanters, and the different colored glasses, and all

the apparatus, are such an adornment; and then the
Follingsbees are such judges of wine.   He imports his
own from Spain."

John's face had been hardening down into a firm,
decided look, while Lillie, stroking his whiskers and
playing with his collar, went on with this address.

At last he said, "Lillie, I have done almost every
thing you ever asked; but this one thing I cannot do,—
it is a matter of principle.   I never drink wine, never
have it on my table, never give it, because I have
pledged myself not to do it."

"Now, John, here is some more of your Quixotism,
isn't it?"

"Well, Lillie, I suppose you will call it so," said
John; "but listen to me patiently.   My father and I
labored for a long time to root out drinking from
our village at Spindlewood.   It seemed, for the time, as
if it would be the destruction of every thing there.
The fact was, there was rum in every family; the
parents took it daily, the children learned to love
and long after it, by seeing the parents, and drinking
little sweetened remains at the bottoms of tumblers.
There were, every year, families broken up and destroyed, and fine fellows going to the very devil, with
this thing; and so we made a movement to form a
temperance society.   I paid lecturers, and finally lec-
tured myself.   At last they said to me: 'It's all very
well for you rich people, that have twice as fine houses
and twice as many pleasures as we poor folks, to pick on
us for having a little something comfortable to drink in

our houses. If we could afford your fine nice wines, and all that, we wouldn't drink whiskey. You must all have your wine on the table; whiskey is the poor man's wine.'"

"I think," said Lillie, "they were abominably impertinent to talk so to you. I should have told them so."

"Perhaps they thought I was impertinent in talking to them about their private affairs," said John; "but I will tell you what I said to them. I said, 'My good fellows, I will clear my house and table of wine, if you will clear yours of rum.' On this agreement I formed a temperance society; my father and I put our names at the head of the list, and we got every man and boy in Spindlewood. It was a complete victory; and, since then, there hasn't been a more temperate, thrifty set of people in these United States."

"Didn't your mother object?"

"My mother! no, indeed; I wish you could have known my mother. It was no small sacrifice to her and father. Not that they cared a penny for the wine itself; but the poetry and hospitality of the thing, the fine old cheery associations connected with it, were a real sacrifice. But when we told my mother how it was, she never hesitated a moment. All our cellar of fine old wines was sent round as presents to hospitals, except a little that we keep for sickness."

"Well, really!" said Lillie, in a dry, cool tone, "I suppose it was very good of you, perfectly saintlike and all that; but it does seem a great pity. Why couldn't these people take care of themselves? I

don't see why you should go on denying yourself, just
to keep them in the ways of virtue."

"Oh, it's no self-denial now! I'm quite used to
it," said John, cheerily. "I am young and strong, and
just as well as I can be, and don't need wine; in fact,
I never think of it. The Fergusons, who are with
us in the Spindlewood business, took just the same
view of it, and did just as we did; and the Wilcoxes
joined us; in fact, all the good old families of our set
came into it."

"Well, couldn't you, just while the Follingsbees are
here, do differently?"

"No, Lillie; there's my pledge, you see. No: it's
really impossible."

Lillie frowned and looked disconsolate.

"John, I really do think you are selfish; you don't
seem to have any consideration for me at all. It's
going to make it so disagreeable and uncomfortable for
me. The Follingsbees are accustomed to wine every
day. I'm perfectly ashamed not to give it to them."

"Do 'em good to fast awhile, then," said John,
laughing like a hard-hearted monster. "You'll see
they won't suffer materially. Bridget makes splendid
coffee."

"It's a shame to laugh at what troubles me, John.
The Follingsbees are my friends, and of course I want
to treat them handsomely."

"We will treat them just as handsomely as we treat
ourselves," said John, "and mortal man or woman
ought not to ask more."

"I don't care," said Lillie, after a pause. "I hate all these moral movements and society questions. They are always in the way of people's having a good time; and I believe the world would wag just as well as it does, if nobody had ever thought of them. People will call you a real muff, John."

"How very terrible!" said John, laughing. "What shall I do if I am called a muff? and what a jolly little Mrs. Muff you will be!" he said, pinching her cheek.

"You needn't laugh, John," said Lillie, pouting. "You don't know how things look in fashionable circles. The Follingsbees are in the very highest circle. They have lived in Paris, and been invited by the Emperor."

"I haven't much opinion of Americans who live in Paris and are invited by the Emperor," said John. "But, be that as it may, I shall do the best I can for them, and Mr. Young says, 'angels could no more;' so, good-by, puss: I must go to my office; and don't let 's talk about this any more."

And John put on his cap and squared his broad shoulders, and, marching off with a resolute stride, went to his office, and had a most uncomfortable morning of it. You see, my dear friends, that though Nature has set the seal of sovereignty on man, in broad shoulders and bushy beard; though he fortify and incase himself in rough overcoats and heavy boots, and walk with a dashing air, and whistle like a freeman, we all know it is not an easy thing to wage a warfare with a pretty little creature in lace cap and tiny slippers, who has a faculty of looking very pensive and grieved, and making up a sad little mouth, as if her heart were breaking.

John never doubted that he was right, and in the way of duty; and yet, though he braved it out so stoutly with Lillie, and though he marched out from her presence victoriously, as it were, with drums beating and colors flying, yet there was a dismal sinking of heart under it.

"I'm right; I know I am. Of course I can't give up here; it's a matter of principle, of honor," he said over and over to himself. "Perhaps if Lillie had been here I never should have taken such a pledge; but as I have, there's no help for it."

Then he thought of what Lillie had suggested about it's looking niggardly in hospitality, and was angry with himself for feeling uncomfortable. "What do I care what Dick Follingsbee thinks?" said he to himself: "a man that I despise; a cheat, and a swindler, — a man of no principle. Lillie doesn't know the sacrifice it is to me to have such people in my house at all. Hang it all! I wish Lillie was a little more like the women I've been used to, — like Grace and Rose and my mother. But, poor thing, I oughtn't to blame her, after all, for her unfortunate bringing up. But it's so nice to be with women that can understand the grounds you go on. A man never wants to fight a woman. I'd rather give up, hook and line, and let Lillie have her own way in every thing. But then it won't do; a fellow must stop somewhere. Well,

I 'll make it up in being a model of civility to these
confounded people that I wish were in the Red Sea.
Let 's see, I 'll ask Lillie if she don't want to give
a party for them when they come. By George! she
shall have every thing her own way there, — send to
New York for the supper, turn the house topsy-turvy,
illuminate the grounds, and do any thing else she
can think of. Yes, yes, she shall have *carte blanche*
for every thing!"

All which John told Mrs. Lillie when he returned to
dinner and found her enacting the depressed wife in a
most becoming lace cap and wrapper that made her
look like a suffering angel; and the treaty was sealed
with many kisses.

"You shall have *carte blanche*, dearest," he said, "for
every thing but what we were speaking of; and that
will content you, won't it?"

And Lillie, with lingering pensiveness, very gracious-
ly acknowledged that it would; and seemed so touchingly resigned, and made such a merit of her resigna-
tion, that John told her she was an angel; in fact, he
had a sort of indistinct remorseful feeling that he was a
sort of cruel monster to deny her any thing. Lillie had
sense enough to see when she could do a thing, and
when she couldn't. She had given up the case when
John went out in the morning, and so accepted the
treaty of peace with a good degree of cheerfulness; and
she was soon busy discussing the matter. "You see,
we 've been invited everywhere, and haven't given any
thing," she said; "and this will do up our social obli-

gations to everybody here. And then we can show off
our rooms; they really are made to give parties in."

"Yes, so they are," said John, delighted to see her
smile again; "they seem adapted to that, and I don't
doubt you'll make a brilliant affair of it, Lillie."

"Trust me for that, John," said Lillie. I'll show the
Follingsbees that something can be done here in
Springdale as well as in New York." And so the great
question was settled.

CHAPTER XV.

THE FOLLINGSBEES ARRIVE.

The Follingsbees.

NEXT week the Follingsbees alighted, so to speak, from a cloud of glory. They came in their own

11

carriage, and with their own horses; all in silk and
silver, purple and fine linen, "with rings on their
fingers and bells on their toes," as the old song has it.
We pause to caution our readers that this last clause
is to be interpreted metaphorically.

Springdale stood astonished. The quiet, respectable
old town had not seen any thing like it for many a long
day; the ostlers at the hotel talked of it; the boys
followed the carriage, and hung on the slats of the fence
to see the party alight, and said to one another in their
artless vocabulary, "Golly! ain't it bully?"

There was Mr. Dick Follingsbee, with a pair of
waxed, tow-colored moustaches like the French emper-
or's, and ever so much longer. He was a little, thin,
light-colored man, with a yellow complexion and sandy
hair; who, with the appendages aforesaid, looked like
some kind of large insect, with very long *antennæ*.
There was Mrs. Follingsbee, — a tall, handsome, dark-
eyed, dark-haired, dashing woman, French dressed from
the tip of her lace parasol to the toe of her boot.
There was Mademoiselle Thérèse, the French maid, an
inexpressibly fine lady; and there was *la petite* Marie,
Mrs. Follingsbee's three-year-old hopeful, a lean, bright-
eyed little thing, with a great scarlet bow on her back
that made her look like a walking butterfly. On the
whole, the tableau of arrival was so impressive, that
Bridget and Annie, Rosa and all the kitchen cabinet,
were in a breathless state of excitement.

"How do I find you, *ma chère?*" said Mrs. Follingsbee, folding Lillie rapturously to her breast. "I've

been just dying to see you! How lovely every thing looks! Oh, *ciel!* how like dear Paris!" she said, as she was conducted into the parlor, and sunk upon the sofa.

"Pretty well done, too, for America!" said Mr. Follingsbee, gazing round, and settling his collar. Mr. Follingsbee was one of the class of returned travellers who always speak condescendingly of any thing American; as, "so-so," or "tolerable," or "pretty fair,"—a considerateness which goes a long way towards keeping up the spirits of the country.

"I say, Dick," said his lady, "have you seen to the bags and wraps?"

"All right, madam."

"And my basket of medicines and the books?"

"O. K.," replied Dick, sententiously.

"Oh! how often must I tell you not to use those odious slang terms?" said his wife, reprovingly.

"Oh! Mrs. John Seymour knows *me* of old," said Mr. Follingsbee, winking facetiously at Lillie. "We've had many a jolly lark togewner; haven't we, Lill?"

"Certainly we have," said Lillie, affably. "But come, darling," she added to Mrs Follingsbee, "don't you want to be shown your room?"

"Go it, then, my dearie; and I'll toddle up with the fol-de-rols and what-you-may-calls," said the incorrigible Dick. "There, wife, Mrs. John Seymour shall go first, so that you shan't be jealous of her and me. You know we came pretty near being in interesting relations ourselves at one time; didn't we, now?" he said with another wink.

It is said that a thorough-paced naturalist can reconstruct a whole animal from one specimen bone. In like manner, we imagine that, from these few words of dialogue, our expert readers can reconstruct Mr. and Mrs. Follingsbee: he, vulgar, shallow, sharp, keen at a bargain, and utterly without scruples; with a sort of hilarious, animal good nature that was in a state of constant ebullition. He was, as Richard Baxter said of a better man, "always in that state of hilarity that another would be in when he hath taken a cup too much."

Dick Follingsbee began life as a peddler. He was now reputed to be master of untold wealth, kept a yacht and race-horses, ran his own theatre, and patronized the whole world and creation in general with a jocular freedom. Mrs. Follingsbee had been a country girl, with small early advantages, but considerable ambition. She had married Dick Follingsbee, and helped him up in the world, as a clever, ambitious woman may. The last few years she had been spending in Paris, improving her mind and manners in reading Dumas' and Madame George Sand's novels, and availing herself of such outskirt advantages of the court of the Tuileries as industrious, pains-taking Americans, not embarrassed by self-respect, may command.

Mrs. Follingsbee, like many another of our republicans who besieged the purlieus of the late empire, felt that a residence near the court, at a time when every thing good and decent in France was hiding in obscure corners, and every thing *parvenu* was wide awake and active, entitled her to speak as one having authority concerning French character, French manners and customs. This lady assumed the sentimental literary *rôle.* She was always cultivating herself in her own way; that is to say, she was assiduous in what she called keeping up her French.

In the opinion of many of her class of thinkers, French is the key of the kingdom of heaven; and, of course, it is worth one's while to sell all that one has to be possessed of it. Mrs. Follingsbee had not been in the least backward to do this; but, as to getting the golden key, she had not succeeded. She had formed the acquaintance of many disreputable people; she had read French novels and French plays such as no well-bred French woman would suffer in her family; she had lost such innocence and purity of mind as she had to lose, and, after all, had *not* got the French language.

However, there are losses that do not trouble the subject of them, because they bring insensibility. Just as Mrs. Follingsbee's ear was not delicate enough to perceive that her rapid and confident French was not Parisian, so also her conscience and moral sense were not delicate enough to know that she had spent her labor for "that which was not bread." She had only succeeded in acquiring such an air that, on a careless survey, she might have been taken for one of the *demimonde* of Paris; while secretly she imagined herself the fascinating heroine of a French romance.

The friendship between Mrs. Follingsbee and Lillie

was of the most impassioned nature; though, as both
of them were women of a good solid perception in
regard to their own material interests, there were
excellent reasons on both sides for this enthusiasm.

Notwithstanding the immense wealth of the Follingsbees, there were circles to which Mrs. Follingsbee
found it difficult to be admitted. With the usual
human perversity, these, of course, became exactly the
ones, and the only ones, she particularly cared for.
Her ambition was to pass beyond the ranks of the
"shoddy" aristocracy to those of the old-established
families. Now, the Seymours, the Fergusons, and the
Wilcoxes were families of this sort; and none of them
had ever cared to conceal the fact, that they did not
intend to know the Follingsbees. The marriage of
Lillie into the Seymour family was the opening of a
door; and Mrs. Follingsbee had been at Lillie's feet
during her Newport campaign. On the other hand,
Lillie, having taken the sense of the situation at
Springdale, had cast her thoughts forward like a discreet young woman, and perceived in advance of her
a very dull domestic winter, enlivened only by reading-circles and such slow tea-parties as unsophisticated
Springdale found agreeable. The idea of a long visit
to the New-York alhambra of the Follingsbees in the
winter, with balls, parties, unlimited opera-boxes, was
not a thing to be disregarded; and so, when Mrs. Follingsbee "*ma chèred*" Lillie, Lillie "my deared" Mrs.
Follingsbee: and the pair are to be seen at this blessed
moment sitting with their arms tenderly round each

other's waists on a *causeuse* in Mrs. Follingsbee's dressing-room.

"You don't know, *mignonne*," said Mrs. Follingsbee, "how perfectly *ravissante* these apartments are! I'm so glad poor Charlie did them so well for you. I laid my commands on him, poor fellow!"

"Pray, how does your affair with him get on?" said Lillie.

"O dearest! you've no conception what a trial it is to me to keep him in the bounds of reason. He has such struggles of mind about that stupid wife of his. Think of it, my dear! a man like Charlie Ferrola, all poetry, romance, ideality, tied to a woman who thinks of nothing but her children's teeth and bowels, and turns the whole house into a nursery! Oh, I've no patience with such people."

"Well, poor fellow! it's a pity he ever got married," said Lillie.

"Well, it would be all well enough if this sort of woman ever would be reasonable; but they won't. They don't in the least comprehend the necessities of genius. They want to yoke Pegasus to a cart, you see. Now, I understand Charlie perfectly. I could give him that which he needs. I appreciate him. I make a bower of peace and enjoyment for him, where his artistic nature finds the repose it craves."

"And she pitches into him about you," said Lillie, not slow to perceive the true literal rendering of all this.

"Of course, *ma chère*,—tears him, rends him, lacer-

ates his soul; sometimes he comes to me in the most
dreadful states. Really, dear, I have apprehended
something quite awful! I shouldn't in the least be
surprised if he should blow his brains out!"

And Mrs. Follingsbee sighed deeply, gave a glance at
herself in an opposite mirror, and smoothed down a
bow pensively, as the prima donna at the grand opera
generally does when her lover is getting ready to stab
himself.

"Oh! I don't think he's going to kill himself," said
Mrs. Lillie, who, it must be understood, was secretly
somewhat sceptical about the power of her friend's
charms, and looked on this little French romance with
the eye of an outsider: "never you believe that, dearest. These men make dreadful tearings, and shocking
eyes and mouths; but they take pretty good care to
keep in the world, after all. You see, if a man's dead,
there's an end of all things; and I fancy they think of
that before they quite come to any thing decisive."

"*Chère étourdie*," said Mrs. Follingsbee, regarding
Lillie with a pensive smile: "you are just your old self, I
see; you are now at the height of your power, — '*jeune
Madame, un mari qui vous adore*,' ready to put all
things under your feet. How can you feel for a worn,
lonely heart like mine, that sighs for congeniality?"

"Bless me, now," said Lillie, briskly; "you don't tell
me that you're going to be so silly as to get in love
with Charlie yourself! It's all well enough to keep
these fellows on the tragic high ropes; but, if a woman
falls in love herself, there's an end of her power. And,

darling, just think of it: you wouldn't have married that creature if you could; he's poor as a rat, and always will be; these desperately interesting fellows always are. Now you have money without end; and of course you have position; and your husband is a man you can get any thing in the world out of."

"Oh! as to that, I don't complain of Dick," said Mrs. Follingsbee: "he's coarse and vulgar, to be sure, but he never stands in my way, and I never stand in his; and, as you say, he's free about money. But still, darling, sometimes it seems to me such a weary thing to live without sympathy of soul! A marriage without congeniality, *mon Dieu*, what is it? And then the harsh, cold laws of human society prevent any relief. They forbid natures that are made for each other from being to each other what they can be."

"You mean that people will talk about you," said Lillie. "Well, I assure you, dearest, they *will* talk awfully, if you are not very careful. I say this to you frankly, as your friend, you know."

"Ah, *ma petite!* you don't need to tell me that. I *am* careful," said Mrs. Follingsbee. "I am always lecturing Charlie, and showing him that we must keep up *les convenances;* but is it not hard on us poor women to lead always this repressed, secretive life?"

"What made you marry Mr. Follingsbee?" said Lillie, with apparent artlessness.

"Darling, I was but a child. I was ignorant of the mysteries of my own nature, of my capabilities. As Charlie said to me the other day, we never learn what

we are till some congenial soul unlocks the secret **door**
of our hearts. The fact is, dearest, that American society, with its strait-laced, puritanical notions, bears
terribly hard on woman's heart. Poor Charlie! he is
no less one of the victims of society."

"Oh, nonsense!" said Lillie. "You take it too much
to heart. You mustn't mind all these men say. They
are always being desperate and tragic. Charlie has
talked just so to me, time and time again. I understand it all. He talked exactly so to me when he came
to Newport last summer. You must take matters easy,
my dear, — you, with your beauty, and your style, and
your money. Why, you can lead all New York captive! Forty fellows like Charlie are not worth spoiling
one's dinner for. Come, cheer up; positively I shan't
let you be blue, *ma reine.* Let me ring for your maid
to dress you for dinner. *Au revoir.*"

The fact was, that Mrs. Lillie, having formerly set
down this lovely Charlie on the list of her own adorers,
had small sympathy with the sentimental romance of her
friend.

"What a fool she makes of herself!" she thought, as
she contemplated her own sylph-like figure and wonderful freshness of complexion in the glass. "Don't I
know Charlie Ferrola? he wants her to get him into
fashionable life, and knows the way to do it. To think
of that stout, middle-aged party imagining that Charlie
Ferrola's going to die for her charms! it's too funny!
How stout the dear old thing does get, to be sure!"

It will be observed here that our dear Lillie did not

want for perspicacity. There is nothing so absolutely clear-sighted, in certain directions, as selfishness. Entire want of sympathy with others clears up one's vision astonishingly, and enables us to see all the weak points and ridiculous places of our neighbors in the most accurate manner possible.

MR. CHARLIE FERROLA.

As to Mr. Charlie Ferrola, our Lillie was certainly in the right in respect to him. He was one of those blossoms of male humanity that seem as expressly de-s'gned by nature for the ornamentation of ladies' boudoirs, as an Italian greyhound: he had precisely the same graceful, shivery adaptation to live by petting and caresses. His tastes were all so exquisite that it was the most difficult thing in the world to keep him out of misery a moment. He was in a chronic state of disgust with something or other in our lower world from morning till night.

His profession was nominally that of architecture and landscape gardening; but, in point of fact, consisted in telling certain rich, *blasé*, stupid, fashionable people how they could quickest get rid of their money. He ruled despotically in the Follingsbee halls: he bought and rejected pictures and jewelry, ordered and sent off furniture, with the air of an absolute master; amusing himself meanwhile with running a French romance with the handsome mistress of the establishment. As a consequence, he had not only opportunities for much quiet feathering of his own nest, but the *éclat* of always having the use of the Follingsbees' carriages, horses, and opera-boxes, and being the acknowledged and supreme head of fashionable dictation. Ladies sometimes pull caps for such charming individuals, as we have seen in the case of Mrs. Follingsbee and Lillie.

For it is not to be supposed that Mrs. Follingsbee, though she had assumed the gushing style with her young friend, wanted spirit or perception on her part. Her darling Lillie had left a nettle in her bosom which rankled there.

"The vanity of these thin, light, watery blondes!"
she said to herself, as she looked into her own great
dark eyes in the mirror,—"thinking Charlie Ferrola
cares for her! I know just what he thinks of *her*, thank
heaven! Poor thing! Don't you think Mrs. John Seymour has gone off astonishingly since her marriage?"
she said to Thérèse.

" *Mon Dieu, madame, q'oui*," said the obedient tire-
woman, scraping the very back of her throat in her
zeal. "Madame Seymour has the real American
maigreur. These thin women, madame, they have no
substance; there is noting to them. For young girl,
they are charming; but, as woman, they are just noting
at all. Now, you will see, madame, what I tell you.
In a year or two, people shall ask, 'Was she ever handsome?' But *you*, madame, you come to your prime
like great rose! Oh, dere is no comparison of you to
Mrs. John Seymour!"

And Thérèse found her words highly acceptable,
after the·manner of all her tribe, who prophesy smooth
things unto their mistresses.

It may be imagined that the entertaining of Dick
Follingsbee was no small strain on the conjugal endurance of our faithful John; but he was on duty, and
endured without flinching that gentleman's free and
easy jokes and patronizing civilities.

"I do wish, darling, you'd teach that creature not to
call you 'Lillie' in that abominably free manner," he
said to his wife, the first day, after dinner.

"Mercy on us, John! what can I do? All the world

knows that Dick Follingsbee's an oddity; and everybody agrees to take what he says for what it's worth. If I should go to putting on any airs, he'd behave ten times worse than he does: the only way is, to pass it over quietly, and not to seem to notice any thing he says or does. My way is, to smile, and look gracious, and act as if I hadn't heard any thing but what is perfectly proper."

"It's a tremendous infliction, Lillie!"

"Poor man! is it?" said Lillie, putting her arm round his neck, and stroking his whiskers. "Well, now, he's a good man to bear it so well, so he is; and they shan't plague him long. But, John, you must confess Mrs. Follingsbee is nice: poor woman! she is mortified with the way Dick will go on; but she can't do any thing with him."

"Yes, I can get on with her," said John. In fact, John was one of the men so loyal to women that his path of virtue in regard to them always ran down hill. Mrs. Follingsbee was handsome, and had a gift in language, and some considerable tact in adapting herself to her society; and, as she put forth all her powers to win his admiration, she succeeded.

Grace had done her part to assist John in his hospitable intents, by securing the prompt co-operation of the Fergusons. The very first evening after their arrival, old Mrs. Ferguson, with Letitia and Rose, called, not formally but socially, as had always been the custom of the two families. Dick Follingsbee was out, enjoying an evening cigar, — a circumstance on which John secretly congratulated himself as a favorable feature in the case. He felt instinctively a sort of uneasy responsibility for his guests; and, judging the Fergusons by himself, felt that their call was in some sort an act of self-abnegation on his account; and he was anxious to make it as easy as possible. Mrs. Follingsbee was presentable, so he thought; but he dreaded the irrepressible Dick, and had much the same feeling about him that one has on presenting a pet spaniel or pointer in a lady's parlor, — there was no answering for what he might say or do.

The Fergusons were disposed to make themselves most amiable to Mrs. Follingsbee; and, with this intent, Miss Letitia started the subject of her Parisian experiences, as being probably one where she would feel herself especially at home. Mrs. Follingsbee of course expanded in rapturous description, and was quite clever and interesting.

"You must feel quite a difference between that country and this, in regard to facilities of living," said Miss Letitia.

"Ah, indeed! do I not?" said Mrs. Follingsbee, casting up her eyes. "Life here in America is in a state of perfect disorganization."

"We are a young people here, madam," said John. "We haven't had time to organize the smaller conveniences of life."

"Yes, that's what I mean," said Mrs. Follingsbee. "Now, you men don't feel it so very much; but it bears hard on us poor women. Life here in America is perfect slavery to women, — a perfect dead grind. You see there 's no career at all for a married woman in this country, as there is in France. Marriage there opens a brilliant prospect before a girl : it introduces her to the world; it gives her wings. In America, it is clipping her wings, chaining her down, shutting her up, — no more gayety, no more admiration; nothing but cradles and cribs, and bibs and tuckers, little narrowing, wearing, domestic cares, hard, vulgar domestic slaveries: and so our women lose their bloom and health and freshness, and are moped to death."

"I can't see the thing in that light, Mrs. Follingsbee," said old Mrs. Ferguson. "I don't understand this modern talk. I am sure, for one, I can say I have had all the career I wanted ever since I married. You know, dear, when one begins to have children, one's heart goes into them: we find nothing hard that we do for the dear little things. I 've heard that the Parisian ladies never nurse their own babies. From my very heart, I pity them."

"Oh, my dear madam!" said Mrs. Follingsbee, "why insist upon it that a cultivated, intelligent woman shall waste some of the most beautiful years of her life in a mere animal function, that, after all, any healthy peasant can perform better than she? The French are a philosophical nation; and, in Paris, you see, this thing is all systematic: it 's altogether better for the child. It 's taken to the country, and put to nurse with a good strong woman, who makes that her only business. She just lives to be a good animal, you see, and so is a better one than a more intellectual being can be; thus she gives the child a strong constitution, which is the main thing."

"Yes," said Miss Letitia; "I was told, when in Paris, that this system is universal. The dressmaker, who works at so much a day, sends her child out to nurse as certainly as the woman of rank and fashion. There are no babies, as a rule, in French households."

"And you see how good this is for the mother," said Mrs. Follingsbee. "The first year or two of a child's life it is nothing but a little animal; and one person can do for it about as well as another: and all this time, while it is growing physically, the mother has for art, for self-cultivation, for society, and for literature. Of course she keeps her eye on her child, and visits it often enough to know that all goes right with it."

"Yes," said Miss Letitia; "and the same philosophical spirit regulates the education of the child throughout. An American gentleman, who wished to live in Paris, told me that, having searched all over it, he could not accommodate his family, including himself and wife and two children, without taking *two* of the suites that are usually let to one family. The reason, he inferred, was the perfection of the system which keeps the French family reduced in numbers. The babies are out at nurse, sometimes till two, and sometimes till three years of age; and, at seven or eight, the girl goes into a pension, and the boy into a college, till they are ready to be taken out, — the girl to be married, and the

12

boy to enter a profession: so the leisure of parents for literature, art, and society is preserved."

"It seems to me the most perfectly dreary, dreadful way of living I ever heard of," said Mrs. Ferguson, with unwonted energy. "How I pity people who know so little of real happiness!"

"Yet the French are dotingly fond of children," said Mrs. Follingsbee. "It's a national peculiarity; you can see it in all their literature. Don't you remember Victor Hugo's exquisite description of a mother's feelings for a little child in 'Notre Dame de Paris'? I never read any thing more affecting; it's perfectly subduing."

"They can't love their children as I did mine," said Mrs. Ferguson: "it's impossible; and, if that's what's called organizing society, I hope our society in America never will be organized. It can't be that children are well taken care of on that system. I always attended to every thing for my babies *myself;* because I felt God had put them into my hands perfectly helpless; and, if there is any thing difficult or disagreeable in the case, how can I expect to *hire* a woman for money to be faithful in what I cannot do for love?"

"But don't you think, dear madam, that this system of personal devotion to children may be carried too far?" said Mrs. Follingsbee. "Perhaps in France they may go to an extreme; but don't our American women, as a rule, sacrifice themselves too much to their families?"

"*Sacrifice!*" said Mrs. Ferguson. "How can we? Our children are our new life. We live in them a thousand times more than we could in ourselves. No, I think a mother that doesn't take care of her own baby misses the greatest happiness a woman can know. A baby isn't a mere animal; and it is a great and solemn thing to see the coming of an immortal soul into it from day to day. My very happiest hours have been spent with my babies in my arms."

" There may be women constituted so as to enjoy it," said Mrs. Follingsbee; " but you must allow that there is a vast difference among women."

"There certainly is," said Mrs. Ferguson, as she rose with a frigid courtesy, and shortened the call. "My dear girls," said the old lady to her daughters, when they returned home, "I disapprove of that woman. I am very sorry that pretty little Mrs. Seymour has so bad a friend and adviser. Why, the woman talks like a Fejee Islander! Baby a mere animal, to be sure! it puts me out of temper to hear such talk. The woman talks as if she had never heard of such a thing as love in her life, and don't know what it means."

" Oh, well, mamma!" said Rose, "you know we are old-fashioned folks, and not up to modern improvements."

"Well," said Miss Letitia, " I should think that that poor little weird child of Mrs. Follingsbee's, with the great red bow on her back, had been brought up on this system. Yesterday afternoon I saw her in the garden, with that maid of hers, apparently enjoying a free fight. They looked like a pair of goblins, — an old and a young one. I never saw any thing like it."

"What a pity!" said Rose; "for she's a smart, bright little thing; and it's cunning to hear her talk French."

"Well," said Mrs. Ferguson, straightening her back, and sitting up with a grand air: "I am one of eight children that my mother nursed herself at her own breast, and lived to a good honorable old age after it. People called her a handsome woman at sixty: she could ride and walk and dance with the best; and nobody kept up a keener interest in reading or general literature. Her conversation was sought by the most eminent men of the day as something remarkable. She was always with her children: we always knew we had her to run to at any moment; and we were the first thing with her. She lived a happy, loving, useful life; and her children rose up and called her blessed."

"As we do you, dear mamma," said Rose, kissing her: "so don't be oratorical, darling mammy; because we are all of your mind here."

CHAPTER XVI.

MRS. JOHN SEYMOUR'S PARTY, AND WHAT CAME OF IT.

MRS. JOHN SEYMOUR'S party marked an era in the annals of Springdale. Of this, you may be sure, my dear reader, when you consider that it was projected and arranged by Mrs. Lillie, in strict counsel with her friend Mrs. Follingsbee, who had lived in Paris, and been to balls at the Tuileries. Of course, it was a tip-top New-York-Paris party, with all the new, fashionable, unspeakable crinkles and wrinkles, all the high, divine, spick and span new ways of doing things; which, however, like the Eleusinian mysteries, being in their very nature incommunicable except to the elect, must be left to the imagination.

A French *artiste*, whom Mrs. Follingsbee patronized as "my confectioner," came in state to Springdale, with a retinue of appendages and servants sufficient for a circus; took formal possession of the Seymour mansion, and became, for the time being, absolute dictator, as was customary in the old Roman Republic in times of emergency.

Mr. Follingsbee was forward, fussy, and advisory, in

his own peculiar free-and-easy fashion; and Mrs. Follingsbee was instructive and patronizing to the very last degree. Lillie had bewailed in her sympathizing bosom John's unaccountable and most singular moral Quixotism in regard to the wine question, and been comforted by her appreciative discourse. Mrs. Follingsbee had a sort of indefinite faith in French phrases for mending all the broken places in life. A thing said partly in French became at once in her view elucidated, even though the words meant no more than the same in English; so she consoled Lillie as follows:—

"Oh, *ma chère!* I understand perfectly: your husband may be '*un peu borné,*' as they say in Paris, but still '*un homme très respectable,*' (Mrs. Follingsbee here scraped her throat emphatically, just as her French maid did),—a sublime example of the virtues; and let me tell you, darling, you are very fortunate to get such a man. It is not often that a woman can get an establishment like yours, and a good man into the bargain; so, if the goodness is a little *ennuyeuse,* one must put up with it. Then, again, people of old established standing may do about what they like socially: their position is made. People only say, 'Well, that is their way; the Seymours will do so and so.' Now, we have to do twice as much of every thing to make our position, as certain other people do. We might flood our place with champagne and Burgundy, and get all the young fellows drunk, as we generally do; and yet people will call our parties '*bourgeois,*' and yours '*recherché,*' if you give them nothing but tea and biscuit. Now,

there's my Dick: he respects your husband; you can
see he does. In his odious slang way, he says he's
'some,' and 'a brick;' and he's a little anxious to please
him, though he professes not to care for anybody. Now,
Dick has pretty sharp sense, after all, or he'd never
have been just where he is."

Our friend John, during these days preceding the
party, the party itself, and the clearing up after it,
enacted submissively that part of unconditional sur-
render which the master of the house, if well trained,
generally acts on such occasions. He resembled the
prize ox, which is led forth adorned with garlands,
ribbons, and docility, to grace a triumphal procession.
He went where he was told, did as he was bid, marched
to the right, marched to the left, put on gloves and
cravat, and took them off, entirely submissive to the
word of his little general; and exhibited, in short, an
edifying spectacle of that pleasant domestic animal, a
tame husband. He had to make atonement for being
a reformer, and for endeavoring to live like a Christian,
by conceding to his wife all this latitude of indulgence;
and he meant to go through it like a man and a philosopher. To be sure, in his eyes, it was all so much
unutterable bosh and nonsense; and bosh and nonsense
for which he was eventually to settle the bills: but he
armed himself with the patient reflection that all things
have their end in time, — that fireworks and Chinese
lanterns, bands of music and kid gloves, ruffs and puffs,
and pinkings and quillings, and all sorts of unspeakable
eatables with French names, would ere long float down

the stream of time, and leave their record only in a few bad colds and days of indigestion, which also time would mercifully cure.

So John steadied his soul with a view of that comfortable future, when all this fuss should be over, and the coast cleared for something better. Moreover, John found this good result of his patience: that he learned a little something in a Christian way by it. Men of elevated principle and moral honesty often treat themselves to such large slices of contempt and indignation, in regard to the rogues of society, as to forget a common brotherhood of pity. It is sometimes wholesome for such men to be obliged to tolerate a scamp to the extent of exchanging with him the ordinary benevolences of social life.

John, in discharging the duty of a host to Dick Follingsbee, found himself, after a while, looking on him with pity, as a poor creature, like the rich fool in the Gospels, without faith, or love, or prayer; spending life as a moth does,—in vain attempts to burn himself up in the candle, and knowing nothing better. In fact, after a while, the stiff, tow-colored moustache, smart stride, and flippant air of this poor little man struck him somewhere in the region between a smile and a tear; and his enforced hospitality began to wear a tincture of real kindness. There is no less pathos in moral than in physical imbecility.

It is an observable social phenomenon that, when any family in a community makes an advance very greatly ahead of its neighbors in style of living or splendor of entertainments, the fact causes great searchings of spirit in all the region round about, and abundance of talk, wherein the thoughts of many hearts are revealed.

Springdale was a country town, containing a choice knot of the old, respectable, true-blue, Boston-aristocracy families. Two or three of them had winter houses in Beacon Street, and went there, after Christmas, to enjoy the lectures, concerts, and select gayeties of the modern Athens; others, like the Fergusons and Seymours, were in intimate relationship with the same circle.

Now, it is well known that the real old true-blue, Simon-pure, Boston family is one whose claims to be considered "the thing," and the only thing, are somewhat like the claim of apostolic succession in ancient churches. It is easy to see why certain affluent, cultivated, and eminently well-conducted people should be considered "the thing" in their day and generation; but why they should be considered as the "only thing" is the point insoluble to human reason, and to be received by faith alone; also, why certain other people, equally affluent, cultivated, and well-conducted are *not* "the thing" is one of the divine mysteries, about which whoso observes Boston society will do well not too curiously to exercise his reason.

These "true-blue" families, however, have claims to respectability; which make them, on the whole, quite a venerable and pleasurable feature of society in our young, topsy-turvy, American community. Some of

them have family records extending clearly back to the
settlement of Massachusetts Bay; and the family estate
is still on grounds first cleared up by aboriginal settlers.
Being of a Puritan nobility, they have an ancestral
record, affording more legitimate subject of family self-
esteem than most other nobility. Their history runs
back to an ancestry of unworldly faith and prayer and
self-denial, of incorruptible public virtue, sturdy resist-
ance of evil, and pursuit of good.

There is also a literary aroma pervading their circles.
Dim suggestions of "The North American Review," of
"The Dial," of Cambridge, — a sort of vague "*miel-
fleur*" of authorship and poetry, — is supposed to float
in the air around them; and it is generally understood
that in their homes exist tastes and appreciations denied
to less favored regions. Almost every one of them has
its great man, — its father, grandfather, cousin, or great
uncle, who wrote a book, or edited a review, or was a
president of the United States, or minister to England,
whose opinions are referred to by the family in any
discussion, as good Christians quote the Bible.

It is true that, in some few instances, the *pleroma*
of aristocratic dignity undergoes a sort of acetic fer-
mentation, and comes out in ungenial qualities. Now
and then, at a public watering-place, a man or woman
appears no otherwise distinguished than by a remarkable talent for being disagreeable; and it is amusing to
find, on inquiry, that this repulsiveness of demeanor
is entirely on account of belonging to an ancient
family.

Such is the tendency of democracy to a general mingling of elements, that this frigidity is deemed necessary by these good souls to prevent the commonalty from being attracted by them, and sticking to them, as straws and bits of paper do to amber. But more generally the "true-blue" old families are simple and urbane in their manners; and their pretensions are, as Miss Edgeworth says, presented rather *intaglio* than in cameo. Of course, they most thoroughly believe in themselves, but in a bland and genial way. "*Noblesse oblige*" is with them a secret spring of gentle address and social suavity. They prefer their own set and their own ways, and are comfortably sure that what they do not know is not worth knowing, and what they have not been in the habit of doing is not worth doing; but still they are indulgent of the existence of human nature outside of their own circle.

The Seymours and the Fergusons belonged to this sort of people; and, of course, Mr. John Seymour's marriage afforded them opportunity for some wholesome moral discipline. The Ferguson girls were frank, social, magnanimous young women; of that class, to whom the saying or doing of a rude or unhandsome thing by any human being was an utter impossibility, and whose cheeks would flush at the mere idea of asserting personal superiority over any one. Nevertheless, they trod the earth firmly, as girls who felt that they were born to a certain position. Judge Ferguson was a gentleman of the old school, devoted to past ideas, fond of the English classics, and with small faith

in any literature later than Dr. Johnson. He confessed
to a toleration for Scott's novels, and had been detected
by his children both laughing and crying over the
stories of Charles Dickens; for the amiable weaknesses
of human nature still remain in the best regulated
mind. To women and children, the judge was benig-
nity itself, imitating the Grand Monarque, who bowed
even to a chambermaid. He believed in good, orderly,
respectable, old ways and entertainments, and had a
quiet horror of all that is loud or noisy or pretentious;
which sometimes made his social duties a trial to
him, as was the case in regard to the Seymour party.

The arrangements of the party, including the preparations for an extensive illumination of the grounds,
and fireworks, were on so unusual a scale as to rouse
the whole community of Springdale to a fever of
excitement; of course, the Wilcoxes and the Lennoxes
were astonished and disgusted. When had it been
known that any of their set had done any thing of
the kind? How horribly out of taste! Just the result
of John Seymour's marrying into that class of society!
Mrs. Lennox was of opinion that she ought not to
go. She was of the determined and spicy order of
human beings, and often, like a certain French countess,
felt disposed to thank Heaven that she generally succeeded in being rude when the occasion required. Mrs.
Lennox regarded "snubbing" in the light of a moral
duty devolving on people of condition, when the foundations of things were in danger of being removed by
the inroads of the vulgar commonalty. On the present

occasion, Mrs. Lennox was of opinion that quiet, respectable people, of good family, ought to ignore this kind of proceeding, and not think of encouraging such things by their presence.

Mrs. Wilcox generally shaped her course by Mrs. Lennox: still she had promised Letitia Ferguson to be gracious to the Seymours in their exigency, and to call on the Follingsbees; so there was a confusion all round. The young people of both families declared that *they* were going, just to see the fun. Bob Lennox, with the usual vivacity of Young America, said he didn't "care a hang who set a ball rolling, if only something was kept stirring." The subject was discussed when Mrs. Lennox and Mrs. Wilcox were making a morning call upon the Fergusons.

"For my part," said Mrs. Lennox, "I'm principled on this subject. Those Follingsbees are not proper people. They are of just that vulgar, pushing class, against which I feel it my duty to set my face like a flint; and I'm astonished that a man like John Seymour should go into relations with them. You see it puts all his friends in a most embarrassing position."

"Dear Mrs. Lennox," said Rose Ferguson, "indeed, it is not Mr. Seymour's fault. These persons are invited by his wife."

"Well, what business has he to allow his wife to invite them? A man should be master in his own house."

"But, my dear Mrs. Lennox," said Mrs. Ferguson, "such a pretty young creature, and just married! of

course it would be unhandsome not to allow her to
have her friends."

"Certainly," said Judge Ferguson, "a gentleman
cannot be rude to his wife's invited guests; for my
part, I think Seymour is putting the best face he can
on it; and we must all do what we can to help him.
We shall all attend the Seymour party."

"Well," said Mrs. Wilcox, "I think we shall go.
To be sure, it is not what I should like to do. I don't
approve of these Follingsbees. Mr. Wilcox was saying,
this morning, that his money was made by frauds
on the government, which ought to have put him in
the State Prison."

"Now, I say," said Mrs. Lennox, "such people ought
to be put down socially: I have no patience with
their airs. And that Mrs. Follingsbee, I have heard
that she was a milliner, or shop-girl, or some such
thing; and to see the airs she gives herself! One
would think it was the Empress Eugénie herself, come
to queen it over us in America. I can't help thinking
we ought to take a stand. I really do."

"But, dear Mrs. Lennox, we are not obliged to
cultivate further relations with people, simply from
exchanging ordinary civilities with them on one evening," said Judge Ferguson.

"But, my dear sir, these pushing, vulgar, rich people
take advantage of every opening. Give them an inch,
and they will take an ell," said Mrs Lennox. "Now, if I
go, they will be claiming acquaintance with me in Newport next summer. Well, I shall cut them, — dead."

"Trust you for that," said Miss Letitia, laughing; "indeed, Mrs. Lennox, I think you may go wherever you please with perfect safety. People will never saddle themselves on you longer than you want them; so you might as well go to the party with the rest of us."

"And besides, you know," said Mrs. Wilcox, "all our young people will go, whether we go or not. Your Tom was at my house yesterday; and he is going with my girls: they are all just as wild about it as they can be, and say that it is the greatest fun that has been heard of this summer."

In fact, there was not a man, woman, or child, in a circle of fifteen miles round, who could show shade or color of an invitation, who was not out in full dress at Mrs. John Seymour's party. People in a city may pick and choose their entertainments, and she who gives a party there may reckon on a falling off of about one-third, for various other attractions; but in the country, where there is nothing else stirring, one may be sure that not one person able to stand on his feet will be missing. A party in a good old sleepy, respectable country place is a godsend. It is equal to an earthquake, for suggesting materials of conversation; and in so many ways does it awaken and vivify the community, that one may doubt whether, after all, it is not a moral benefaction, and the giver of it one to be ranked in the noble army of martyrs.

Everybody went. Even Mrs. Lennox, when she had sufficiently swallowed her moral principles, sent in all haste to New York for an elegant spick and span new dress from Madame de Tullegig's, expressly for the occasion. Was she to be outshone by unprincipled upstarts? Perish the thought! It was treason to the cause of virtue, and the standing order of society. Of course, the best thing to be done is to put certain people down, if you can; but, if you cannot do that, the next best thing is to outshine them in their own way. It may be very naughty for them to be so dressy and extravagant, and very absurd, improper, immoral, unnecessary, and in bad taste; but still, if you cannot help it, you may as well try to do the same, and do a little more of it. Mrs. Lennox was in a feverish state till all her trappings came from New York. The bill was something stunning; but, then, it was voted by the young people that she had never looked so splendidly in her life; and she comforted herself with marking out a certain sublime distance and reserve of manner to be observed towards Mrs. Seymour and the Follingsbees.

The young people, however, came home delighted. Tom, aged twenty-two, instructed his mother that Follingsbee was a brick, and a real jolly fellow; and he had accepted an invitation to go on a yachting cruise with him the next month. Jane Lennox, moreover, began besetting her mother to have certain details in their house rearranged, with an eye to the Seymour glorification.

"Now, Jane dear, that's just the result of allowing you to visit in this flash, vulgar genteel society," said the troubled mamma.

"Bless your heart, mamma, the world moves on, you

know; and we must move with it a little, or be left
behind. For my part, I'm perfectly ashamed of the
way we let things go at our house. It really is not
respectable. Now, I like Mrs. Follingsbee, for my part:
she's clever and amusing. It was fun to hear all about
the balls at the Tuileries, and the opera and things in
Paris. Mamma, when are we going to Paris?"

"Oh! I don't know, my dear; you must ask your
father. He is very unwilling to go abroad."

"Papa is so slow and conservative in his notions!"
said the young lady. "For my part, I cannot see
what is the use of all this talk about the Follingsbees.
He is good-natured and funny; and, I am sure, I think
she's a splendid woman: and, by the way, she gave me
the address of lots of places in New York where we
can get French things. Did you notice her lace? It
is superb; and she told me where lace just like it could
be bought one-third less than they sell at Stewart's."

Thus we see how the starting-out of an old, respectable family in any new ebullition of fancy and fashion
is like a dandelion going to seed. You have not only
the airy, fairy globe; but every feathery particle thereof
bears a germ which will cause similar feather bubbles
all over the country; and thus old, respectable grass-
plots become, in time, half dandelion. It is to be
observed that, in all questions of life and fashion, "the
world and the flesh," to say nothing of the third partner of that ancient firm, have us at decided advantage.
It is easy to see the flash of jewelry, the dazzle of color,
the rush and glitter of equipage, and to be dizzied by

the babble and gayety of fashionable life; while it is not easy to see justice, patience, temperance, self-denial. These are things belonging to the invisible and the eternal, and to be seen with other eyes than those of the body.

Then, again, there is no one thing in all the items which go to make up fashionable extravagance, which, taken separately and by itself, is not in some point of view a good or pretty or desirable thing; and so, whenever the forces of invisible morality begin an encounter with the troops of fashion and folly, the world and the flesh, as we have just said, generally have the best of it.

It may be very shocking and dreadful to get money by cheating and lying; but when the money thus got is put into the forms of yachts, operas, pictures, statues, and splendid entertainments, of which you are freely offered a share if you will only cultivate the acquaintance of a sharper, will you not then begin to say, "Everybody is going, why not I? As to countenancing Dives, why he is countenanced; and my holding out does no good. What is the use of my sitting in my corner and sulking? Nobody minds me." Thus Dives gains one after another to follow his chariot, and make up his court.

Our friend John, simply by being a loving, indulgent husband, had come into the position, in some measure, of demoralizing the public conscience, of bringing in luxury and extravagance, and countenancing people who really ought not to be countenanced. He had a sort of uneasy perception of this fact; yet, at each particular step, he seemed to himself to be doing no more than was right or reasonable. It was a fact that, through all Springdale, people were beginning to be uneasy and uncomfortable in houses that used to seem to them nice enough, and ashamed of a style of dress and entertainment and living that used to content them perfectly, simply because of the changes of style and living in the John-Seymour mansion.

Of old, the Seymour family had always been a bulwark on the side of a temperate self-restraint and reticence in worldly indulgence; of a kind that parents find most useful to strengthen their hands when children are urging them on to expenses beyond their means: for they could say, "The Seymours are richer than we are, and you see they don't change their carpets, nor get new sofas, nor give extravagant parties; and they give simple, reasonable, quiet entertainments, and do not go into any modern follies." So the Seymours kept up the Fergusons, and the Fergusons the Seymours; and the Wilcoxes and the Lennoxes encouraged each other in a style of quiet, reasonable living, saving money for charity, and time for reading and self-cultivation, and by moderation and simplicity keeping up the courage of less wealthy neighbors to hold their own with them.

The John-Seymour party, therefore, was like the bursting of a great dam, which floods a whole region. There was not a family who had not some trouble with the inundation, even where, like Rose and Letitia

Ferguson, they swept it out merrily, and thought no more of it.

"It was all very pretty and pleasant, and I'm glad it went off so well," said Rose Ferguson the next day; "but I have not the smallest desire to repeat any thing of the kind. We who live in the country, and have such a world of beautiful things around us every day, and so many charming engagements in riding, walking, and rambling, and so much to do, cannot afford to go into this sort of thing: we really have not time for it."

"That pretty creature," said Mrs. Ferguson, speaking of Lillie, "is really a charming object. I hope she will settle down now to domestic life. She will soon find better things to care for, I trust: a baby would be her best teacher. I am sure I hope she will have one."

"A baby is mamma's infallible recipe for strengthening the character," said Rose, laughing.

"Well, as the saying is, they bring love with them," said Mrs. Ferguson; "and love always brings wisdom."

CHAPTER XVII.

AFTER THE BATTLE.

"WELL, Grace, the Follingsbees are gone at last, I am thankful to say," said John, as he stretched himself out on the sofa in Grace's parlor with a sigh of relief. "If ever I am caught in such a scrape again, I shall know it."

"Yes, it is all well over," said Grace.

"Over! I wish you would look at the bills. Why, Gracie! I had not the least idea, when I gave Lillie leave to get what she chose, what it would come to, with those people at her elbow, to put things into her head. I could not interfere, you know, after the thing was started; and I thought I would not spoil Lillie's pleasure, especially as I had to stand firm in not allowing wine. It was well I did; for if wine had been given, and taken with the reckless freedom that all the rest was, it might have ended in a general riot."

"As some of the great fashionable parties do, where young women get merry with champagne, and young men get drunk," said Grace.

"Well," said John, "I don't exactly like the whole

turn of the way things have been going at our house lately. I don't like the influence of it on others. It is not in the line of the life I want to lead, and that we have all been trying to lead."

"Well," said Gracie, "things will be settled now quietly, I hope."

"I say," said John, "could not we start our little reading sociables, that were so pleasant last year? You know we want to keep some little pleasant thing going, and draw Lillie in with us. When a girl has been used to lively society, she can't come down to mere nothing; and I am afraid she will be wanting to rush off to New York, and visit the Follingsbees."

"Well," said Grace, "Letitia and Rose were speaking the other day of that, and wanting to begin. You know we were to read Froude together, as soon as the evenings got a little longer."

"Oh, yes! that will be capital," said John.

"Do you think Lillie will be interested in Froude?" asked Grace.

"I really can't say," said John, with some doubting of heart; "perhaps it would be well to begin with something a little lighter at first."

"Any thing you please, John. What shall it be?"

"But I don't want to hold you all back on my account," said John.

"Well, then again, John, there's our old study-club. The Fergusons and Mr. Mathews were talking it over the other night, and wondering when you would be ready to join us. We were going to take up Lecky's

'History of Morals,' and have our sessions Tuesday evenings, — one Tuesday at their house, and the other at mine, you know."

"I should enjoy that, of all things," said John; "but I know it is of no use to ask Lillie: it would only be the most dreadful bore to her."

"And you couldn't come without her, of course," said Grace.

"Of course not; that would be too cruel, to leave the poor little thing at home alone."

"Lillie strikes me as being naturally clever," said Grace; "if she only would bring her mind to enter into your tastes a little, I 'm sure you would find her capable."

"But, Gracie, you 've no conception how very different her sphere of thought is, how entirely out of the line of our ways of thinking. I 'll tell you," said John, "don't wait for me. You have your Tuesdays, and go on with your Lecky; and I will keep a copy at home, and read up with you. And I will bring Lillie in the evening, after the reading is over; and we will have a little music and lively talk, and a dance or charade, you know: then perhaps her mind will wake up by degrees."

SCENE. — *After tea in the Seymour parlor. John at a table, reading. Lillie in a corner, embroidering.*

Lillie. "Look here, John, I want to ask you something."

John, — putting down his book, and crossing to her, "Well, dear?"

Lillie. " There, would you make a green leaf there, or a brown one ? "

John, — endeavoring to look wise, " Well, a brown one."

Lillie. " That's just like you, John ; now, don't you see that a brown one would just spoil the effect ? "

"Oh! would it ? " said John, innocently. " Well, what did you ask me for ? "

" Why, you tiresome creature ! I wanted you to say something. What are you sitting moping over a book for ? You don't entertain me a bit."

"Dear Lillie, I have been talking about every thing I could think of," said John, apologetically.

" Well, I want you to keep on talking, and put up that great heavy book. What is it, any way ? "

" Lecky's ' History of Morals,' " said John.

" How dreadful! do you really mean to read it ? "

" Certainly ; we are all reading it."

" Who all ? "

" Why, Gracie, and Letitia and Rose Ferguson."

" Rose Ferguson ? I don't believe it. Why, Rose isn't twenty yet! She cannot care about such stuff."

" She does care, and enjoys it too," said John, eagerly.

" It is a pity, then, you didn't get her for a wife instead of me," said Lillie, in a tone of pique.

Now, this sort of thing does well enough occasionally, said by a pretty woman, perfectly sure of her ground, in the early days of the honey-moon ; but for steady domestic diet is not to be recommended. Husbands get tired of swearing allegiance over and over ; and John returned to his book quietly, without reply. He did not like the suggestion; and he thought that it was in very poor taste. Lillie embroidered in silence a few minutes, and then threw down her work pettishly.

"How close this room is!"

John read on.

"John, do open the door!"

John rose, opened the door, and returned to his book.

"Now, there's that draft from the hall-window. John, you'll have to shut the door."

John shut it, and read on.

"Oh, dear me!" said Lillie, throwing herself down with a portentous yawn. "I do think this is dreadful!"

"What is dreadful?" said John, looking up.

"It is dreadful to be buried alive here in this gloomy town of Springdale, where there is nothing to see, and nowhere to go, and nothing going on."

"We have always flattered ourselves that Springdale was a most attractive place," said John. "I don't know of any place where there are more beautiful walks and rambles."

"But I detest walking in the country. What is there to see? And you get your shoes muddy, and burrs on your clothes, and don't meet a creature! I got so tired the other day when Grace and Rose Ferguson would drag me off to what they call 'the glen.' They kept oh-ing and ah-ing and exclaiming to each other about some stupid thing every step of the way,— old pokey nutgalls, bare twigs of trees, and red and yellow leaves, and ferns! I do wish you could have seen the armful of trash that those two girls carried into their respective houses. I would not have such stuff in mine for any thing. I am tired of all this talk about Nature. I am free to confess that I don't like Nature, and do like art; and I wish we only lived in New York, where there is something to amuse one."

"But I detest walking in the country."

"Well, Lillie dear, I am sorry; but we don't live in New York, and are not likely to," said John.

"Why can't we? Mrs. Follingsbee said that a man

in your profession, and with your talents, could command a fortune in New York."

"If it would give me the mines of Golconda, I would not go there," said John.

"How stupid of you! You know you would, though."

"No, Lillie; I would not leave Springdale for any money."

"That is because you think of nobody but yourself," said Lillie. "Men are always selfish."

"On the contrary, it is because I have so many here depending on me, of whom I am bound to think more than myself," said John.

"That dreadful mission-work of yours, I suppose," said Lillie; "that always stands in the way of having a good time."

"Lillie," said John, shutting his book, and looking at her, "what is your ideal of a good time?"

"Why, having something amusing going on all the time, — something bright and lively, to keep one in good spirits," said Lillie.

"I thought that you would have enough of that with your party and all," said John.

"Well, now it's all over, and duller than ever," said Lillie. "I think a little spirt of gayety makes it seem duller by contrast."

"Yet, Lillie," said John, "you see there are women, who live right here in Springdale, who are all the time busy, interested, and happy, with only such sources of enjoyment as are to be found here. Their time does not hang heavy on their hands; in fact, it is too short for all they wish to do."

"They are different from me," said Lillie.

"Then, since you must live here," said John, "could you not learn to be like them? could you not acquire some of these tastes that make simple country life agreeable?"

"No, I can't; I never could," said Lillie, pettishly.

"Then," said John, "I don't see that anybody can help your being unhappy." And, opening his book, he sat down, and began to read.

Lillie pouted awhile, and then drew from under the sofa-pillow a copy of "Indiana;" and, establishing her feet on the fender, she began to read.

Lillie had acquired at school the doubtful talent of reading French with facility, and was soon deep in the fascinating pages, whose theme is the usual one of French novels, — a young wife, tired of domestic monotony, with an unappreciative husband, solacing herself with the devotion of a lover. Lillie felt a sort of pique with her husband. He was evidently unappreciative: he was thinking of all sorts of things more than of her, and growing stupid, as husbands in French romances generally do. She thought of her handsome Cousin Harry, the only man that she ever came anywhere near being in love with; and the image of his dark, handsome eyes and glossy curls gave a sort of piquancy to the story.

John got deeply interested in his book; and, looking up from time to time, was relieved to find that Lillie had something to employ her.

"I may as well make a beginning," he said to himself. "I must have my time for reading; and she must learn to amuse herself."

After a while, however, he peeped over her shoulder. "Why, darling!" he said, "where did you get that?"

"It is Mrs. Follingsbee's," said Lillie.

"Dear, it is a bad book," said John. "Don't read it."

"It amuses me, and helps pass away time," said Lillie; "and I don't think it is bad: it is beautiful. Besides, you read what amuses you; and it is a pity if I can't read what amuses me."

"I am glad to see you like to read French," continued John; "and I can get you some delightful French stories, which are not only pretty and witty, but have nothing in them that tend to pull down one's moral principles. Edmond About's ' Mariages de Paris' and 'Tolla' are charming French things; and, as he says, they might be read aloud by a man between his mother and his sister, without a shade of offence."

"Thank you, sir," said Mrs. Lillie. "You had better go to Rose Ferguson, and get her to give you a list of the kinds of books she prefers."

"Lillie!" said John, severely, "your remarks about Rose are in bad taste. I must beg you to discontinue them. There are subjects that never ought to be jested about."

" Thank you, sir, for your moral lessons," said Lillie, turning her back on him defiantly, putting her feet on the fender, and going on with her reading.

John seated himself, and went on with his book in silence.

Now, this mode of passing a domestic evening is certainly not agreeable to either party; but we sustain the thesis that in this sort of interior warfare the woman has generally the best of it. When it comes to the science of annoyance, commend us to the lovely sex! Their methods have a *finesse*, a suppleness, a universal adaptability, that does them infinite credit; and man, with all his strength, and all his majesty, and his commanding talent, is about as well off as a buffalo or a bison against a tiny, rainbow-winged gnat or mosquito, who bites, sings, and stings everywhere at once, with an infinite grace and facility.

A woman without magnanimity, without generosity, who has no love, and whom a man loves, is a terrible antagonist. To give up or to fight often seems equally impossible.

How is a man going to make a woman have a good time, who is determined not to have it? Lillie had sense enough to see, that, if she settled down into enjoyment of the little agreeablenesses and domesticities of the winter society in Springdale, she should lose her battle, and John would keep her there for life. The only way was to keep him as uncomfortable as possible without really breaking her power over him.

In the long-run, in these encounters of will, the woman has every advantage. The constant dropping that wears away the stone has passed into a proverb.

Lillie meant to go to New York, and have a long campaign at the Follingsbees. The thing had been all promised and arranged between them; and it was necessary that she should appear sufficiently miserable, and that John should be made sufficiently uncomfortable, to consent with effusion, at last, when her intentions were announced.

These purposes were not distinctly stated to herself; for, as we have before intimated, uncultivated natures, who have never thought for a serious moment on self-education, or the way their character is forming, act purely from a sort of instinct, and do not even in their own minds fairly and squarely face their own motives and purposes; if they only did, their good angel would wear a less dejected look than he generally must.

Lillie had power enough, in that small circle, to stop and interrupt almost all its comfortable literary culture. The reading of Froude was given up. John could not go to the study club; and, after an evening or two of trying to read up at home, he used to stay an hour later at his office. Lillie would go with him on Tuesday evening, after the readings were over; and then it was understood that all parties were to devote themselves to making the evening pass agreeable to her. She was to be put forward, kept in the foreground, and every thing arranged to make her appear the queen of the *fête.* They had tableaux, where Rose made Lillie into marvellous pictures, which all admired and praised. They had little dances, which Lillie thought rather stupid and humdrum, because they were not *en grande toilette;* yet Lillie always made a great merit of putting up with her life at Springdale. A pleasant English writer has a lively paper on the advantages of being a " cantankerous fool," in which he goes to show that men or women of inferior moral parts, little self-control, and great selfishness, often acquire an absolute dominion over the circle in which they move, merely by the exercise of these traits.   Every one being anxious to please and pacify them, and keep the peace with them, there is a constant succession of anxious compliances and compromises going on around them; by all of which they are benefited in getting their own will and way.

The one person who will not give up, and cannot be expected to be considerate or accommodating, comes at last to rule the whole circle.   He is counted on like the fixed facts of nature; everybody else must turn out for him.   So Lillie reigned in Springdale.   In every little social gathering where she appeared, the one uneasy question was, would she have a good time, and anxious provision made to that end.   Lillie had declared that reading aloud was a bore, which was definitive against reading-parties.   She liked to play and sing; so that was always a part of the programme.   Lillie sang well, but needed a great deal of urging.   Her throat was apt to be sore; and she took pains to say that the harsh winter weather in Springdale was ruining her voice.   A good part of an evening was often spent in supplications before she could be induced to make the endeavor.

Lillie had taken up the whim of being jealous of Rose. Jealousy is said to be a sign of love.   We hold another theory, and consider it more properly a sign of selfishness.   Look at noble-hearted, unselfish women, and ask if they are easily made jealous.   Look, again,

at a woman who in her whole life shows no disposition
to deny herself for her husband, or to enter into his
tastes and views and feelings: are not such as she the
most frequently jealous?

Her husband, in her view, is a piece of her property;
every look, word, and thought which he gives to any
body or thing else is a part of her private possessions,
unjustly withheld from her.

Independently of that, Lillie felt the instinctive
jealousy which a *passée* queen of beauty sometimes
has for a young rival.

She had eyes to see that Rose was daily growing
more and more beautiful; and not all that young girl's
considerateness, her self-forgetfulness, her persistent
endeavors to put Lillie forward, and make her the
queen of the hour, could disguise this fact. Lillie
was a keen-sighted little body, and saw, at a glance,
that, once launched into society together, Rose would
carry the day; all the more that no thought of any day
to be carried was in her head.

Rose Ferguson had one source of attraction which
is as great a natural gift as beauty, and which, when
it is found with beauty, makes it perfectly irresistible;
to wit, perfect unconsciousness of self. This is a
wholly different trait from unselfishness: it is not a
moral virtue, attained by voluntary effort, but a con-
stitutional gift, and a very great one. Fénelon praises
it as a Christian grace, under the name of simplicity;
but we incline to consider it only as an advantage of
natural organization. There are many excellent Chris-

tians who are haunted by themselves, and in some form or other are always busy with themselves; either conscientiously pondering the right and wrong of their actions, or approbatively sensitive to the opinions of others, or æsthetically comparing their appearance and manners with an interior standard; while there are others who have received the gift, beyond the artist's eye or the musician's ear, of perfect self-forgetfulness. Their religion lacks the element of conflict, and comes to them by simple impulse.

> "Glad souls, without reproach or blot,
> Who do His will, and know it not."

Rose had a frank, open joyousness of nature, that shed around her a healthy charm, like fine, breezy weather, or a bright morning; making every one feel as if to be good were the most natural thing in the world. She seemed to be thinking always and directly of matters in hand, of things to be done, and subjects under discussion, as much as if she were an impersonal being.

She had been educated with every solid advantage which old Boston can give to her nicest girls; and that is saying a good deal. Returning to a country home at an early age, she had been made the companion of her father; entering into all his literary tastes, and receiving constantly, from association with him, that manly influence which a woman's mind needs to develop its completeness. Living the whole year in the country, the Fergusons developed within themselves a multiplicity of resources. They read and studied, and discussed subjects with their father; for, as we all know, the discussion of moral and social questions has been from the first, and always will be, a prime source of amusement in New-England families; and many of them keep up, with great spirit, a family debating society, in which whoever hath a psalm, a doctrine, or an interpretation, has free course.

Rose had never been into fashionable life, technically so called. She had not been brought out: there never had been a mile-stone set up to mark the place where "her education was finished;" and so she had gone on unconsciously, — studying, reading, drawing, and cultivating herself from year to year, with her head and hands always so full of pleasurable schemes and plans, that there really seemed to be no room for any thing else. We have seen with what interest she co-operated with Grace in the various good works of the factory village in which her father held shares, where her activity found abundant scope, and her beauty and grace of manner made her a sort of idol.

Rose had once or twice in her life been awakened to self-consciousness, by applicants rapping at the front door of her heart; but she answered with such a kind, frank, earnest, "No, I thank you, sir," as made friends of her lovers; and she entered at once into pleasant relations with them. Her nature was so healthy, and free from all morbid suggestion; her yes and no so perfectly frank and positive, that there seemed no possibility of any tragedy caused by her.

Why did not John fall in love with Rose? Why did not he, O most sapient senate of womanhood? why did not your brother fall in love with that nice girl you know of, who grew up with you all at his very elbow, and was, as everybody else could see, just the proper person for him?

Well, why didn't he? There is the doctrine of election. "The election hath obtained it; and the rest were blinded." John was some six years older than Rose. He had romped with her as a little girl, drawn her on his sled, picked up her hair-pins, and worn her tippet, when they had skated together as girl and boy. They had made each other Christmas and New Year's presents all their lives; and, to say the truth, loved each other honestly and truly: nevertheless, John fell in love with Lillie, and married her. Did you ever know a case like it?

CHAPTER XVIII.

A BRICK TURNS UP.

THE snow had been all night falling silently over the long elm avenues of Springdale.

It was one of those soft, moist, dreamy snow-falls, which come down in great loose feathers, resting in magical frost-work on every tree, shrub, and plant, and seeming to bring down with it the purity and peace of upper worlds.

Grace's little cottage on Elm Street was imbosomed, as New-England cottages are apt to be, in a tangle of shrubbery, evergreens, syringas, and lilacs; which, on such occasions, become bowers of enchantment when the morning sun looks through them.

Grace came into her parlor, which was cheery with the dazzling sunshine, and, running to the window, began to examine anxiously the state of her various greeneries, pausing from time to time to look out admiringly at the wonderful snow-landscape, with its many tremulous tints of rose, lilac, and amethyst.

The only thing wanting was some one to speak to about it; and, with a half sigh, she thought of the good old times when John would come to her chamber-door in the morning, to get her out to look on scenes like this.

"Positively," she said to herself, "I must invite some one to visit me. One wants a friend to help one enjoy solitude." The stock of social life in Springdale, in fact, was running low. The Lennoxes and the Wilcoxes had gone to their Boston homes, and Rose Ferguson was visiting in New York, and Letitia found so much to do to supply her place to her father and mother, that she had less time than usual to share with Grace. Then, again, the Elm-street cottage was a walk of some considerable distance; whereas, when Grace lived at the old homestead, the Fergusons were so near as to seem only one family, and were dropping in at all hours of the day and evening.

"Whom can I send for?" thought Grace to herself; and she ran over mentally, in a moment, the list of available friends and acquaintances. Reader, perhaps you have never really estimated your friends, till you have tried them by the question, which of them you could ask to come and spend a week or fortnight with you, alone in a country-house, in the depth of winter. Such an invitation supposes great faith in your friend, in yourself, or in human nature.

Grace, at the moment, was unable to think of anybody whom she could call from the approaching festivities of holiday life in the cities to share her snow Patmos with her; so she opened a book for company, and turned to where her dainty breakfast-table, with its

hot coffee and crisp rolls, stood invitingly waiting
for her before the cheerful open fire.

At this moment, she saw, what she had not noticed
before, a letter lying on her breakfast plate. Grace
took it up with an exclamation of surprise; which,
however, was heard only by her canary birds and
her plants.

Years before, when Grace was in the first summer
of her womanhood, she had been very intimate with
Walter Sydenham, and thoroughly esteemed and liked
him; but, as many another good girl has done, about
those days she had conceived it her duty not to think
of marriage, but to devote herself to making a home
for her widowed father and her brother. There was a
certain romance of self-abnegation in this disposition of
herself which was rather pleasant to Grace, and in which
both the gentlemen concerned found great advantage.
As long as her father lived, and John was unmarried
and devoted to her, she had never regretted it.

Sydenham had gone to seek his fortune in California.
He had begged to keep up intercourse by correspondence; but Grace was not one of those women who
are willing to drain the heart of the man they refuse
to marry, by keeping up with him just that degree of
intimacy which prevents his seeking another. Grace
had meant her refusal to be final, and had sincerely
hoped that he would find happiness with some other
woman; and to that intent had rigorously denied herself and him a correspondence: yet, from time to time,
she had heard of him through an occasional letter

to John, or by a chance Californian newspaper. Since John's marriage had so altered her course of life, Grace had thought of him more frequently, and with some questionings as to the wisdom of her course.

This letter was from him; and we shall give our readers the benefit of it:—

"DEAR GRACE,— You must pardon me this beginning,— in the old style of other days; for though many years have passed, in which I have been trying to walk in your ways, and keep all your commandments, I have never yet been able to do as you directed, and forget you: and here I am, beginning 'Dear Grace,'—just where I left off on a certain evening long, long ago. I wonder if you remember it as plainly as I do. I am just the same fellow that I was then and there. If you remember, you admitted that, were it not for other duties, you might have considered my humble supplication. I gathered that it would not have been impossible *per se*, as metaphysicians say, to look with favor on your humble servant.

"Gracie, I have been living, I trust, not unworthily of you. Your photograph has been with me round the world,— in the miner's tent, on shipboard, among scenes where barbarous men do congregate; and everywhere it has been a presence, 'to warn, to comfort, to command;' and if I have come out of many trials firmer, better, more established in right than before; if I am more believing in religion, and in every way grounded and settled in the way you would have me,—it has been your spiritual presence and your power over me that has done it. Besides that, I may as well tell you, I have never given up the hope that by and by you would see all this, and in some hour give me a different answer.

"When, therefore, I learned of your father's death, and afterwards of John's marriage, I thought it was time for me to return again. I have come to New York, and, if you do not forbid, shall come to Springdale.

"Will you be a little glad to see me, Gracie? Why not? We are both alone now. Let us take hands, and walk the same path together. Shall we?

"Yours till death, and after,

"WALTER SYDENHAM."

Would she? To say the truth, the question as asked now had a very different air from the question as asked years before, when, full of life and hope and enthusiasm, she had devoted herself to making an ideal home for her father and brother. What other sympathy or communion, she had asked herself then, should she ever need than these friends, so very dear: and, if she needed more, there, in the future, was John's ideal wife, who, somehow, always came before her in the likeness of Rose Ferguson, and John's ideal children, whom she was sure she should love and pet as if they were her own.

And now here she was, in a house all by herself, coming down to her meals, one after another, without the excitement of a cheerful face opposite to her, and

with all possibility of confidential intercourse with
her brother entirely cut off. Lillie, in this matter,
acted, with much grace and spirit, the part of the dog
in the manger; and, while she resolutely refused to
enter into any of John's literary or intellectual tastes,
seemed to consider her wifely rights infringed upon
by any other woman who would. She would absolutely refuse to go up with her husband and spend an
evening with Grace, alleging it was "pokey and stupid,"
and that they always got talking about things that
she didn't care any thing about. If, then, John went
without her to spend the evening, he was sure to be
received, on his return, with a dead and gloomy silence,
more fearful, sometimes, than the most violent of objur-
gations. That look of patient, heart-broken woe, those
long-drawn sighs, were a reception that he dreaded, to
say the truth, a great deal more than a direct attack,
or any fault-finding to which he could have replied ;
and so, on the whole, John made up his mind that the
best thing he could do was to stay at home and rock the
cradle of this fretful baby, whose wisdom-teeth were so
hard to cut, and so long in coming. It was a pretty
baby; and when made the sole and undivided object of
attention, when every thing possible was done for it by
everybody in the house, condescended often to be very
graceful and winning and playful, and had numberless
charming little ways and tricks. The difference between Lillie in good humor and Lillie in bad humor
was a thing which John soon learned to appreciate as
one of the most powerful forces in his life. If you

knew, my dear reader, that by pursuing a certain course
you could bring upon yourself a drizzling, dreary, north-
east rain-storm, and by taking heed to your ways you
could secure sunshine, flowers, and bird-singing, you
would be very careful, after a while, to keep about you
the right atmospheric temperature; and, if going to see
the very best friend you had on earth was sure to bring
on a fit of rheumatism or tooth-ache, you would soon
learn to be very sparing of your visits. For this reason it was that Grace saw very little of John; that she
never now had a sisterly conversation with him; that
she preferred arranging all those little business matters,
in which it would be convenient to have a masculine
appeal, solely and singly by herself. The thing was
never referred to in any conversation between them.
It was perfectly understood without words. There are
friends between whom and us has shut the coffin-lid;
and there are others between whom and us stand sacred
duties, considerations never to be enough reverenced,
which forbid us to seek their society, or to ask to lean
on them either in joy or sorrow: the whole thing as
regards them must be postponed until the future life.
Such had been Grace's conclusion with regard to her
brother. She well knew that any attempt to restore
their former intimacy would only diminish and destroy
what little chance of happiness yet remained to him;
and it may therefore be imagined with what changed
eyes she read Walter Sydenham's letter from those
of years ago.

There was a sound of stamping feet at the front door;

and John came in, all ruddy and snow-powdered, but looking, on the whole, uncommonly cheerful.

"Well, Gracie," he said, "the fact is, I shall have to let Lillie go to New York for a week or two, to see those Follingsbees. Hang them! But what's the matter, Gracie? Have you been crying, or sitting up all night reading, or what?"

The fact was, that Gracie had for once been indulging in a good cry, rather pitying herself for her loneliness, now that the offer of relief had come. She laughed, though; and, handing John her letter, said,—

"Look here, John! here's a letter I have just had from Walter Sydenham."

John broke out into a loud, hilarious laugh.

"The blessed old brick!" said he. "Has he turned up again?"

"Read the letter, John," said Grace. "I don't know exactly how to answer it."

John read the letter, and seemed to grow more and more quiet as he read it. Then he came and stood by Grace, and stroked her hair gently.

"I wish, Gracie dear," he said, "you had asked my advice about this matter years ago. You loved Walter, —I can see you did; and you sent him off on my account. It is just too bad! Of all the men I ever knew, he was the one I should have been best pleased to have you marry!"

"It was not wholly on your account, John. You know there was our father," said Grace.

"Yes, yes, Gracie; but he would have preferred to

see you well married.   He would not have been so selfish, nor I either.   It is your self-abnegation, you dear
over-good women, that makes us men seem selfish.
We should be as good as you are, if you would give us
the chance.   I think, Gracie, though you're not aware
of it, there is a spice of Pharisaism in the way in which
you good girls allow us men to swallow you up without ever telling us what you are doing.   I often wondered about your intimacy with Sydenham, and why it
never came to any thing; and I can but half forgive
you.   How selfish I must have seemed!"

"Oh, no, John! indeed not."

"Come, you needn't put on these meek airs.   I insist upon it, you have been feeling self-righteous and
abused," said John, laughing; "but 'all's well that
ends well.'   Sit down, now, and write him a real sensible letter, like a nice honest woman as you are."

"And say, 'Yes, sir, and thank you too'?" said
Grace, laughing.

"Well, something in that way," said John.   "You
can fence it in with as many make-believes as is proper.
And now, Gracie, this is deuced lucky!   You see Sydenham will be down here at once; and it wouldn't be
exactly the thing for you to receive him at this house,
and our only hotel is perfectly impracticable in winter;
and that brings me to what I am here about.   Lillie is
going to New York to spend the holidays; and I wanted
you to shut up, and come up and keep house for us.
You see you have only one servant, and we have four
to be looked after.   You can bring your maid along,

and then I will invite Walter to our house, where he will have a clear field; and you can settle all your matters between you."

"So Lillie is going to the Follingsbees'?" said Grace.

"Yes: she had a long, desperately sentimental letter from Mrs. Follingsbee, urging, imploring, and entreating, and setting forth all the splendors and glories of New York. Between you and me, it strikes me that that Mrs. Follingsbee is an affected goose; but I couldn't say so to Lillie, 'by no manner of means.' She professes an untold amount of admiration and friendship for Lillie, and sets such brilliant prospects before her, that I should be the most hard-hearted old Turk in existence if I were to raise any objections; and, in fact, Lillie is quite brilliant in anticipation, and makes herself so delightful that I am almost sorry that I agreed to let her go."

"When shall you want me, John?"

"Well, this evening, say; and, by the way, couldn't you come up and see Lillie a little while this morning? She sent her love to you, and said she was so hurried with packing, and all that, that she wanted you to excuse her not calling."

"Oh, yes! I'll come," said Grace, good-naturedly, "as soon as I have had time to put things in a little order."

"And write your letter," said John, gayly, as he went out. "Don't forget that."

Grace did not forget the letter; but we shall not indulge our readers with any peep over her shoulder, only saying that, though written with an abundance of precaution, it was one with which Walter Syndenham was well satisfied.

Then she made her few arrangements in the house-keeping line, called in her grand vizier and prime minister from the kitchen, and held with her a counsel of ways and means; put on her india-rubbers and Polish boots, and walked up through the deep snow-drifts to the Springdale post-office, where she dropped the fateful letter with a good heart on the whole; and then she went on to John's, the old home, to offer any parting services to Lillie that might be wanted.

It is rather amusing, in any family circle, to see how some one member, by dint of persistent exactions, comes to receive always, in all the exigencies of life, an amount of attention and devotion which is never rendered back. Lillie never thought of such a thing as offering any services of any sort to Grace. Grace might have packed her trunks to go to the moon, or the Pacific Ocean, quite alone for matter of any help Lillie would ever have thought of. If Grace had headache or toothache or a bad cold, Lillie was always "so sorry;" but it never occurred to her to go and sit with her, to read to her, or offer any of a hundred little sisterly offices. When she was in similar case, John always summoned Grace to sit with Lillie during the hours that his business necessarily took him from her. It really seemed to be John's impression that a toothache or headache of Lillie's was something entirely different from the same thing with Grace, or any other person in the world; and Lillie fully shared the impression.

Grace found the little empress quite bewildered in her multiplicity of preparations, and neglected details, all of which had been deferred to the last day; and Rosa and Anna and Bridget, in fact the whole staff, were all busy in getting her off.

"So good of you to come, Gracie!" and, "If you would do this;" and, "Won't you see to that?" and, "If you could just do the other!" and Grace both could and would, and did what no other pair of hands could in the same time. John apologized for the lack of any dinner. "The fact is, Gracie, Bridget had to be getting up a lot of her things that were forgotten till the last moment; and I told her not to mind, we could do on a cold lunch." Bridget herself had become so wholly accustomed to the ways of her little mistress, that it now seemed the most natural thing in the world that the whole house should be upset for her.

But, at last, every thing was ready and packed; the trunks and boxes shut and locked, and the keys sorted; and John and Lillie were on their way to the station.

"I shall find out Walter in New York, and bring him back with me," said John, cheerily, as he parted from Grace in the hall. "I leave you to get things all to rights for us."

It would not have been a very agreeable or cheerful piece of work to tidy the disordered house and take command of the domestic forces under any other circumstances; but now Grace found it a very nice

diversion to prevent her thoughts from running too
curiously on this future meeting. "After all," she
thought to herself, "he is just the same venturesome,
imprudent creature that he always was, jumping to
conclusions, and insisting on seeing every thing in
his own way. How could he dare write me such a
letter without seeing me? Ten years make great
changes. How could he be sure he would like me?"
And she examined herself somewhat critically in the
looking-glass.

"Well," she said, "he may thank me for it that
we are not engaged, and that he comes only as an
old friend, and perfectly free, for all he has said, to
be nothing more, unless on seeing each other we are so
agreed. I am so sorry the old place is all demolished
and be-Frenchified. It won't look natural to him; and
I am not the kind of person to harmonize with these
cold, polished, glistening, slippery surroundings, that
have no home life or association in them."

But Grace had to wake from these reflections to culinary counsels with Bridget, and to arrangements of
apartments with Rosa. Her own exacting carefulness
followed the careless footsteps of the untrained hand-
maids, and rearranged every plait and fold; so that by
nightfall the next day she was thoroughly tired.

She beguiled the last moments, while waiting for the
coming of the cars, in arranging her hair, and putting
on one of those wonderful Parisian dresses, which
adapt themselves so precisely to the air of the wearer
that they seem to be in themselves works of art. Then

15

she stood with a fluttering color to see the carriage drive up to the door, and the two get out of it.

It is almost too bad to spy out such meetings, and certainly one has no business to describe them; but Walter Sydenham carried all before him, by an old habit which he had of taking all and every thing for granted, as, from the first moment, he did with Grace. He had no idea of hesitations or holdings off, and would have none; and met Gracie as if they had parted only yesterday, and as if her word to him always had been yes, instead of no.

In fact, they had not been together five minutes before the whole life of youth returned to them both,— that indestructible youth which belongs to warm hearts and buoyant spirits.

Such a merry evening as they had of it! When John, as the wood fire burned low on the hearth, with some excuse of letters to write in his library, left them alone together, Walter put on her finger a diamond ring, saying,—

"There, Gracie! now, when shall it be? You see you've kept me waiting so long that I can't spare you much time. I have an engagement to be in Montreal the first of February, and I couldn't think of going 'alone. They have merry times there in midwinter; and I'm sure it will be ever so much nicer for you than keeping house alone here."

Grace said, of course, that it was impossible; but Walter declared that doing the impossible was precisely in his line, and pushed on his various advantages with

such spirit and energy that, when they parted for
the night, Grace said she would think of it: which
promise, at the breakfast-table next morning, was
interpreted by the unblushing Walter, and reported
to John, as a full consent. Before noon that day,
Walter had walked up with John and Grace to take
a survey of the cottage, and had given John indefinite
power to engage workmen and artificers to rearrange
and enlarge and beautify it for their return after the
wedding journey. For the rest of the visit, all the
three were busy with pencil and paper, projecting
balconies, bow-windows, pantries, library, and dining-
room, till the old cottage so blossomed out in imagination as to leave only a germ of its former self.

Walter's visit brought back to John a deal of the
warmth and freedom which he had not known since he
married. We often live under an insensible pressure
of which we are made aware only by its removal.
John had been so much in the habit lately of watching
to please Lillie, of measuring and checking his words
or actions, that he now bubbled over with a wild,
free delight in finding himself alone with Grace and
Walter. He laughed, sang, whistled, skipped upstairs
two at a time, and scarcely dared to say even to
himself why he was so happy. He did not face himself
with that question, and went dutifully to the library at
stated times to write to Lillie, and made much of her
little letters.

CHAPTER XIX.

THE CASTLE OF INDOLENCE.

IF John managed to be happy without Lillie in Springdale, Lillie managed to be blissful without him in New York.

"The bird let loose in Eastern skies" never hastened more fondly home than she to its glitter and gayety, its life and motion, dash and sensation. She rustled in all her bravery of curls and frills, pinkings and quillings,— a marvellous specimen of Parisian frostwork, without one breath of reason or philosophy or conscience to melt it.

The Follingsbees' house might stand for the original of the Castle of Indolence.

> "Halls where who can tell
> What elegance and grandeur wide expand,—
> The pride of Turkey and of Persia's land?
> Soft quilts on quilts; on carpets, carpets spread;
> And couches stretched around in seemly band;
> And endless pillows rise to prop the head:
> So that each spacious room was one full swelling bed."

It was not without some considerable profit that Mrs. Follingsbee had read Balzac and Dumas, and had

Charlie Ferrola for master of arts in her establishment. The effect of the whole was perfect; it transported one, bodily, back to the times of Montespan and Pompadour, when life was all one glittering upper-crust, and pretty women were never troubled with even the shadow of a duty.

It was with a rebound of joyousness that Lillie found herself once more with a crowded list of invitations, calls, operas, dancing, and shopping, that kept her pretty little head in a perfect whirl of excitement, and gave her not one moment for thought.

Mrs. Follingsbee, to say the truth, would have been a little careful about inviting a rival queen of beauty into the circle, were it not that Charlie Ferrola, after an attentive consideration of the subject, had assured her that a golden-haired blonde would form a most complete and effective tableau, in contrast with her own dark rich style of beauty. Neither would lose by it, so he said; and the impression, as they rode together in an elegant open barouche, with ermine carriage robes, would be "stunning." So they called each other *ma sœur*, and drove out in the park in a ravishing little pony-phaeton all foamed over with ermine, drawn by a lovely pair of cream-colored horses, whose harness glittered with gold and silver, after the fashion of the Count of Monte Cristo. In truth, if Dick Follingsbee did not remind one of Solomon in all particulars, he was like him in one, that he " made silver and gold as the stones of the street" in New York.

Lillie's presence, however, was all desirable ; because

it would draw the calls of two or three old New York families who had hitherto stood upon their dignity, and refused to acknowledge the shoddy aristocracy. The beautiful Mrs. John Seymour, therefore, was no less useful than ornamental, and advanced Mrs. Follingsbee's purposes in her "Excelsior" movements.

"Now, I suppose," said Mrs. Follingsbee to Lillie one day, when they had been out making fashionable calls together, "we really must call on Charlie's wife, just to keep her quiet."

"I thought you didn't like her," said Lillie.

"I don't; I think she is dreadfully common," said Mrs. Follingsbee: "she is one of those women who can't talk any thing but baby, and bores Charlie half to death. But then, you know, when there is a *liaison* like mine with Charlie, one can't be too careful to cultivate the wives. *Les convenances*, you know, are the all-important things. I send her presents constantly, and send my carriage around to take her to church or opera, or any thing that is going on, and have her children at my fancy parties: yet, for all that, the creature has not a particle of gratitude; those narrow-minded women never have. You know I am very susceptible to people's atmospheres; and I always feel that that creature is just as full of spite and jealousy as she can stick in her skin."

It will be remarked that this was one of those idiomatic phrases which got lodged in Mrs. Follingsbee's head in a less cultivated period of her life, as a rusty needle sometimes hides in a cushion, coming out unexpectedly when excitement gives it an honest squeeze.

"Now, I should think," pursued Mrs. Follingsbee, "that a woman who really loved her husband would be thankful to have him have such a rest from the disturbing family cares which smother a man's genius, as a house like ours offers him. How can the artistic nature exercise itself in the very grind of the thing, when this child has a cold, and the other the croup; and there is fussing with mustard-paste and ipecac and paregoric, — all those realities, you know? Why, Charlie tells me he feels a great deal more affection for his children when he is all calm and tranquil in the little boudoir at our house; and he writes such lovely little poems about them, I must show you some of them. But this creature doesn't appreciate them a bit: she has no poetry in her."

"Well, I must say, I don't think I should have," said Lillie, honestly. "I should be just as mad as I could be, if John acted so."

"Oh, my dear! the cases are different: Charlie has such peculiarities of genius. The artistic nature, you know, requires soothing." Here they stopped, and rang at the door of a neat little house, and were ushered into a pair of those characteristic parlors which show that they have been arranged by a home-worshipper, and a mother. There were plants and birds and flowers, and little *genre* pictures of children, animals, and household interiors, arranged with a loving eye and hand.

"Did you ever see any thing so perfectly characteristic?" said Mrs. Follingsbee, looking around her as if she were going to faint.

"This woman drives Charlie perfectly wild, because she has no appreciation of high art. Now, I sent her photographs of Michel Angelo's 'Moses,' and 'Night and Morning;' and I really wish you would see where she hung them, — away in yonder dark corner!"

"I think myself they are enough to scare the owls," said Lillie, after a moment's contemplation.

"But, my dear, you know they are the thing," said Mrs. Follingsbee: "people never like such things at first, and one must get used to high art before one forms a taste for it. The thing with her is, she has no docility. She does not try to enter into Charlie's tastes."

The woman with "no docility" entered at this moment, — a little snow-drop of a creature, with a pale, pure, Madonna face, and that sad air of hopeless firmness which is seen unhappily in the faces of so many women.

"I had to bring baby down," she said. "I have no nurse to-day, and he has been threatened with croup."

"The dear little fellow!" said Mrs. Follingsbee, with officious graciousness. "So glad you brought him down; come to his aunty?" she inquired lovingly, as the little fellow shrank away, and regarded her with round, astonished eyes. "Why will you not come to my next reception, Mrs. Ferrola?" she added. "You make yourself quite a stranger to us. You ought to give yourself some variety."

"The fact is, Mrs. Follingsbee," said Mrs. Ferrola, "receptions in New York generally begin about my bed-time; and, if I should spend the night out, I should have no strength to give to my children the next day."

" I had to bring baby down."

"But, my dear, you ought to have some amusement."

"My children amuse me, if you will believe it," said Mrs. Ferrola, with a remarkably quiet smile.

Mrs. Follingsbee was not quite sure whether this was meant to be sarcastic or not. She answered, however, "Well! your husband will come, at all events."

"You may be quite sure of that," said Mrs. Ferrola, with the same quietness.

"Well!" said Mrs. Follingsbee, rising, with patronizing cheerfulness, "delighted to see you doing so well; and, if it is pleasant, I will send the carriage round to take you a drive in the park this afternoon. Good-morning."

And, like a rustling cloud of silks and satins and perfumes, she bent down and kissed the baby, and swept from the apartment.

Mrs. Ferrola, with a movement that seemed involuntary, wiped the baby's cheek with her handkerchief, and, folding it closer to her bosom, looked up as if asking patience where patience is to be found for the asking.

"There! didn't I tell you?" said Mrs. Follingsbee when she came out; "just one of those provoking, meek, obstinate, impracticable creatures, with no adaptation in her."

"Oh, gracious me!" said Lillie: "I can't imagine more dire despair than to sit all day tending baby."

"Well, so you would think; and Charlie has offered to hire competent nurses, and wants her to dress herself up and go into society; and she just won't do it, and sticks right down by the cradle there, with her children running over her like so many squirrels."

"Oh! I hope and trust I never shall have children," said Lillie, fervently, "because, you see, there's an end of every thing. No more fun, no more frolics, no more admiration or good times; nothing but this frightful baby, that you can't get rid of."

Yet, as Lillie spoke, she knew, in her own slippery little heart, that the shadow of this awful cloud of maternity was resting over her; though she laced and danced, and bid defiance to every law of nature, with a blind and ignorant wilfulness, not caring what consequences she might draw down on herself, if only she might escape this.

And was there, then, no soft spot in this woman's heart anywhere? Generally it is thought that the throb of the child's heart awakens a heart in the mother, and that the mother is born again with her child. It is so with unperverted nature, as God meant it to be; and you shall hear from the lips of an Irish washer-woman a genuine poetry of maternal feeling, for the little one who comes to make her toil more toilsome, that is wholly withered away out of luxurious circles, where there is every thing to make life easy. Just as the Chinese have contrived fashionable monsters, where human beings are constrained to grow in the shape of flower-pots, so fashionable life contrives at last to grow a woman who hates babies, and will risk her life to be rid of the crowning glory of womanhood.

There was a time in Lillie's life, when she was sixteen years of age, which was a turning-point with her, and decided that she should be the heartless woman she was. If at that age, and at that time, she had decided to marry the man she really loved, marriage might indeed have proved to her a sacrament. It might have opened to her a door through which she could have passed out from a career of selfish worldliness into that gradual discipline of unselfishness which a true love-marriage brings.

But she did not. The man was poor, and she was beautiful; her beauty would buy wealth and worldly position, and so she cast him off. Yet partly to gratify her own lingering feeling, and partly because she could not wholly renounce what had once been hers, she kept up for years with him just that illusive simulacrum which such women call friendship; which, while constantly denying, constantly takes pains to attract, and drains the heart of all possibility of loving another.

Harry Endicott was a young man of fine capabilities, sensitive, interesting, handsome, full of generous impulses, whom a good woman might easily have led to a full completeness. He was not really Lillie's cousin, but the cousin of her mother; yet, under the name of cousin, he had constant access and family intimacy.

This winter Harry Endicott suddenly returned to the fashionable circles of New York, — returned from a successful career in India, with an ample fortune. He was handsomer than ever, took stylish bachelor lodgings, set up a most distracting turnout, and became a sort of Marquis of Farintosh in fashionable circles. Was ever any thing so lucky, or so unlucky, for our Lillie? — lucky, if life really does run on the basis of French novels, and if all that is needed is the sparkle and stimulus of new emotions; unlucky, nay, even gravely terrible, if life really is established on a basis of moral responsibility, and dogged by the fatal necessity that "whatsoever man or woman soweth, that shall he or she also reap."

In the most critical hour of her youth, when love was sent to her heart like an angel, to beguile her from selfishness, and make self-denial easy, Lillie's pretty little right hand had sowed to the world and the flesh; and of that sowing she was now to reap all the disquiets, the vexations, the tremors, that go to fill the pages of French novels, — records of women who marry where they cannot love, to serve the purposes of selfishness and ambition, and then make up for it by loving where they cannot marry. If all the women in America who have practised, and are practising, this species of moral agriculture should stand forth together, it would be seen that it is not for nothing that France has been called the society educator of the world.

The apartments of the Follingsbee mansion, with their dreamy voluptuousness, were eminently adapted to be the background and scenery of a dramatic performance of this kind. There were vistas of drawing-rooms, with delicious boudoirs, like side chapels in a temple of Venus, with handsome Charlie Ferrola gliding in and out, or lecturing dreamily from the corner of some sofa on the last most important crinkle of the artistic rose-leaf, demonstrating conclusively that beauty was the only true morality, and that there was no sin but bad taste; and that nobody knew what good taste was but himself and his clique. There was the discussion, far from edifying, of modern improved theories of society, seen from an improved philosophic point of view; of all the peculiar wants and needs of etherealized beings, who have been refined and cultivated till it is the most difficult problem in the world to keep them comfortable, while there still remains the most imperative necessity that they should be made happy, though the whole universe were to be torn down and made over to effect it.

The idea of not being happy, and in all respects as blissful as they could possibly be made, was one always assumed by the Follingsbee clique as an injustice to be wrestled with. Anybody that did not affect them agreeably, that jarred on their nerves, or interrupted the delicious reveries of existence with the sharp saw-setting of commonplace realities, in their view ought to be got rid of summarily, whether that somebody were husband or wife, parent or child.

Natures that affected each other pleasantly were to spring together like dew-drops, and sail off on rosy clouds with each other to the land of Do-just-as-you-have-a-mind-to.

The only thing never to be enough regretted, which prevented this immediate and blissful union of particles, was the impossibility of living on rosy clouds, and making them the means of conveyance to the desirable country before mentioned. Many of the fair *illuminatæ*, who were quite willing to go off with a kindred spirit, were withheld by the necessities of infinite pairs of French kid gloves, and gallons of cologne-water, and indispensable clouds of mechlin and point lace, which were necessary to keep around them the poetry of existence.

Although it was well understood among them that the religion of the emotions is the only true religion, and that nothing is holy that you do not feel exactly like doing, and every thing is holy that you do; still these fair confessors lacked the pluck of primitive Christians, and could not think of taking joyfully the spoiling of their goods, even for the sake of a kindred spirit. Hence the necessity of living in deplored marriage-bonds with husbands who could pay rent and taxes, and stand responsible for unlimited bills at Stewart's and Tiffany's. Hence the philosophy which allowed the possession of the body to one man, and of the soul to another, which one may see treated of at large in any writings of the day.

As yet Lillie had been kept intact from all this sort of thing by the hard, brilliant enamel of selfishness. That little shrewd, gritty common sense, which enabled her to see directly through other people's illusions, has, if we mistake not, by this time revealed itself to our readers as an element in her mind : but now there is to come a decided thrust at the heart of her womanhood; and we shall see whether the paralysis is complete, or whether the woman is alive.

If Lillie had loved Harry Endicott poor, had loved him so much that at one time she had seriously balanced the possibility of going to housekeeping in a little unfashionable house, and having only one girl, and hand in hand with him walking the paths of economy, self-denial, and prudence, — the reader will see that Harry Endicott rich, Harry Endicott enthroned in fashionable success, Harry Endicott plus fast horses, splendid equipages, a fine city house, and a country house on the Hudson, was something still more dangerous to her imagination.

But more than this was the stimulus of Harry Endicott out of her power, and beyond the sphere of her charms. She had a feverish desire to see him, but he never called. Forthwith she had a confidential conversation with her bosom friend, who entered into the situation with enthusiasm, and invited him to her receptions. But he didn't come.

The fact was, that Harry Endicott hated Lillie now, with that kind of hatred which is love turned wrong-side out. He hated her for the misery she had caused him, and was in some danger of feeling it incumbent on himself to go to the devil in a wholly unnecessary manner on that account.

He had read the story of Monte Cristo, with its highly wrought plot of vengeance, and had determined to avenge himself on the woman who had so tortured him, and to make her feel, if possible, what he had felt.

So, when he had discovered the hours of driving observed by Mrs. Follingsbee and Lillie in the park, he took pains, from time to time, to meet them face to face, and to pass Lillie with an unrecognizing stare. Then he dashed in among Mrs. Follingsbee's circle, making himself everywhere talked of, till they were beset on all

hands by the inquiry, "Don't you know young Endicott? why, I should think you would want to have him
visit here."

After this had been played far enough, he suddenly
showed himself one evening at Mrs. Follingsbee's, and
apologized in an off-hand manner to Lillie, when reminded
of passing her in the park, that really he wasn't thinking of meeting her, and didn't recognize her, she was so
altered; it had been so many years since they had met,
&c. All in a tone of cool and heartless civility, every
word of which was a dagger's thrust not only into her
vanity, but into the poor little bit of a real heart which
fashionable life had left to Lillie.

Every evening, after he had gone, came a long, confidential conversation with Mrs. Follingsbee, in which
every word and look was discussed and turned, and
all possible or probable inferences therefrom reported;
after which Lillie often laid a sleepless head on a hot
and tumbled pillow, poor, miserable child! suffering her
punishment, without even the grace to know whence it
came, or what it meant. Hitherto Lillie had been walking only in the limits of that kind of permitted wickedness, which, although certainly the remotest thing
possible from the Christianity of Christ, finds a great
deal of tolerance and patronage among communicants
of the altar. She had lived a gay, vain, self-pleasing
life, with no object or purpose but the simple one to get
each day as much pleasurable enjoyment out of existence as possible. Mental and physical indolence and
inordinate vanity had been the key-notes of her life.

She hated every thing that required protracted thought, or that made trouble, and she longed for excitement. The passion for praise and admiration had become to her like the passion of the opium-eater for his drug, or of the brandy-drinker for his dram. But now she was heedlessly steering to what might prove a more palpable sin.

Harry the serf, once half despised for his slavish devotion, now stood before her, proud and free, and tantalized her by the display he made of his indifference, and preference for others. She put forth every art and effort to recapture him. But the most dreadful stroke of fate of all was, that Rose Ferguson had come to New York to make a winter visit, and was much talked of in certain circles where Harry was quite intimate; and he professed himself, indeed, an ardent admirer at her shrine.

CHAPTER XX.

THE VAN ASTRACHANS.

THE Van Astrachans, a proud, rich old family, who took a certain defined position in New-York life on account of some ancestral passages in their family history, had invited Rose to spend a month or two with them; and she was therefore moving as a star in a very high orbit.

Now, these Van Astrachans were one of those cold, glittering, inaccessible pinnacles in Mrs. Follingsbee's fashionable Alp-climbing which she would spare no expense to reach if possible. It was one of the families for whose sake she had Mrs. John Seymour under her roof; and the advent of Rose, whom she was pleased to style one of Mrs. Seymour's most intimate friends, was an unhoped-for stroke of good luck; because there was the necessity of calling on Rose, of taking her out to drive in the park, and of making a party on her account, from which, of course, the Van Astrachans could not stay away.

It will be seen here that our friend, Mrs. Follingsbee, like all ladies whose watch-word is "Excelsior," had a peculiar, difficult, and slippery path to climb.

The Van Astrachans were good old Dutch-Reformed Christians, unquestioning believers in the Bible in general, and the Ten Commandments in particular,— persons whose moral constitutions had been nourished on the great stocky beefsteaks and sirloins of plain old truths which go to form English and Dutch nature. Theirs was a style of character which rendered them utterly hopeless of comprehending the etherealized species of holiness which obtained in the innermost circles of the Follingsbee *illuminati.* Mr. Van Astrachan buttoned under his coat not only many solid inches of what Carlyle calls "good Christian fat," but also a pocket-book through which millions of dollars were passing daily in an easy and comfortable flow, to the great advantage of many of his fellow-creatures no less than himself; and somehow or other he was pig-headed in the idea that the Bible and the Ten Commandments had something to do with that stability of things which made this necessary flow easy and secure.

He was slow-moulded, accurate, and fond of security; and was of opinion that nineteen centuries of Christianity ought to have settled a few questions so that they could be taken for granted, and were not to be kept open for discussion.

Moreover, Mr. Van Astrachan having read the accounts of the first French revolution, and having remarked all the subsequent history of that country, was confirmed in his idea, that pitching every thing into pi once in fifty years was no way to get on in the affairs of this world.

He had strong suspicions of every thing French, and a mind very ill adapted to all those delicate reasonings and shadings and speculations of which Mr. Charlie Ferrola was particularly fond, which made every thing in morals and religion an open question.

He and his portly wife planted themselves, like two canons of the sanctuary, every Sunday, in the tip-top highest-priced pew of the most orthodox old church in New York; and if the worthy man sometimes indulged in gentle slumbers in the high-padded walls of his slip, it was because he was so well assured of the orthodoxy of his minister that he felt that no interest of society would suffer while he was off duty. But may Heaven grant us, in these days of dissolving views and general undulation, large armies of these solid-planted artillery on the walls of our Zion!

Blessed be the people whose strength is to sit still! Much needed are they when the activity of free inquiry seems likely to chase us out of house and home, and leave us, like the dove in the deluge, no rest for the sole of our foot.

Let us thank God for those Dutch-Reformed churches; great solid breakwaters, that stand as the dykes in their ancestral Holland to keep out the muddy waves of that sea whose waters cast up mire and dirt.

But let us fancy with what quakings and shakings of heart Mrs. Follingsbee must have sought the alliance of these tremendously solid old Christians. They were precisely what she wanted to give an air of solidity to the cobweb glitter of her state. And we can also see how necessary it was that she should ostentatiously visit Charlie Ferrola's wife, and speak of her as a darling creature, her particular friend, whom she was doing her very best to keep out of an early grave.

Chârlie Ferrola said that the Van Astrachans were obtuse; and so, to a certain degree, they were. In social matters they had a kind of confiding simplicity. They were so much accustomed to regard positive morals in the light of immutable laws of Nature, that it would not have been easy to have made them understand that sliding scale of estimates which is in use nowadays. They would probably have had but one word, and that a very disagreeable one, to designate a married woman who was in love with anybody but her husband. Consequently, they were the very last people whom any gossip of this sort could ever reach, or to whose ears it could have been made intelligible.

Mr. Van Astrachan considered Dick Follingsbee a swindler, whose proper place was the State's prison, and whose morals could only be mentioned with those of Sodom and Gomorrah.

Nevertheless, as Mrs. Follingsbee made it a point of rolling up her eyes and sighing deeply when his name was mentioned,—as she attended church on Sunday with conspicuous faithfulness, and subscribed to charitable societies and all manner of good works,—as she had got appointed directress on the board of an orphan asylum where Mrs. Van Astrachan figured in association with her, that good lady was led to look upon her with compassion, as a worthy woman who was making the best of her way to heaven, notwithstanding the opposition of a dissolute husband.

As for Rose, she was as fresh and innocent and dewy, in the hot whirl and glitter and glare of New York, as a waving spray of sweet-brier, brought in fresh with all the dew upon it.

She really had for Lillie a great deal of that kind of artistic admiration which nice young girls sometimes have for very beautiful women older than themselves; and was, like almost every one else, somewhat bejuggled and taken in by that air of infantine sweetness and simplicity which had survived all the hot glitter of her life, as if a rose, fresh with dew, should lie unwilted in the mouth of a furnace.

Moreover, Lillie's face had a beauty this winter it had never worn: the softness of a real feeling, the pathos of real suffering, at times touched her face with something that was always wanting in it before. The bitter waters of sin that she would drink gave a strange feverish color to her cheek; and the poisoned perfume she would inhale gave a strange new brightness to her eyes.

Rose sometimes looked on her and wondered; so innocent and healthy and light-hearted in herself, she could not even dream of what was passing. She had been brought up to love John as a brother, and opened her heart at once to his wife with a sweet and loyal faithfulness. When she told Mrs. Van Astrachan that Mrs. John Seymour was one of her friends from Springdale, married into a family with which she had grown up with great intimacy, it seemed the most natural thing in the world to the good lady that Rose should want to visit her; that she should drive with her, and call on her, and receive her at their house; and with her of course must come Mrs. Follingsbee.

Mr. Van Astrachan made a dead halt at the idea of Dick Follingsbee. He never would receive *that* man under his roof, he said, and he never would enter his house; and when Mr. Van Astrachan once said a thing of this kind, as Mr. Hosea Biglow remarks, "a meeting-house wasn't sotter."

But then Mrs. Follingsbee's situation was confidentially stated to Lillie, and by Lillie confidentially stated to Rose, and by Rose to Mrs. Van Astrachan; and it was made to appear how Dick Follingsbee had entirely abandoned his wife, going off in the ways of Balaam the son of Bosor, and all other bad ways mentioned in Scripture, habitually leaving poor Mrs. Follingsbee to entertain company alone, so that he was never seen at her parties, and had nothing to do with her.

"So much the better for them," remarked Mr. Van Astrachan.

"In that case, my dear, I don't see that it would do any harm for you to go to Mrs. Follingsbee's party on Rose's account. I never go to parties, as you know; and I certainly should not begin by going there. But still I see no objection to your taking Rose."

If Mr. Van Astrachan had seen objections, you never would have caught Mrs. Van Astrachan going; for she was one of your full-blooded women, who never in her life engaged to do a thing she didn't mean to do: and having promised in the marriage service to obey her husband, she obeyed him plumb, with the air of a person who is fulfilling the prophecies; though her chances in this way were very small, as Mr. Van Astrachan generally called her "ma," and obeyed all her orders with a stolid precision quite edifying to behold. He took her advice always, and was often heard naively to remark that Mrs. Van Astrachan and he were always of the same opinion, — an expression happily defining that state in which a man does just what his wife tells him to.

CHAPTER XXI.

MRS. FOLLINGSBEE'S PARTY, AND WHAT CAME OF IT.

OUR vulgar idea of a party is a week or fortnight of previous discomfort and chaotic tergiversation, and the mistress of it all distracted and worn out with endless cares. Such a party bursts in on a well-ordered family state as a bomb bursts into a city, leaving confusion and disorder all around. But it would be a pity if such a life-long devotion to the arts and graces as Mrs. Follingsbee had given, backed by Dick Follingsbee's fabulous fortune, and administered by the exquisite Charlie Ferrola, should not have brought forth some appreciable results. One was, that the great Castle of Indolence was prepared for the *fête*, with no more ripple of disturbance than if it had been a Nereid's bower, far down beneath the reach of tempests, where the golden sand is never ruffled, and the crimson and blue sea flowers never even dream of commotion.

Charlie Ferrola wore, it is true, a brow somewhat oppressed with care, and was kept tucked up on a rose-colored satin sofa, and served with lachrymæ Christi,

and Montefiascone, and all other substitutes for the
dews of Hybla, while he draughted designs for the
floral arrangements, which were executed by obsequious
attendants in felt slippers; and the whole process of
arrangement proceeded like a dream of the lotus-eaters'
paradise.

Madame de Tullegig was of course retained primarily
for the adornment of Mrs. Follingsbee's person. It
was understood, however, on this occasion, that the
composition of the costumes was to embrace both hers
and Lillie's, that they might appear in a contrasted
tableau, and bring out each other's points. It was a
subject worthy a Parisian artiste, and drew so seriously
on Madame de Tullegig's brain-power, that she assured
Mrs. Follingsbee afterwards that the effort of composition had sensibly exhausted her.

Before we relate the events of that evening, as they
occurred, we must give some little idea of the position
in which the respective parties now stood.

Harry Endicott, by his mother's side, was related
to Mrs. Van Astrachan. Mr. Van Astrachan had been,
in a certain way, guardian to him; and his success in
making his fortune was in consequence of capital advanced and friendly patronage thus accorded. In the
family, therefore, he had the *entrée* of a son, and
had enjoyed the opportunity of seeing Rose with a
freedom and frequency that soon placed them on the
footing of old acquaintanceship. Rose was an easy
person to become acquainted with in an ordinary and
superficial manner. She was like those pellucid waters

whose great clearness deceives the eye as to their
depth. Her manners had an easy and gracious frankness; and she spoke right on, with an apparent simplicity
and fearlessness that produced at first the impression
that you knew all her heart. A longer acquaintance,
however, developed depths of reserved thought and
feeling far beyond what at first appeared.

Harry, at first, had met her only on those superficial
grounds of banter and *badinage* where a gay young
gentleman and a gay young lady may reconnoitre, before either side gives the other the smallest peep of the
key of what Dr. Holmes calls the side-door of their
hearts.

Harry, to say the truth, was in a bad way when
he first knew Rose: he was restless, reckless, bitter.
Turned loose into society with an ample fortune and
nothing to do, he was in danger, according to the
homely couplet of Dr. Watts, of being provided with
employment by that undescribable personage who
makes it his business to look after idle hands.

Rose had attracted him first by her beauty, all the
more attractive to him because in a style entirely different from that which hitherto had captivated his imagination. Rose was tall, well-knit, and graceful, and
bore herself with a sort of slender but majestic light-
ness, like a meadow-lily. Her well-shaped, classical head
was set finely on her graceful neck, and she had a stag-
like way of carrying it, that impressed a stranger sometimes as haughty; but Rose could not help that, it was
a trick of nature. Her hair was of the glossiest black,

her skin fair as marble, her nose a little, nicely-turned aquiline affair, her eyes of a deep violet blue and shadowed by long dark lashes, her mouth a little larger than the classical proportion, but generous in smiles and laughs which revealed perfect teeth of dazzling whiteness. There, gentlemen and ladies, is Rose Ferguson's picture: and, if you add to all this the most attractive impulsiveness and self-unconsciousness, you will not wonder that Harry Endicott at first found himself admiring her, and fancied driving out with her in the park; and that when admiring eyes followed them both, as a handsome pair, Harry was well pleased.

Rose, too, liked Harry Endicott. A young girl of twenty is not a severe judge of a handsome, lively young man, who knows far more of the world than she does; and though Harry's conversation was a perfect Catherine-wheel of all sorts of wild talk, — sneering, bitter, and sceptical, and giving expression to the most heterodox sentiments, with the evident intention of shocking respectable authorities, — Rose rather liked him than otherwise; though she now and then took the liberty to stand upon her dignity, and opened her great blue eyes on him with a grave, inquiring look of surprise, — a look that seemed to challenge him to stand and defend himself. From time to time, too, she let fall little bits of independent opinion, well poised and well turned, that hit exactly where she meant they should; and Harry began to stand a little in awe of her.

Harry had never known a woman like Rose; a wo-

man so poised and self-centred, so cultivated, so capable
of deep and just reflections, and so religious. His experience with women had not been fortunate, as has been
seen in this narrative; and, insensibly to himself, Rose
was beginning to exercise an influence over him. The
sphere around her was cool and bright and wholesome,
as different from the hot atmosphere of passion and
sentiment and flirtation to which he had been accustomed, as a New-England summer morning from a
sultry night in the tropics. Her power over him was
in the appeal to a wholly different part of his nature,—
intellect, conscience, and religious sensibility; and once
or twice he found himself speaking to her quietly, seriously, and rationally, not from the purpose of pleasing
her, but because she had aroused such a strain of thought
in his own mind. There was a certain class of brilliant
sayings of his, of a cleverly irreligious and sceptical
nature, at which Rose never laughed: when this sort of
firework was let off in her presence, she opened her
eyes upon him, wide and blue, with a calm surprise
intermixed with pity, but said nothing; and, after trying the experiment several times, he gradually felt this
silent kind of look a restraint upon him.

At the same time, it must not be conjectured that, at
present, Harry Endicott was thinking of falling in love
with Rose. In fact, he scoffed at the idea of love,
and professed to disbelieve in its existence. And,
beside all this, he was gratifying an idle vanity, and
the wicked love of revenge, in visiting Lillie; sometimes professing for days an exclusive devotion to her,

in which there was a little too much reality on both
sides to be at all safe or innocent; and then, when he
had wound her up to the point where even her involuntary looks and words and actions towards him must
have compromised her in the eyes of others, he would
suddenly recede for days, and devote himself exclu-
sively to Rose; driving ostentatiously with her in the
park, where he would meet Lillie face to face, and bow
triumphantly to her in passing. All these proceed-
ings, talked over with Mrs. Follingsbee, seemed to
give promise of the most impassioned French romance
possible.

Rose walked through all her part in this little drama,
wrapped in a veil of sacred ignorance. Had she known
the whole, the probability is that she would have refused Harry's acquaintance; but, like many another
niçe girl, she tripped gayly near to pitfalls and chasms
of which she had not the remotest conception.

Lillie's want of self-control, and imprudent conduct,
had laid her open to reports in certain circles where
such reports find easy credence; but these were circles
with which the Van Astrachans never mingled. The
only accidental point of contact was the intimacy of
Rose with the Seymour family; and Rose was the last
person to understand an allusion if she heard it. The
reading of Rose had been carefully selected by her
father, and had not embraced any novels of the French
romantic school; neither had she, like some modern
young ladies, made her mind a highway for the tramp-
ing of every kind of possible fictitious character which

a novelist might choose to draw, nor taken an interest in the dissections of morbid anatomy. In fact, she was old-fashioned enough to like Scott's novels; and though she was just the kind of girl Thackeray would have loved, she never could bring her fresh young heart to enjoy his pictures of world-worn and decaying natures.

The idea of sentimental flirtations and love-making on the part of a married woman was one so beyond her conception of possibilities that it would have been very difficult to make her understand or believe it.

On the occasion of the Follingsbee party, therefore, Rose accepted Harry as an escort in simple good faith. She was by no means so wise as not to have a deal of curiosity about it, and not a little of dazed and dazzled sense of enjoyment in prospect of the perfect labyrinth of fairy-land which the Follingsbee mansion opened before her.

On the eventful evening, Mrs. Follingsbee and Lillie stood together to receive their guests,—the former in gold color, with magnificent point lace and diamond tiara; while Lillie in heavenly blue, with wreaths of misty tulle and pearl ornaments, seemed like a filmy cloud by the setting sun.

Rose, entering on Harry Endicott's arm, in the full bravery of a well-chosen toilet, caused a buzz of admiration which followed them through the rooms; but Rose was nothing to the illuminated eyes of Mrs. Follingsbee compared with the portly form of Mrs. Van Astrachan entering beside her, and spreading over her the wings of motherly protection. That much-desired matron,

scrcne in her point lace and diamonds, beamed around
her with an innocent kindliness, shedding respectability
wherever she moved, as a certain Russian prince was
said to shed diamonds.

"Rose, entering on Harry Endicott's arm."

"Why, that is Mrs. Van Astrachan!"

"You don't tell me so!   Is it possible?"

"Which?"   "Where is she?"   "How in the world
did she get here?" were the whispered remarks that

followed her wherever she moved; and Mrs. Follingsbee, looking after her, could hardly suppress an exulting
Te Deum. It was done, and couldn't be undone.

Mrs. Van Astrachan might not appear again at a
salon of hers for a year; but that could not do away
the patent fact, witnessed by so many eyes, that she
had been there once. Just as a modern newspaper or
magazine wants only one article of a celebrated author
to announce him as among their stated contributors for
all time, and to flavor every subsequent issue of the
journal with expectancy, so Mrs. Follingsbee exulted
in the idea that this one evening would flavor all her
receptions for the winter, whether the good lady's
diamonds ever appeared there again or not. In her
secret heart, she always had the perception, when striving to climb up on this kind of ladder, that the time
might come when she should be found out; and she
well knew the absolute and uncomprehending horror
with which that good lady would regard the French
principles and French practice of which Charlie Ferrola
and Co. were the expositors and exemplars.

This was what Charlie Ferrola meant when he said
that the Van Astrachans were obtuse. They never
could be brought to the niceties of moral perspective
which show one exactly where to find the vanishing
point for every duty.

Be that as it may, there, at any rate, she was, safe
and sound; surrounded by people whom she had never
met before, and receiving introductions to the right and
left with the utmost graciousness. The arrangements

for the evening had been made at the tea-table of the
Van Astrachans with an innocent and trustful simplicity.

"You know, dear," said Mrs. Van Astrachan to
Rose, "that I never like to stay long away from papa"
(so the worthy lady called her husband); "and so, if
it's just the same to you, you shall let me have the
carriage come for me early, and then you and Harry
shall be left free to see it out. I know young folks
must be young," she said, with a comfortable laugh.
"There was a time, dear, when my waist was not bigger

THE VAN ASTRACHANS.

than yours, that I used to dance all night with the best
of them; but I've got bravely over that now."

"Yes, Rose," said Mr. Van Astrachan, "you mayn't

believe it, but ma there was the spryest dancer of any of the girls. You are pretty nice to look at, but you don't quite come up to what she was in those days. I tell you, I wish you could have seen her," said the good man, warming to his subject. "Why, I've seen the time when every fellow on the floor was after her."

"Papa," says Mrs. Van Astrachan, reprovingly, "I wouldn't say such things if I were you."

"Yes, I would," said Rose. "Do tell us, Mr. Van Astrachan."

"Well, I'll tell you," said Mr. Van Astrachan: "you ought to have seen her in a red dress she used to wear."

"Oh, come, papa! what nonsense! Rose, I never wore a red dress in my life; it was a pink silk; but you know men never do know the names for colors."

"Well, at any rate," said Mr. Van Astrachan, hardily, "pink or red, no matter; but I'll tell you, she took all before her that evening. There were Stuyvesants and Van Rennselaers and Livingstons, and all sorts of grand fellows, in her train; but, somehow, I cut 'em out. There is no such dancing nowadays as there was when wife and I were young. I've been caught once or twice in one of their parties; and I don't call it dancing. I call it draggle-tailing. They don't take any steps, and there is no spirit in it."

"Well," said Rose, "I know we moderns are very much to be pitied. Papa always tells me the same story about mamma, and the days when he was young. But, dear Mrs. Van Astrachan, I hope you won't stay a mo-

ment, on my account, after you get tired. I suppose if
you are just seen with me there in the beginning of the
evening, it will matronize me enough; and then I have
engaged to dance the 'German' with Mr. Endicott,
and I believe they keep that up till nobody knows when.
But I am determined to see the whole through."

"Yes, yes! see it all through," said Mr. Van Astrachan.
"Young people must be young. It's all right enough,
and you won't miss my Polly after you get fairly into
it near so much as I shall. I 'll sit up for her till twelve
o'clock, and read my paper."

Rose was at first, to say the truth, bewildered and
surprised by the perfect labyrinth of fairy-land which
Charlie Ferrola's artistic imagination had created in the
Follingsbee mansion.

Initiated people, who had travelled in Europe, said it
put them in mind of the "Jardin Mabille;" and those
who had not were reminded of some of the wonders of
"The Black Crook." There were apartments turned
into bowers and grottoes, where the gas-light shim-
mered behind veils of falling water, and through pen-
dant leaves of all sorts of strange water-plants of
tropical regions. There were all those wonderful leaf-
plants of every weird device of color, which have been
conjured up by tricks of modern gardening, as Rappa-
cini is said to have created his strange garden in Padua.
There were beds of hyacinths and crocuses and tulips,
made to appear like living gems by the jets of gas-light
which came up among them in glass flowers of the same
form. Far away in recesses were sofas of soft green

velvet turf, overshadowed by trailing vines, and illuminated with moonlight-softness by hidden alabaster lamps. The air was heavy with the perfume of flowers, and the sound of music and dancing from the ball-room came to these recesses softened by distance.

The Follingsbee mansion occupied a whole square of the city; and these enchanted bowers were created by temporary enlargements of the conservatory covering the ground of the garden. With money, and the Croton Water-works, and all the New-York greenhouses at disposal, nothing was impossible.

There was in this reception no vulgar rush or crush or jam. The apartments opened were so extensive, and the attractions in so many different directions, that there did not appear to be a crowd anywhere.

There was no general table set, with the usual liabilities of rush and crush; but four or five well-kept rooms, fragrant with flowers and sparkling with silver and crystal, were ready at any hour to minister to the guest whatever delicacy or dainty he or she might demand; and light-footed waiters circulated with noiseless obsequiousness through all the rooms, proffering dainties on silver trays.

Mrs. Van Astrachan and Rose at first found themselves walking everywhere, with a fresh and lively interest. It was something quite out of the line of the good lady's previous experience, and so different from any thing she had ever seen before, as to keep her in a state of placid astonishment. Rose, on the other hand, was delighted and excited; the more so that she could not help perceiving that she herself amid all these objects of beauty was followed by the admiring glances of many eyes.

It is not to be supposed that a girl so handsome as Rose comes to her twentieth year without having the pretty secret made known to her in more ways than one, or that thus made known it is any thing but agreeable; but, on the present occasion, there was a buzz of inquiry and a crowd of applicants about her; and her dancing-list seemed in a fair way to be soon filled up for the evening, Harry telling her laughingly that he would let her off from every thing but the " German; " but that she might consider her engagement with him as a standing one whenever troubled with an application which for any reason she did not wish to accept.

Harry assumed towards Rose that air of brotherly guardianship which a young man who piques himself on having seen a good deal of the world likes to take with a pretty girl who knows less of it. Besides, he rather valued himself on having brought to the reception the most brilliant girl of the evening.

Our friend Lillie, however, was in her own way as entrancingly beautiful this evening as the most perfect mortal flesh and blood could be made; and Harry went back to her when Rose went off with her partners as a moth flies to a candle, not with any express intention of burning his wings, but simply because he likes to be dazzled, and likes the bitter excitement. He felt now that he had power over her, — a bad, a dangerous power he knew, with what of conscience was left in him; but he thought, " Let her take her own risk." And so, many busy gossips saw the handsome young man, his great dark eyes kindled with an evil light, whirling in dizzy mazes with this cloud of flossy mist; out of which looked up to him an impassioned woman's face, and eyes that said what those eyes had no right to say.

There are times, in such scenes of bewilderment, when women are as truly out of their own control by nervous excitement as if they were intoxicated; and Lillie's looks and words and actions towards Harry were as open a declaration of her feelings as if she had spoken them aloud to every one present.

The scandals about them were confirmed in the eyes of every one that looked on; for there were plenty of people present in whose view of things the worst possible interpretation was the most probable one.

Rose was in the way, during the course of the evening, of hearing remarks of the most disagreeable and startling nature with regard to the relations of Harry and Lillie to each other. They filled her with a sort of horror, as if she had come to an unwholesome place; while she indignantly repelled them from her thoughts, as every uncontaminated woman will the first suspicion of the purity of a sister woman. In Rose's view it was monstrous and impossible. Yet when she stood at one time in a group to see them waltzing, she started, and felt a cold shudder, as a certain instinctive conviction of something not right forced itself on her. She closed her eyes, and wished herself away; wished that she had not let Mrs. Van Astrachan go home without her; wished that somebody would speak to Lillie and caution her; felt an indignant rising of her heart against Harry, and was provoked at herself that she was engaged to him for the "German."

She turned away; and, taking the arm of the gentleman with her, complained of the heat as oppressive, and they sauntered off together into the bowery region beyond.

"Oh, now! where can I have left my fan?" she said, suddenly stopping.

"Let me go back and get it for you," said he of the whiskers who attended her. It was one of the dancing young men of New York, and it is no particular matter what his name was.

"Thank you," said Rose: "I believe I left it on the sofa in the yellow drawing-room." He was gone in a moment.

Rose wandered on a little way, through the labyrinth of flowers and shadowy trees and fountains, and sat down on an artificial rock where she fell into a deep reverie. Rising to go back, she missed her way, and became quite lost, and went on uneasily, conscious that she had committed a rudeness in not waiting for her attendant.

At this moment she looked through a distant alcove of shrubbery, and saw Harry and Lillie standing together, — she with both hands laid upon his arm, looking up to him and speaking rapidly with an imploring accent. She saw him, with an angry frown, push Lillie from him so rudely that she almost fell backward, and sat down with her handkerchief to her eyes; he came forward hurriedly, and met the eyes of Rose fixed upon him.

"She saw him, with an angry frown, push Lillie from him."

"Mr. Endicott," she said, "I have to ask a favor of you. Will you be so good as to excuse me from the 'German' to-night, and order my carriage?"

"Why, Miss Ferguson, what is the matter?" he said: "what has come over you? I hope I have not had the misfortune to do any thing to displease you?"

Without replying to this, Rose answered, "I feel very unwell. My head is aching violently, and I cannot go through the rest of the evening. I must go home at once." She spoke it in a decided tone that admitted of no question.

Without answer, Harry Endicott gave her his arm, accompanied her through the final leave-takings, went with her to the carriage, put her in, and sprang in after her.

Rose sank back on her seat, and remained perfectly silent; and Harry, after a few remarks of his had failed to elicit a reply, rode by her side equally silent through the streets homeward.

He had Mr. Van Astrachan's latch-key; and, when the carriage stopped, he helped Rose to alight, and went up the steps of the house.

"Miss Ferguson," he said abruptly, "I have something I want to say to you."

"Not now, not to-night," said Rose, hurriedly. "I am too tired; and it is too late."

"To-morrow then," he said: "I shall call when you will have had time to be rested. Good-night!"

CHAPTER XXII.

THE SPIDER-WEB BROKEN.

HARRY did not go back, to lead the "German," as he had been engaged to do. In fact, in his last apologies to Mrs. Follingsbee, he had excused himself on account of his partner's sudden indisposition,— a thing which made no small buzz and commotion ; though the missing gap, like all gaps great and little in human society, soon found somebody to step into it : and the dance went on just as gayly as if they had been there.

Meanwhile, there were in this good city of New York a couple of sleepless individuals, revolving many things uneasily during the night-watches, or at least that portion of the night-watches that remained after they reached home, — to wit, Mr. Harry Endicott and Miss Rose Ferguson.

What had taken place in that little scene between Lillie and Harry, the termination of which was seen by Rose ? We are not going to give a minute description. The public has already been circumstantially instructed by such edifying books as "Cometh up as a Flower," and others of a like turn, in what manner and in what terms married women can abdicate the dignity of their sex, and degrade themselves so far as to offer their whole life, and their whole selves, to some reluctant man, with too much remaining conscience or prudence to accept the sacrifice.

It was from some such wild, passionate utterances of Lillie that Harry felt a recoil of mingled conscience, fear, and that disgust which man feels when she, whom God made to be sought, degrades herself to seek. There is no edification and no propriety in highly colored and minute drawing of such scenes of temptation and degradation, though they are the stock and staple of some French novels, and more disgusting English ones made on their model. Harry felt in his own conscience that he had been acting a most unworthy part, that no advances on the part of Lillie could excuse his conduct; and his thoughts went back somewhat regretfully to the days long ago, when she was a fair, pretty, innocent girl, and he had loved her honestly and truly. Unperceived by himself, the character of Rose was exerting a powerful influence over him; and, when he met that look of pain and astonishment which he had seen in her large blue eyes the night before, it seemed to awaken many things within him. It is astonishing how blindly people sometimes go on as to the character of their own conduct, till suddenly, like a torch in a dark place, the light of another person's opinion is thrown in upon them, and they begin to judge themselves under the quickening influence of another person's moral magnetism. Then, indeed, it often happens that the graves give up their dead, and that there is a sort of interior resurrection and judgment.

Harry did not seem to be consciously thinking of Rose, and yet the undertone of all that night's uneasiness was a something that had been roused and quickened in him by his acquaintance with her. How he loathed himself for the last few weeks of his life! How he loathed that hot, lurid, murky atmosphere of flirtation and passion and French sentimentality in which he had been living! — atmosphere as hard to draw healthy breath in as the odor of wilting tuberoses the day after a party.

Harry valued Rose's good opinion as he had never valued it before; and, as he thought of her in his restless tossings, she seemed to him something as pure, as wholesome, and strong as the air of his native New-England hills, as the sweet-brier and sweet-fern he used to love to gather when he was a boy. She seemed of a piece with all the good old ways of New England, — its household virtues, its conscientious sense of right, its exact moral boundaries ; and he felt somehow as if she belonged to that healthy portion of his life which he now looked back upon with something of regret.

Then, what would she think of him? They had been friends, he said to himself; they had passed over those boundaries of teasing unreality where most young gentlemen and young ladies are content to hold converse with each other, and had talked together reasonably and seriously, saying in some hours what they really thought and felt. And Rose had impressed him at times by her silence and reticence in certain connections, and on certain subjects, with a sense of something hidden and veiled, — a reserved force that he longed still further to penetrate. But now, he said to himself, he must have fallen in her opinion. Why was she so cold, so almost haughty, in her treatment of him the night before? He felt in the atmosphere around her, and in the touch of her hand, that she was quivering like a galvanic battery with the suppressed force of some powerful emotion; and his own conscience dimly interpreted to him what it might be.

To say the truth, Rose was terribly aroused. And there was a great deal in her to be aroused, for she had a strong nature; and the whole force of womanhood in her had never received such a shock.

Whatever may be scoffingly said of the readiness of women to pull one another down, it is certain that the highest class of them have the feminine *esprit de corps* immensely strong. The humiliation of another woman seems to them their own humiliation; and man's lordly contempt for another woman seems like contempt of themselves.

The deepest feeling roused in Rose by the scenes which she saw last night was concern for the honor of womanhood; and her indignation at first did not strike where we are told woman's indignation does, on the woman, but on the man. Loving John Seymour as a brother from her childhood, feeling in the intimacy in which they had grown up as if their families had been one, the thoughts that had been

forced upon her of his wife the night before had struck
to her heart with the weight of a terrible affliction.
She judged Lillie as a pure woman generally judges
another,—out of herself,—and could not and would
not believe that the gross and base construction which
had been put upon her conduct was the true one. She
looked upon her as led astray by inordinate vanity, and
the hopeless levity of an undeveloped, unreflecting
habit of mind. She was indignant with Harry for the
part that he had taken in the affair, and indignant
and vexed with herself for the degree of freedom and
intimacy which she had been suffering to grow up
between him and herself. Her first impulse was to
break it off altogether, and have nothing more to say to
or do with him. She felt as if she would like to take
the short course which young girls sometimes take out
of the first serious mortification or trouble in their life,
and run away from it altogether. She would have
liked to have packed her trunk, taken her seat on board
the cars, and gone home to Springdale the next day,
and forgotten all about the whole of it; but then, what
should she say to Mrs. Van Astrachan? what account
could she give for the sudden breaking up of her
visit?

Then, there was Harry going to call on her the next
day! What ought she to say to him? On the whole,
it was a delicate matter for a young girl of twenty
to manage alone. How she longed to have the counsel
of her sister or her mother! She thought of Mrs. Van
Astrachan; but then, again, she did not wish to disturb

that good lady's pleasant, confidential relations with Harry, and tell tales of him out of school: so, on the whole, she had a restless and uncomfortable night of it.

Mrs. Van Astrachan expressed her surprise at seeing Rose take her place at the breakfast-table the next morning. "Dear me!" she said, "I was just telling Jane to have some breakfast kept for you. I had no idea of seeing you down at this time."

"But," said Rose, "I gave out entirely, and came away only an hour after you did. The fact is, we country girls can't stand this sort of thing. I had such a terrible headache, and felt so tired and exhausted, that I got Mr. Endicott to bring me away before the 'German.'"

"Bless me!" said Mr. Van Astrachan; "why, you're not at all up to snuff! Why, Polly, you and I used to stick it out till daylight! didn't we?"

"Well, you see, Mr. Van Astrachan, I hadn't anybody like you to stick it out with," said Rose. "Perhaps that made the difference."

"Oh, well, now, I am sure there's our Harry! I am sure a girl must be difficult, if he doesn't suit her for a beau," said the good gentleman.

"Oh, Mr. Endicott is all well enough!" said Rose; "only, you observe, not precisely to me what you were to the lady you call Polly,—that's all."

"Ha, ha!" laughed Mr. Van Astrachan. "Well, to be sure, that does make a difference; but Harry's a nice fellow, nice fellow, Miss Rose: not many fellows like him, as I think."

18

"Yes, indeed," chimed in Mrs. Van Astrachan. "I haven't a son in the world that I think more of than I do of Harry; he has such a good heart."

Now, the fact was, this eulogistic strain that the worthy couple were very prone to fall into in speaking of Harry to Rose was this morning most especially annoying to her; and she turned the subject at once, by chattering so fluently, and with such minute details of description, about the arrangements of the rooms and the flowers and the lamps and the fountains and the cascades, and all the fairy-land wonders of the Follingsbee party, that the good pair found themselves constrained to be listeners during the rest of the time devoted to the morning meal.

It will be found that good young ladies, while of course they have all the innocence of the dove, do display upon emergencies a considerable share of the wisdom of the serpent. And on this same mother wit and wisdom, Rose called internally, when that day, about eleven o'clock, she was summoned to the library, to give Harry his audience.

Truth to say, she was in a state of excited womanhood vastly becoming to her general appearance, and entered the library with flushed cheeks and head erect, like one prepared to stand for herself and for her sex.

Harry, however, wore a mortified, semi-penitential air, that, on the first glance, rather mollified her. Still, however, she was not sufficiently clement to give him the least assistance in opening the conversation, by the suggestions of any of those nice little oily nothings with which ladies, when in a gracious mood, can smooth the path for a difficult confession.

She sat very quietly, with her hands before her, while Harry walked tumultuously up and down the room.

"Miss Ferguson," he said at last, abruptly, "I know you are thinking ill of me."

Miss Ferguson did not reply.

"I had hoped," he said, "that there had been a little something more than mere acquaintance between us. I had hoped you looked upon me as a friend."

"I did, Mr. Endicott," said Rose.

"And you do not now?"

"I cannot say that," she said, after a pause; "but, Mr. Endicott, if we are friends, you must give me the liberty to speak plainly."

"That's exactly what I want you to do!" he said impetuously; "that is just what I wish."

"Allow me to ask, then, if you are an early friend and family connection of Mrs. John Seymour?"

"I was an early friend, and am somewhat of a family connection."

"That is, I understand there has been a ground in your past history for you to be on a footing of a certain family intimacy with Mrs. Seymour; in that case, Mr. Endicott, I think you ought to have considered yourself the guardian of her honor and reputation, and not allowed her to be compromised on your account."

The blood flushed into Harry's face; and he stood abashed and silent. Rose went on, —

"I was shocked, I was astonished, last night, because I could not help overhearing the most disagreeable, the most painful remarks on you and her, — remarks most unjust, I am quite sure, but for which I fear you have given too much reason!"

"Miss Ferguson," said Harry, stopping as he walked up and down, "I confess I have been wrong and done wrong; but, if you knew all, you might see how I have been led into it. That woman has been the evil fate of my life. Years ago, when we were both young, I loved her as honestly as man could love a woman; and she professed to love me in return. But I was poor; and she would not marry me. She sent me off, yet she would not let me forget her. She would always write to me just enough to keep up hope and interest; and she knew for years that all my object in striving for fortune was to win her. At last, when a lucky stroke made me suddenly rich, and I came home to seek her, I found her married, — married, as she owns, without love, — married for wealth and ambition. I don't justify myself, — I don't pretend to; but when she met me with her old smiles and her old charms, and told me she loved me still, it roused the very devil in me. I wanted revenge. I wanted to humble her, and make her suffer all she had made me; and I didn't care what came of it."

Harry spoke, trembling with emotion; and Rose felt almost terrified with the storm she had raised.

"O Mr. Endicott!" she said, "was this worthy of you? was there nothing better, higher, more manly

than this poor revenge? You men are stronger than
we: you have the world in your hands; you have a
thousand resources where we have only one. And you
ought to be stronger and nobler according to your
advantages; you ought to rise superior to the temptations that beset a poor, weak, ill-educated woman,
whom everybody has been flattering from her cradle,
and whom you, I dare say, have helped to flatter,
turning her head with compliments, like all the rest
of them. Come, now, is not there something in
that?"

"Well, I suppose," said Harry, "that when Lillie and
I were girl and boy together, I did flatter her, sincerely
that is. Her beauty made a fool of me; and I helped
make a fool of her."

"And I dare say," said Rose, "you told her that all
she was made for was to be charming, and encouraged
her to live the life of a butterfly or canary-bird. Did
you ever try to strengthen her principles, to educate
her mind, to make her strong? On the contrary, haven't
you been bowing down and adoring her for being weak?
It seems to me that Lillie is exactly the kind of woman
that you men educate, by the way you look on women,
and the way you treat them."

Harry sat in silence, ruminating.

"Now," said Rose, "it seems to me it's the most
cowardly and unmanly thing in the world for men, with
every advantage in their hands, with all the strength
that their kind of education gives them, with all their
opportunities, — a thousand to our one, — to hunt down

these poor little silly women, whom society keeps stunted and dwarfed for their special amusement."

"Miss Ferguson, you are very severe," said Harry, his face flushing.

"Well," said Rose, "you have this advantage, Mr. Endicott: you know, if I am, the world will not be. Everybody will take your part; everybody will smile on you, and condemn her. That is generous, is it not? I think, after all, Noah Claypole isn't so very uncommon a picture of the way that your lordly sex turn round and cast all the blame on ours. You will never make me believe in a protracted flirtation between a gentleman and lady, where at least half the blame does not lie on his lordship's side. I always said that a woman had no need to have offers made her by a man she could not love, if she conducted herself properly; and I think the same is true in regard to men. But then, as I said before, you have the world on your side; nine persons out of ten see no possible harm in a man's taking every advantage of a woman, if she will let him."

"But I care more for the opinion of the tenth person than of the nine," said Harry; "I care more for what you think than any of them. Your words are severe; but I think they are just."

"O Mr. Endicott!" said Rose, "live for something higher than for what I think,—than for what any one thinks. Think how many glorious chances there are for a noble career for a young man with your fortune, with your leisure, with your influence! is it for you to waste life in this unworthy way? If I had your chances, I would try to do something worth doing."

Rose's face kindled with enthusiasm; and Harry looked at her with admiration.

"Tell me what I ought to do!" he said.

"I cannot tell you," said Rose; "but where there is a will there is a way: and, if you have the will, you will find the way. But, first, you must try and repair the mischief you have done to Lillie. By your own account of the matter, you have been encouraging and keeping up a sort of silly, romantic excitement in her. It is worse than silly; it is sinful. It is trifling with her best interests in this life and the life to come. And I think you must know that, if you had treated her like an honest, plain-spoken brother or cousin, without any trumpery of gallantry or sentiment, things would have never got to be as they are. You could have prevented all this; and you can put an end to it now."

"Honestly, I will try," said Harry. "I will begin, by confessing my faults like a good boy, and take the blame on myself where it belongs, and try to make Lillie see things like a good girl. But she is in bad surroundings; and, if I were her husband, I wouldn't let her stay there another day. There are no morals in that circle; it's all a perfect crush of decaying garbage."

"I think," said Rose, "that, if this thing goes no farther, it will gradually die out even in that circle; and, in the better circles of New York, I trust it will not be heard of. Mrs. Van Astrachan and I will appear publicly with Lillie; and if she is seen with us, and at this house, it will be sufficient to contradict a dozen slanders. She has the noblest, kindest husband, — one of the best men and truest gentlemen I ever knew."

"I pity him then," said Harry.

"He is to be pitied," said Rose; "but his work is before him. This woman, such as she is, with all her faults, he has taken for better or for worse; and all true friends and good people, both his and hers, should help both sides to make the best of it."

"I should say," said Harry, "that there is in this no best side."

"I think you do Lillie injustice," said Rose. "There is, and must be, good in every one; and gradually the good in him will overcome the evil in her."

"Let us hope so," said Harry. "And now, Miss Ferguson, may I hope that you won't quite cross my name out of your good book? You'll be friends with me, won't you?"

"Oh, certainly!" said Rose, with a frank smile.

"Well, let's shake hands on that," said Harry, rising to go.

Rose gave him her hand, and the two parted in all amity.

CHAPTER XXIII.

COMMON-SENSE ARGUMENTS.

HARRY went straightway from the interview to call upon Lillie, and had a conversation with her; in which he conducted himself like a sober, discreet, and rational man. It was one of those daylight, matter-of-fact kinds of talks, with no nonsense about them, in which things are called by their right names. He confessed his own sins, and took upon his own shoulders the blame that properly belonged there; and, having thus cleared his conscience, took occasion to give Lillie a deal of grandfatherly advice, of a very sedative tendency.

They had both been very silly, he said; and the next step to being silly very often was to be wicked. For his part, he thought she ought to be thankful for so good a husband; and, for his own part, he should lose no time in trying to find a good wife, who would help him to be a good man, and do something worth doing in the world. He had given people occasion to say ill-natured things about her; and he was sorry for it. But, if they stopped being imprudent, the world would in time stop talking. He hoped, some of these days, to bring his wife down to see her, and to make the acquaintance of her husband, whom he knew to be a capital fellow, and one that she ought to be proud of.

Thus, by the intervention of good angels, the little paper-nautilus bark of Lillie's fortunes was prevented from going down in the great ugly maelstrom, on the verge of which it had been so heedlessly sailing.

Harry was not slow in pushing the advantage of his treaty of friendship with Rose to its utmost limits; and, being a young gentleman of parts and proficiency, he made rapid progress.

The interview of course immediately bred the necessity for at least a dozen more; for he had to explain this thing, and qualify that, and, on reflection, would find by the next day that the explanation and qualification required a still further elucidation. Rose also, after the first conversation was over, was troubled at her own boldness, and at the things that she in her state of excitement had said; and so was only too glad to accord interviews and explanations as often as sought, and, on the whole, was in the most favorable state towards her penitent.

Hence came many calls, and many conferences with Rose in the library, to Mrs. Van Astrachan's great satisfaction, and concerning which Mr. Van Astrachan had many suppressed chuckles and knowing winks at Polly.

"Now, pa, don't you say a word," said Mrs. Van Astrachan.

"Oh, no, Polly! catch me! I see a great deal, but I say nothing," said the good gentleman, with a jocular quiver of his portly person. "I don't say any thing, — oh, no! by no manner of means."

Neither at present did Harry; neither do we.

CHAPTER XXIV.

SENTIMENT v. SENSIBILITY.

THE poet has feelingly sung the condition of

> " The banquet hall deserted,
>   Whose lights are fled, and garlands dead," &c.,

and so we need not cast the daylight of minute description on the Follingsbee mansion.

Charlie Ferrola, however, was summoned away at early daylight, just as the last of the revellers were dispersing, by a hurried messenger from his wife; and, a few moments after he entered his house, he was standing beside his dying baby, — the little fellow whom we have seen brought down on Mrs. Ferrola's arm, to greet the call of Mrs. Follingsbee.

It is an awful thing for people of the flimsy, vain, pain-shunning, pleasure-seeking character of Charlie Ferrola, to be taken at times, as such people will be, in the grip of an inexorable power, and held face to face with the sternest, the most awful, the most frightful realities of life. Charlie Ferrola was one of those whose softness and pitifulness, like that of sentimentalists generally, was only one form of intense selfishness. The

sight of suffering pained him; and his first impulse was
to get out of the way of it. Suffering that he did not
see was nothing to him; and, if his wife or children
were in any trouble, he would have liked very well to
have known nothing about it.

But here he was, by the bedside of this little creature, dying in the agonies of slow suffocation, rolling
up its dark, imploring eyes, and lifting its poor little
helpless hands; and Charlie Ferrola broke out into
the most violent and extravagant demonstrations of
grief.

The pale, firm little woman, who had watched all
night, and in whose tranquil face a light as if from
heaven was beaming, had to assume the care of him, in
addition to that of her dying child. He was another
helpless burden on her hands.

There came a day when the house was filled with
white flowers, and people came and went, and holy
words were spoken; and the fairest flower of all was
carried out, to return to the house no more.

"That woman is a most unnatural and peculiar
woman!" said Mrs. Follingsbee, who had been most
active and patronizing in sending flowers, and attending to the scenic arrangements of the funeral. "It is
just what I always said: she is a perfect statue; she's
no kind of feeling. There was Charlie, poor fellow! so
sick that he had to go to bed, perfectly overcome, and
have somebody to sit up with him; and there was that
woman never shed a tear,—went round attending to
every thing, just like a piece of clock-work. Well, I

suppose people are happier for being made so; people
that have no sensibility are better fitted to get through
the world. But, gracious me! I can't understand such
people. There she stood at the grave, looking so calm,
when Charlie was sobbing so that he could hardly
hold himself up. Well, it really wasn't respectable. I
think, at least, I would keep my veil down, and keep
my handkerchief up. Poor Charlie! he came to me at
last; and I gave way. I was completely broken down,
I must confess. Poor fellow! he told me there was no
conceiving his misery. That baby was the very idol of
his soul; all his hopes of life were centred in it. He
really felt tempted to rebel at Providence. He said
that he really could not talk with his wife on the subject. He could not enter into her submission at all;
it seemed to him like a want of feeling. He said of
course it wasn't her fault that she was made one way
and he another."

In fact, Mr. Charlie Ferrola took to the pink satin
boudoir with a more languishing persistency than ever,
requiring to be stayed with flagons, and comforted with
apples, and receiving sentimental calls of condolence
from fair admirers, made aware of the intense poignancy
of his grief. A lovely poem, called "My Withered
Blossom," which appeared in a fashionable magazine
shortly after, was the out-come of this experience, and
increased the fashionable sympathy to the highest
degree.

Honest Mrs. Van Astrachan, however, though not
acquainted with Mrs. Ferrola, went to the funeral with

Rose; and the next day her carriage was seen at Mrs. Ferrola's door.

"You poor little darling!" she said, as she came up and took Mrs. Ferrola in her arms. "You must let me come, and not mind me; for I know all about it. I lost the dearest little baby once; and I have never forgotten it. There! there, darling!" she said, as the little woman broke into sobs in her arms. "Yes, yes; do cry! it will do your little heart good."

There are people who, wherever they move, freeze the hearts of those they touch, and chill all demonstration of feeling; and there are warm natures, that unlock every fountain, and bid every feeling gush forth. The reader has seen these two types in this story.

"Wife," said Mr. Van Astrachan, coming to Mrs. V. confidentially a day or two after, "I wonder if you remember any of your French. What is a *liaison?*"

"Really, dear," said Mrs. Van Astrachan, whose reading of late years had been mostly confined to such memoirs as that of Mrs. Isabella Graham, Doddridge's "Rise and Progress," and Baxter's "Saint's Rest," "it's a great while since I read any French. What do you want to know for?"

"Well, there's Ben Stuyvesant was saying this morning, in Wall Street, that there's a great deal of talk about that Mrs. Follingsbee and that young fellow whose baby's funeral you went to. Ben says there's a *liaison* between her and him. I didn't ask him what 'twas;

but it's something or other with a French name that
makes talk, and I don't think it's respectable! I'm
sorry that you and Rose went to her party; but then
that can't be helped now. I'm afraid this Mrs. Follingsbee is no sort of a woman, after all."

"But, pa, I've been to call on Mrs. Ferrola, poor
little afflicted thing!" said Mrs. Van Astrachan. "I
couldn't help it! You know how we felt when little
Willie died."

"Oh, certainly, Polly! call on the poor woman by all
means, and do all you can to comfort her; but, from all
I can find out, that handsome jackanapes of a husband
of hers is just the poorest trash going. They say this
Follingsbee woman half supports him. The time was
in New York when such doings wouldn't be allowed;
and I don't think calling things by French names makes
them a bit better. So you just be careful, and steer as
clear of her as you can."

"I will, pa, just as clear as I can; but you know
Rose is a friend of Mrs. John Seymour; and Mrs. Seymour is visiting at Mrs. Follingsbee's."

"Her husband oughtn't to let her stay there another
day," said Mr. Van Astrachan. "It's as much as any
woman's reputation is worth to be staying with her.
To think of that fellow being dancing and capering at
that Jezebel's house the night his baby was dying!"

"Oh, but, pa, he didn't know it."

"Know it? he ought to have known it! What business has a man to get a woman with a lot of babies
round her, and then go capering off? 'Twasn't the way

I did, Polly, you know, when our babies were young. I was always on the spot there, ready to take the baby, and walk up and down with it nights, so that you might get your sleep; and I always had it my side of the bed half the night. I'd like to have seen myself out at a ball, and you sitting up with a sick baby! I tell you, that if I caught any of my boys up to such tricks, I'd cut them out of my will, and settle the money on their wives;—that's what I would!"

"Well, pa, I shall try and do all in my power for poor Mrs. Ferrola," said Mrs. Van Astrachan; "and you may be quite sure I won't take another step towards Mrs. Follingsbee's acquaintance."

"It's a pity," said Mr. Van Astrachan, "that somebody couldn't put it into Mr. John Seymour's head to send for his wife home.

"I don't see, for my part, what respectable women want to be gallivanting and high-flying on their own separate account for, away from their husbands! Goods that are sold shouldn't go back to the shop-windows," said the good gentleman, all whose views of life were of the most old-fashioned, domestic kind.

"Well, dear, we don't want to talk to Rose about any of this scandal," said his wife.

"No, no; it would be a pity to put any thing bad into a nice girl's head," said Mr. Van Astrachan. "You might caution her in a general way, you know; tell her, for instance, that I've heard of things that make me feel you ought to draw off. Why can't some bird of the air tell that little Seymour woman's husband to get her home?"

The little Seymour woman's husband, though not warned by any particular bird of the air, was not backward in taking steps for the recall of his wife, as shall hereafter appear.

CHAPTER XXV.

WEDDING BELLS.

SOME weeks had passed in Springdale while these affairs had been going on in New York. The time for the marriage of Grace had been set; and she had gone to Boston to attend to that preparatory shopping which even the most sensible of the sex discover to be indispensable on such occasions.

Grace inclined, in the centre of her soul, to Bostonian rather than New-York preferences. She had the innocent impression that a classical severity and a rigid reticence of taste pervaded even the rebellious department of feminine millinery in the city of the Pilgrims, — an idea which we rather think young Boston would laugh down as an exploded superstition, young Boston's leading idea at the present hour being apparently to outdo New York in New York's imitation of Paris.

In fact, Grace found it very difficult to find a milliner who, if left to her own devices, would not befeather and beflower her past all self-recognition, giving to her that generally betousled and fly-away air which comes straight from the *demi-monde* of Paris.

We apprehend that the recent storms of tribulation

which have beat upon those fairy islands of fashion
may scatter this frail and fanciful population, and send
them by shiploads on missions of civilization to our
shores; in which case, the bustle and animation and the
brilliant display on the old turnpike, spoken of familiarly
as the "broad road," will be somewhat increased.

Grace however managed, by the exercise of a good
individual taste, to come out of these shopping conflicts
in good order, — a handsome, well-dressed, charming
woman, with everybody's best wishes for, and sympathy
in, her happiness.

Lillie was summoned home by urgent messages from
her husband, calling her back to take her share in wedding festivities.

She left willingly; for the fact is that her last conversation with her cousin Harry had made the situation
as uncomfortable to her as if he had unceremoniously
deluged her with a pailful of cold water.

There is a chilly, disagreeable kind of article, called
common sense, which is of all things most repulsive
and antipathetical to all petted creatures whose life has
consisted in flattery. It is the kind of talk which sisters
are very apt to hear from brothers, and daughters from
fathers and mothers, when fathers and mothers do their
duty by them; which sets the world before them as it
is, and not as it is painted by flatterers. Those women
who prefer the society of gentlemen, and who have the
faculty of bewitching their senses, never are in the way
of hearing from this cold matter-of-fact region; for them
it really does not exist. Every phrase that meets their

ear is polished and softened, guarded and delicately
turned, till there is not a particle of homely truth left
in it. They pass their time in a world of illusions;
they demand these illusions of all who approach them,
as the sole condition of peace and favor. All gentlemen,
by a sort of instinct, recognize the woman who lives by
flattery, and give her her portion of meat in due season;
and thus some poor women are hopelessly buried, as
suicides used to be in Scotland, under a mountain of
rubbish, to which each passer-by adds one stone. It is
only by some extraordinary power of circumstances
that a man can be found to invade the sovereignty of
a pretty woman with any disagreeable tidings; or, as
Junius says, "to instruct the throne in the language of
truth." Harry was brought up to this point only by
such a concurrence of circumstances. He was in love
with another woman, — a ready cause for disenchantment. He was in some sort a family connection; and
he saw Lillie's conduct at last, therefore, through the
plain, unvarnished medium of common sense. Moreover, he felt a little pinched in his own conscience by
the view which Rose seemed to take of his part in the
matter, and, manlike, was strengthened in doing his
duty by being a little galled and annoyed at the woman
whose charms had tempted him into this dilemma. So
he talked to Lillie like a brother; or, in other words,
made himself disagreeably explicit, — showed her her
sins, and told her her duties as a married woman. The
charming fair ones who sentimentally desire gentlemen
to regard them as sisters do not bargain for any of this

sort of brotherly plainness; and yet they might do it with great advantage. A brother, who is not a brother, stationed near the ear of a fair friend, is commonly very careful not to compromise his position by telling unpleasant truths; but, on the present occasion, Harry made a literal use of the brevet of brotherhood which Lillie had bestowed on him, and talked to her as the generality of *real* brothers talk to their sisters, using great plainness of speech. He withered all her poor little trumpery array of hothouse flowers of sentiment, by treating them as so much garbage, as all men know they are. He set before her the gravity and dignity of marriage, and her duties to her husband. Last, and most unkind of all, he professed his admiration of Rose Ferguson, his unworthiness of her, and his determination to win her by a nobler and better life; and then showed himself to be a stupid blunderer by exhorting Lillie to make Rose her model, and seek to imitate her virtues.

Poor Lillie! the world looked dismal and dreary enough to her. She shrunk within herself. Every thing was withered and disenchanted. All her poor little stock of romance seemed to her as disgusting as the withered flowers and crumpled finery and half-melted ice-cream the morning after a ball.

In this state, when she got a warm, true letter from John, who always grew tender and affectionate when she was long away, couched in those terms of admiration and affection that were soothing to her ear, she really longed to go back to him. She shrunk from the dreary plainness of truth, and longed for flattery and petting and caresses once more; and she wrote to John an overflowingly tender letter, full of longings, which brought him at once to her side, the most delighted of men. When Lillie cried in his arms, and told him that she found New York perfectly hateful; when she declaimed on the heartlessness of fashionable life, and longed to go with him to their quiet home, — she was tolerably in earnest; and John was perfectly enchanted.

Poor John! Was he a muff, a spoon? We think not. We understand well that there is not a *woman* among our readers who has the slightest patience with Lillie, and that the most of them are half out of patience with John for his enduring tenderness towards her.

But men were born and organized by nature to be the protectors of women; and, generally speaking, the stronger and more thoroughly manly a man is, the more he has of what phrenologists call the "pet organ," — the disposition which makes him the charmed servant of what is weak and dependent. John had a great share of this quality. He was made to be a protector. He loved to protect; he loved every thing that was help-less and weak, — young animals, young children, and delicate women.

He was a romantic adorer of womanhood, as a sort of divine mystery, — a never-ending poem; and when his wife was long enough away from him to give scope for imagination to work, when she no longer annoyed him with the friction of the sharp little edges of her cold and selfish nature, he was able to see her once more in the ideal light of first love. After all, she was his wife; and in that one word, to a good man, is every thing holy and sacred. He longed to believe in her and trust her wholly; and now that Grace was going from him, to belong to another, Lillie was more than ever his dependence.

On the whole, if we must admit that John was weak, he was weak where strong and noble natures may most gracefully be so, — weak through disinterestedness, faith, and the disposition to make the best of the wife he had chosen.

And so Lillie came home; and there was festivity and rejoicing. Grace found herself floated into matrimony on a tide bringing gifts and tokens of remembrance from everybody that had ever known her; for all were delighted with this opportunity of testifying a sense of her worth, and every hand was ready to help ring her wedding bells.

CHAPTER XXVI.

MOTHERHOOD.

IT is supposed by some that to become a mother is of itself a healing and saving dispensation; that of course the reign of selfishness ends, and the reign of better things begins, with the commencement of maternity.

But old things do not pass away and all things become new by any such rapid process of conversion. A whole life spent in self-seeking and self-pleasing is no preparation for the most august and austere of woman's sufferings and duties; and it is not to be wondered at if the untrained, untaught, and self-indulgent shrink from this ordeal, as Lillie did.

The next spring, while the gables of the new cottage on Elm Street were looking picturesquely through the blossoming cherry-trees, and the smoke was curling up from the chimneys where Grace and her husband were cosily settled down together, there came to John's house another little Lillie.

The little creature came in terror and trembling. For the mother had trifled fearfully with the great laws

of her being before its birth; and the very shadow
of death hung over her at the time the little new
life began.

Lillie's mother, now a widow, was sent for, and by
this event installed as a fixture in her daughter's dwelling; and for weeks the sympathies of all the neighborhood were concentrated upon the sufferer. Flowers
and fruits were left daily at the door. Every one
was forward in offering those kindly attentions which
spring up so gracefully in rural neighborhoods. Everybody was interested for her. She was little and pretty
and suffering; and people even forgot to blame her for
the levities that had made her present trial more
severe. As to John, he watched over her day and
night with anxious assiduity, forgetting every fault and
foible. She was now more than the wife of his youth;
she was the mother of his child, enthroned and glorified
in his eyes by the wonderful and mysterious experiences which had given this new little treasure to their
dwelling.

To say the truth, Lillie was too sick and suffering for
sentiment. It requires a certain amount of bodily
strength and soundness to feel emotions of love; and,
for a long time, the little Lillie had to be banished from
the mother's apartment, as she lay weary in her darkened room, with only a consciousness of a varied succession of disagreeables and discomforts. Her general
impression about herself was, that she was a much
abused and most unfortunate woman; and that all that
could ever be done by the utmost devotion of every-

body in the house was insufficient to make up for such trials as had come upon her.

A nursing mother was found for the little Lillie in the person of a goodly Irish woman, fair, fat, and loving; and the real mother had none of those awakening influences, from the resting of the little head in her bosom, and the pressure of the little helpless fingers, which magnetize into existence the blessed power of love.

She had wasted in years of fashionable folly, and in a life led only for excitement and self-gratification, all the womanly power, all the capability of motherly giving and motherly loving that are the glory of womanhood. Kathleen, the white-armed, the gentle-bosomed, had all the simple pleasures, the tendernesses, the poetry of motherhood; while poor, faded, fretful Lillie had all the prose — the sad, hard, weary prose — of sickness and pain, unglorified by love.

John did not well know what to do with himself in Lillie's darkened room; where it seemed to him he was always in the way, always doing something wrong; where his feet always seemed too large and heavy, and his voice too loud; and where he was sure, in his anxious desire to be still and gentle, to upset something, or bring about some general catastrophe, and to go out feeling more like a criminal than ever.

The mother and the nurse, stationed there like a pair of chief mourners, spoke in tones which experienced feminine experts seem to keep for occasions like these, and which, as Hawthorne has said, give an effect as if the voice had been dyed black. It was a comfort and relief to pass from the funeral gloom to the little pink-ruffled chamber among the cherry-trees, where the birds were singing and the summer breezes blowing, and the pretty Kathleen was crooning her Irish songs, and invoking the holy virgin and all the saints to bless the "darlin'" baby.

"An' it 's a blessin' they brings wid 'em, sir."

"An' it 's a blessin' they brings wid 'em to a house, sir; the angels comes down wid 'em. We can't see 'em, sir; but, bless the darlin', she can. And she smiles in her sleep when she sees 'em."

Rose and Grace came often to this bower with kisses and gifts and offerings, like a pair of nice fairy godmothers. They hung over the pretty little waxen miracle as she opened her great blue eyes with a silent, mysterious wonder; but, alas! all these delicious moments, this artless love of the new baby life, was not for the mother. She was not strong enough to enjoy it. Its cries made her nervous; and so she kept the uncheered solitude of her room without the blessing of the little angel.

People may mourn in lugubrious phrase about the Irish blood in our country. For our own part, we think the rich, tender, motherly nature of the Irish girl an element a thousand times more hopeful in our population than the faded, washed-out indifferentism of fashionable women, who have danced and flirted away all their womanly attributes, till there is neither warmth nor richness nor maternal fulness left in them, — mere paper-dolls, without milk in their bosoms or blood in their veins. Give us rich, tender, warm-hearted Bridgets and Kathleens, whose instincts teach them the real poetry of motherhood; who can love unto death, and bear trials and pains cheerfully for the joy that is set before them. We are not afraid for the republican citizens that such mothers will bear to us. They are the ones that will come to high places in our land, and that will possess the earth by right of the strongest.

Motherhood, to the woman who has lived only to be petted, and to be herself the centre of all things, is a virtual dethronement.   Something weaker, fairer, more delicate than herself comes, — something for her to serve and to care for more than herself.

It would sometimes seem as if motherhood were a lovely artifice of the great Father, to wean the heart from selfishness by a peaceful and gradual process. The babe is self in another form.   It is so interwoven and identified with the mother's life, that she passes by almost insensible gradations from herself to it; and day by day the distinctive love of self wanes as the child-love waxes, filling the heart with a thousand new springs of tenderness.

But that this benignant transformation of nature may be perfected, it must be wrought out in Nature's own way.   Any artificial arrangement that takes the child away from the mother interrupts that wonderful system of contrivances whereby the mother's nature and being shade off into that of the child, and her heart enlarges to a new and heavenly power of loving.

When Lillie was sufficiently recovered to be fond of any thing, she found in her lovely baby only a new toy, — a source of pride and pleasure, and a charming occasion for the display of new devices of millinery. But she found Newport indispensable that summer to the re-establishment of her strength.   "And really," she said, "the baby would be so much better off quietly at home with mamma and Kathleen.   The fact is," she said, "she quite disregards me.   She cries after Kathleen if I take her; so that it's quite provoking."

And so Lillie, free and unencumbered, had her gay

season at Newport with the Follingsbees, and the Simpkinses, and the Tompkinses, and all the rest of the nice people, who have nothing to do but enjoy themselves; and everybody flattered her by being incredulous that one so young and charming could possibly be a mother.

CHAPTER XXVII.

CHECKMATE.

IF ever our readers have observed two chess-players, both ardent, skilful, determined, who have been carrying on noiselessly the moves of a game, they will understand the full significance of this decisive term.

Up to this point, there is hope, there is energy, there is enthusiasm; the pieces are marshalled and managed with good courage. At last, perhaps in an unexpected moment, one, two, three adverse moves follow each other, and the decisive words, *check-mate*, are uttered.

This is a symbol of what often goes on in the game of life.

Here is a man going on, indefinitely, conscious in his own heart that he is not happy in his domestic relations. There is a want of union between him and his wife. She is not the woman that meets his wants or his desires; and in the intercourse of life they constantly cross and annoy each other. But still he does not allow himself to look the matter fully in the face. He goes on and on, hoping that to-morrow will bring something better than to-day, — hoping that this thing or that thing or the other thing will bring a change, and that in some indefinite future all will round and fashion itself to his desires. It is very slowly that a man awakens from the illusions of his first love. It is very unwillingly that he ever comes to the final conclusion that he has made *there* the mistake of a whole lifetime, and that the woman to whom he gave his whole heart not only is not the woman that he supposed her to be, but never in any future time, nor by any change of circumstances, will become that woman,—that the difficulty is radical and final and hopeless.

In "The Pilgrim's Progress," we read that the poor man, Christian, tried to persuade his wife to go with him on the pilgrimage to the celestial city; but that finally he had to make up his mind to go alone without her. Such is the lot of the man who is brought to the conclusion, positively and definitely, that his wife is always to be a hinderance, and never a help to him, in any upward aspiration; that whatever he does that is needful and right and true must be done, not by her influence, but in spite of it; that, if he has to swim against the hard, upward current of the river of life, he must do so with her hanging on his arm, and holding him back, and that he cannot influence and cannot control her.

Such hours of disclosure to a man are among the terrible hidden tragedies of life,—tragedies such as are never acted on the stage. Such a time of disclosure came to John the year after Grace's marriage; and it came in this way:—

The Spindlewood property had long been critically

situated. Sundry financial changes which were going on in the country had depreciated its profits, and affected it unfavorably. All now depended upon the permanency of one commercial house. John had been passing through an interval of great anxiety. He could not tell Lillie his trouble. He had been for months past nervously watching all the in-comings and out-goings of his family, arranged on a scale of reckless expenditure, which he felt entirely powerless to control. Lillie's wishes were importunate. She was nervous and hysterical, wholly incapable of listening to reason; and the least attempt to bring her to change any of her arrangements, or to restrict any of her pleasures, brought tears and faintings and distresses and scenes of domestic confusion which he shrank from. He often tried to set before her the possibility that they might be obliged, for a time at least, to live in a different manner; but she always resisted every such supposition as so frightful, so dreadful, that he was utterly discouraged, and put off and off, hoping that the evil day never might arrive.

But it did come at last. One morning, when he received by mail the tidings of the failure of the great house of Clapham & Co., he knew that the time had come when the thing could no longer be staved off. He was an indorser to a large amount on the paper of this house; and the crisis was inevitable.

It was inevitable also that he must acquaint Lillie with the state of his circumstances; for she was going on with large arrangements and calculations for a Newport campaign, and sending the usual orders to New York, to her milliner and dressmaker, for her summer outfit. It was a cruel thing for him to be obliged to interrupt all this; for she seemed perfectly cheerful and happy in it, as she always was when preparing to go on a pleasure-seeking expedition. But it could not be. All this luxury and indulgence must be cut off at a stroke. He must tell her that she could not go to Newport; that there was no money for new dresses or new finery; that they should probably be obliged to move out of their elegant house, and take a smaller one, and practise for some time a rigid economy.

John came into Lillie's elegant apartments, which glittered like a tulip-bed with many colored sashes and ribbons, with sheeny silks and misty laces, laid out in order to be surveyed before packing.

"Gracious me, John! what on earth is the matter with you to-day? How perfectly awful and solemn you do look!"

"I have had bad news, this morning, Lillie, which I must tell you."

"Oh, dear me, John! what is the matter? Nobody is dead, I hope!"

"No, Lillie; but I am afraid you will have to give up your Newport journey."

"Gracious, goodness, John! what for?"

"To say the truth, Lillie, I cannot afford it."

"Can't afford it? Why not? Why, John, what is the matter?"

"Well, Lillie, just read this letter!"

Lillie took it, and read it with her hands trembling.

"Well, dear me, John! I don't see any thing in this letter. If they have failed, I don't see what that is to you!"

"But, Lillie, I am indorser for them."

"How very silly of you, John! What made you indorse for them? Now that is too bad; it just makes me perfectly miserable to think of such things. I know *I* should not have done so; but I don't see why you need pay it. It is their business, anyhow."

"But, Lillie, I shall have to pay it. It is a matter of honor and honesty to do it; because I engaged to do it."

"Well, I don't see why that should be! It isn't your debt; it is their debt: and why need you do it? I am sure Dick Follingsbee said that there were ways in which people could put their property out of their hands when they got caught in such scrapes as this. Dick knows just how to manage. He told me of plenty of people that had done that, who were living splendidly, and who were received everywhere; and people thought just as much of them."

"O Lillie, Lillie! my child," said John; "you don't know any thing of what you are talking about! That would be dishonorable, and wholly out of the question. No, Lillie dear, the fact is," he said, with a great gulp, and a deep sigh, — "the fact is, I have failed; but I am going to fail honestly. If I have nothing else left, I will have my honor and my conscience. But we shall have to give up this house, and move into a smaller one.

Every thing will have to be given up to the creditors to settle the business. And then, when all is arranged, we must try to live economically some way; and perhaps we can make it up again. But you see, dear, there can be no more of this kind of expenses at present," he said, pointing to the dresses and jewelry on the bed.

"Well, John, I am sure I had rather die!" said Lillie, gathering herself into a little white heap, and tumbling into the middle of the bed. "I am sure if we have got to rub and scrub and starve so, I had rather die and done with it; and I hope I shall."

John crossed his arms, and looked gloomily out of the window.

"Perhaps you had better," he said. "I am sure I should be glad to."

"Yes, I dare say!" said Lillie; "that is all you care for me. Now there is Dick Follingsbee, he would be taking care of his wife. Why, he has failed three or four times, and always come out richer than he was before!"

"He is a swindler and a rascal!" said John; "that is what he is."

"I don't care if he is," said Lillie, sobbing. "His wife has good times, and goes into the very first society in New York. People don't care, so long as you are rich, what you do. Well, I am sure I can't do any thing about it. I don't know how to live without money, —that's a fact! and I can't learn. I suppose you would be glad to see me rubbing around in old calico dresses, wouldn't you? and keeping only one girl, and going into the kitchen, like Miss Dotty Peabody? I

think I see myself! And all just for one of your Quix-
otic notions, when you might just as well keep all your
money as not. That is what it is to marry a reformer!
I never have had any peace of my life on account of
your conscience, always something or other turning up
that you can't act like anybody else. I should think,
at least, you might have contrived to settle this place
on me and poor little Lillie, that we might have a house
to put our heads in."

"Lillie, Lillie," said John, "this is too much! Don't
you think that *I* suffer at all?"

"I don't see that you do," said Lillie, sobbing. "I
dare say you are glad of it; it is just like you. Oh,
dear, I wish I had never been married!"

"I *certainly* do," said John, fervently.

"I suppose so. You see, it is nothing to you men;
you don't care any thing about these things. If you
can get a musty old corner and your books, you are
perfectly satisfied; and you don't know when things
are pretty, and when they are not: and so you can talk
grand about your honor and your conscience and all
that. I suppose the carriages and horses have got to
be sold too?"

"Certainly, Lillie," said John, hardening his heart and
his tone.

"Well, well," she said, "I wish you would go now
and send ma to me. I don't want to talk about it any
more. My head aches as if it would split. Poor ma!
She little thought when I married you that it was going
to come to this."

John walked out of the room gloomily enough. He had received this morning his *check-mate*. All illusion was at an end. The woman that he had loved and idolized and caressed and petted and indulged, in whom he had been daily and hourly disappointed since he was married, but of whom he still hoped and hoped, he now felt was of a nature not only unlike, but opposed to his own. He felt that he could neither love nor respect her further. And yet she was his wife, and the mother of his daughter, and the only queen of his household; and he had solemnly promised at God's altar that "forsaking all others, he would keep only unto her, so long as they both should live, for better, for worse," John muttered to himself, — "for better, for worse. This is the worse; and oh, it is dreadful!"

In all John's hours of sorrow and trouble, the instinctive feeling of his heart was to go back to the memory of his mother; and the nearest to his mother was his sister Grace. In this hour of his blind sorrow, he walked directly over to the little cottage on Elm Street, which Grace and her husband had made a perfectly ideal home.

When he came into the parlor, Grace and Rose were sitting together with an open letter lying between them. It was evident that some crisis of tender confidence had passed between them; for the tears were hardly dry on Rose's cheeks. Yet it was not painful, whatever it was; for her face was radiant with smiles, and John thought he had never seen her look so lovely. At this moment the truth of her beautiful and lovely womanhood, her sweetness and nobleness of nature, came over him, in bitter contrast with the scene he had just passed through, and the woman he had left.

"What do you think, John?" said Grace; "we have some congratulations here to give! Rose is engaged to Harry Endicott."

"Indeed!" said John, "I wish her joy."

"But what is the matter, John?" said both women, looking up, and seeing something unusual in his face.

"Oh, trouble!" said John,—"trouble upon us all. Gracie and Rose, the Spindlewood Mills have failed."

"Is it possible?" was the exclamation of both.

"Yes, indeed!" said John; "you see, the thing has been running very close for the last six months; and the manufacturing business has been looking darker and darker. But still we could have stood it if the house of Clapham & Co. had stood; but they have gone to smash, Gracie. I had a letter this morning, telling me of it."

Both women stood a moment as if aghast; for the Ferguson property was equally involved.

"Poor papa!" said Rose; "this will come hard on him."

"I know it," said John, bitterly. "It is more for others that I feel than for myself,—for all that are involved must suffer with me."

"But, after all, John dear," said Rose, "don't feel so about us at any rate. We shall do very well. People that fail honorably always come right side up at last; and, John, how good it is to think, whatever you lose, you cannot lose your best treasure,—your true noble heart, and your true friends. I feel this minute that we shall all know each other better, and be more precious to each other for this very trouble."

John looked at her through his tears.

"Dear Rose," he said, "you are an angel; and from my soul I congratulate the man that has got *you*. He that has you would be rich, if he lost the whole world."

"You are too good to me, all of you," said Rose. "But now, John, about that bad news—let me break it to papa and mamma; I think I can do it best. I know when they feel brightest in the day; and I don't want it to come on them suddenly: but I can put it in the very best way. How fortunate that I am just engaged to Harry! Harry is a perfect prince in generosity. You don't know what a good heart he has; and it happens so fortunately that we have him to lean on just now. Oh, I'm sure we shall find a way out of these troubles, never fear." And Rose took the letter, and left John and Grace together.

"O Gracie, Gracie!" said John, throwing himself down on the old chintz sofa, and burying his face in his hands, "what a woman there is! O Gracie! I wish I was dead! Life is played out with me. I haven't the least desire to live. I can't get a step farther."

"O John, John! don't talk so!" said Grace, stooping over him. "Why, you will recover from this! You are young and strong. It will be settled; and you can work your way up again."

"It is not the money, Grace; I could let that go. It

is that I have nothing to live for,—nobody and nothing. My wife, Gracie! she is worse than nothing,—worse, oh! infinitely worse than nothing! She is a chain and a shackle. She is my obstacle. She tortures me and hinders me every way and everywhere. There will never be a home for me where she is; and, because she is there, no other woman can make a home for me. Oh, I wish she would go away, and stay away! I would not care if I never saw her face again."

"O Gracie! I wish I was dead!"

There was something shocking and terrible to Grace about this outpouring. It was dreadful to her to be

the recipient of such a confidence, to hear these words spoken, and to more than suspect their truth. She was quite silent for a few moments, as he still lay with his face down, buried in the sofa-pillow.

Then she went to her writing-desk, took out a little ivory miniature of their mother, came and sat down by him, and laid her hand on his head.

"John," she said, "look at this."

He raised his head, took it from her hand, and looked at it. Soon she saw the tears dropping over it.

"John," she said, "let me say to you now what I think our mother would have said. The great object of life is not happiness; and, when we have lost our own personal happiness, we have not lost all that life is worth living for. No, John, the very best of life often lies beyond that. When we have learned to let ourselves go, then we may find that there is a better, a nobler, and a truer life for us."

"I *have* given up," said John in a husky voice, "I have lost *all.*"

"Yes," replied Grace, steadily, "I know perfectly well that there is very little hope of personal and individual happiness for you in your marriage for years to come. Instead of a companion, a friend, and a helper, you have a moral invalid to take care of. But, John, if Lillie had been stricken with blindness, or insanity, or paralysis, you would not have shrunk from your duty to her; and, because the blindness and paralysis are moral, you will not shrink from it, will you? You sacrifice all your property to pay an indorsement for a

debt that is not yours; and why do you do it? Because
society rests on every man's faithfulness to his engagements. John, if you stand by a business engagement
with this faithfulness, how much more should you stand
by that great engagement which concerns all other
families and the stability of all society. Lillie is your
wife. You were free to choose; and you chose her.
She is the mother of your child; and, John, what that
daughter is to be depends very much on the steadiness
with which you fulfil your duties to the mother. I
know that Lillie is a most undeveloped and uncongenial
person; I know how little you have in common: but
your duties are the same as if she were the best and
the most congenial of wives. It is every man's duty to
make the best of his marriage."

"But, Gracie," said John, "is there any thing to be
made of her?"

"You will never make me believe, John, that there
are any human beings absolutely without the capability
of good. They may be very dark, and very slow to
learn, and very far from it; but steady patience and
love and well-doing will at last tell upon any one."

"But, Gracie, if you could have heard how utterly
without principle she is: urging me to put my property
out of my hands dishonestly, to keep her in luxury!"

"Well, John, you must have patience with her. Consider that she has been unfortunate in her associates.
Consider that she has been a petted child all her life,
and that you have helped to pet her. Consider how
much your sex always do to weaken the moral sense

of women, by liking and admiring them for being weak and foolish and inconsequent, so long as it is pretty and does not come in your way. I do not mean you in particular, John; but I mean that the general course of society releases pretty women from any sense of obligation to be constant in duty, or brave in meeting emergencies. You yourself have encouraged Lillie to live very much like a little humming-bird."

"Well, I thought," said John, "that she would in time develop into something better."

"Well, there lies your mistake; you expected too much. The work of years is not to be undone in a moment; and you must take into account that this is Lillie's first adversity. You may as well make up your mind not to expect her to be reasonable. It seems to me that we can make up our minds to bear any thing that we know must come; and you may as well make up yours, that, for a long time, you will have to carry Lillie as a burden. But then, you must think that she is your daughter's mother, and that it is very important for the child that she should respect and honor her mother. You must treat her with respect and honor, even in her weaknesses. We all must. We all must help Lillie as we can to bear this trial, and sympathize with her in it, unreasonable as she may seem; because, after all, John, it is a real trial to her."

"I cannot see, for my part," said John, "that she loves any thing."

"The power of loving may be undeveloped in her, John; but it will come, perhaps, later in life. At all

events take this comfort to yourself, — that, when you
are doing your duty by your wife, when you are holding
her in her place in the family, and teaching her child to
respect and honor her, you are putting her in God's
school of love. If we contend with and'fly from our
duties, simply because they gall us and burden us, we
go against every thing; but if we take them up bravely,
then every thing goes with us. God and good angels
and good men and all good influences are working with
us when we are working for the right. And in this
way, John, you may come to happiness; or, if you do
not come to personal happiness, you may come to something higher and better. You know that you think it
nobler to be an honest man than a rich man; and I
am sure that you will think it better to be a good man
than to be a happy one. Now, dear John, it is not I
that say these things, I think; but it seems to me it
is what our mother would say, if she should speak
to you from where she is. And then, dear brother,
it will all be over soon, this life-battle; and the only
thing is, to come out victorious."

"Gracie, you are right," said John, rising up: "I
see it myself. I will brace up to my duty. Couldn't
you try and pacify Lillie a little, poor girl? I suppose
I have been rough with her."

"Oh, yes, John, I will go up and talk with Lillie,
and condole with her; and perhaps we shall bring her
round. And then when my husband comes home next
week, we'll have a family palaver, and he will find some
ways and means of setting this business straight, that it

won't be so bad as it looks now. There may be arrangements made when the creditors come together. My
impression is that, whenever people find a man really
determined to arrange a matter of this kind honorably,
they are all disposed to help him; so don't be cast
down about the business. As for Lillie's discontent,
treat it as you would the crying of your little daughter
for its sugar-plums, and do not expect any thing more
of her just now than there is."

. . . .

We have brought our story up to this point. We
informed our readers in the beginning that it was not a
novel, but a story with a moral; and, as people pick all
sorts of strange morals out of stories, we intend to put
conspicuously into our story exactly what the moral of
it is.

Well, then, it has been very surprising to us to see
in these our times that some people, who really at heart
have the interest of women upon their minds, have
been so short-sighted and reckless as to clamor for an
easy dissolution of the marriage-contract, as a means of
righting their wrongs. Is it possible that they do not
see that this is a liberty which, once granted, would
always tell against the weaker sex? If the woman
who finds that she has made a mistake, and married a
man unkind or uncongenial, may, on the discovery of
it, leave him and seek her fortune with another, so also
may a man. And what will become of women like
Lillie, when the first gilding begins to wear off, if the
man who has taken one of them shall be at liberty to

cast her off and seek another? Have we not enough now of miserable, broken-winged butterflies, that sink down, down, down into the mud of the street? But are women-reformers going to clamor for having every woman turned out helpless, when the man who has married her, and made her a mother, discovers that she has not the power to interest him, and to help his higher spiritual development? It was because woman is helpless and weak, and because Christ was her great Protector, that he made the law of marriage irrevocable. " Whosoever putteth away his wife causeth her to commit adultery." If the sacredness of the marriage-contract did not hold, if the Church and all good men and all good women did not uphold it with their might and main, it is easy to see where the career of many women like Lillie would end. Men have the power to reflect before the choice is made; and that is the only proper time for reflection. But, when once marriage is made and consummated, it should be as fixed a fact as the laws of nature. And they who suffer under its stringency should suffer as those who endure for the public good. " He that sweareth to his own hurt, and changeth not, he shall enter into the tabernacle of the Lord."

CHAPTER XXVIII.

AFTER THE STORM.

THE painful and unfortunate crises of life often arise and darken like a thunder-storm, and seem for the moment perfectly terrific and overwhelming; but wait a little, and the cloud sweeps by, and the earth, which seemed about to be torn to pieces and destroyed, comes out as good as new. Not a bird is dead; not a flower killed: and the sun shines just as he did before. So it was with John's financial trouble. When it came to be investigated and looked into, it proved much less terrible than had been feared. It was not utter ruin. The high character which John bore for honor and probity, the general respect which was felt for him by all to whom he stood indebted, led to an arrangement by which the whole business was put into his hands, and time given him to work it through. His brother-in-law came to his aid, advancing money, and entering into the business with him. Our friend Harry Endicott was only too happy to prove his devotion to Rose by offers of financial assistance.

In short, there seemed every reason to hope that, after a period of somewhat close sailing, the property

21

might be brought into clear water again, and go on even better than before.

To say the truth, too, John was really relieved by that terrible burst of confidence in his sister. It is a curious fact, that giving full expression to bitterness of feeling or indignation against one we love seems to be such a relief, that it always brings a revulsion of kindliness. John never loved his sister so much as when he heard her plead his wife's cause with him; for, though in some bitter, impatient hour a man may feel, which John did, as if he would be glad to sunder all ties, and tear himself away from an uncongenial wife, yet a good man never can forget the woman that once he loved, and who is the mother of his children. Those sweet, sacred visions and illusions of first love will return again and again, even after disenchantment; and the better and the purer the man is, the more sacred is the appeal to him of woman's weakness. Because he is strong, and she is weak, he feels that it would be unmanly to desert her; and, if there ever was any thing for which John thanked his sister, it was when she went over and spent hours with his wife, patiently listening to her complainings, and soothing her as if she had been a petted child. All the circle of friends, in a like manner, bore with her for his sake.

Thanks to the intervention of Grace's husband and of Harry, John was not put to the trial and humiliation of being obliged to sell the family place, although constrained to live in it under a system of more rigid economy. Lillie's mother, although quite a commonplace woman as a companion, had been an economist in her day; she had known how to make the most of straitened circumstances, and, being put to it, could do it again.

To be sure, there was an end of Newport gayeties; for Lillie vowed and declared that she would not go to Newport and take cheap board, and live without a carriage. She didn't want the Follingsbees and the Tompkinses and the Simpkinses talking about her, and saying that they had failed. Her mother worked like a servant for her in smartening her up, and tidying her old dresses, of which one would think that she had a stock to last for many years. And thus, with everybody sympathizing with her, and everybody helping her, Lillie subsided into enacting the part of a patient, persecuted saint. She was touchingly resigned, and wore an air of pleasing melancholy. John had asked her pardon for all the hasty words he said to her in the terrible interview; and she had forgiven him with edifying meekness. "Of course," she remarked to her mother, "she knew he would be sorry for the way he had spoken to her; and she was very glad that he had the grace to confess it."

So life went on and on with John. He never forgot his sister's words, but received them into his heart as a message from his mother in heaven. From that time, no one could have judged by any word, look, or action of his that his wife was not what she had always been to him.

Meanwhile Rose was happily married, and settled

down in the Ferguson place; where her husband and she formed one family with her parents. It was a pleasant, cosey, social, friendly neighborhood. After all, John found that his cross was not so very heavy to carry, when once he had made up his mind that it must be borne. By never expecting much, he was never disappointed. Having made up his mind that he was to serve and to give without receiving, he did it, and began to find pleasure in it. By and by, the little Lillie, growing up by her mother's side, began to be a compensation for all he had suffered. The little creature inherited her mother's beauty, the dazzling delicacy of her complexion, the abundance of her golden hair; but there had been given to her also her father's magnanimous and generous nature. Lillie was a selfish, exacting mother; and such women often succeed in teaching to their children patience and self-denial. As soon as the little creature could walk, she was her father's constant play-fellow and companion. He took her with him everywhere. He was never weary of talking with her and playing with her; and gradually he relieved the mother of all care of her early training. When, in time, two others were added to the nursery troop, Lillie became a perfect model of a gracious, motherly, little older sister.

Did all this patience and devotion of the husband at last awaken any thing like love in the wife? Lillie was not naturally rich in emotion. Under the best education and development, she would have been rather wanting in the loving power; and the whole course of her education had been directed to suppress what little she had, and to concentrate all her feelings upon herself.

The factitious and unnatural life she had lived so many years had seriously undermined the stamina of her constitution; and, after the birth of her third child, her health failed altogether. Lillie thus became in time a chronic invalid, exacting, querulous, full of troubles and wants which tasked the patience of all around her. During all these trying years, her husband's faithfulness never faltered. As he gradually retrieved his circumstances, she was first in every calculation. Because he knew that here lay his greatest temptation, here he most rigidly performed his duty. Nothing that money could give to soften the weariness of sickness was withheld; and John was for hours and hours, whenever he could spare the time, himself a personal, assiduous, unwearied attendant in the sickroom.

CHAPTER XXIX.

THE NEW LILLIE.

WE have but one scene more before our story closes. It is night now in Lillie's sick-room; and her mother is anxiously arranging the drapery, to keep the fire-light from her eyes, stepping noiselessly about the room. She lies there behind the curtains, on her pillow, — the wreck and remnant only of what was once so beautiful. During all these years, when the interests and pleasures of life have been slowly dropping, leaf by leaf, and

passing away like fading flowers, Lillie has learned to
do much thinking. It sometimes seems to take a stab,
a thrust, a wound, to open in some hearts the capacity
of deep feeling and deep thought. There are things
taught by suffering that can be taught in no other way.
By suffering sometimes is wrought out in a person the
power of loving, and of appreciating love. During the
first year, Lillie had often seemed to herself in a sort of
wild, chaotic state. The coming in of a strange new
spiritual life was something so inexplicable to her that
it agitated and distressed her ; and sometimes, when
she appeared more petulant and fretful than usual, it
was only the stir and vibration on her weak nerves of
new feelings, which she wanted the power to express.
These emotions at first were painful to her. She felt
weak, miserable, and good for nothing. It seemed to
her that her whole life had been a wretched cheat, and
that she had ill repaid the devotion of her husband.
At first these thoughts only made her bitter and angry;
and she contended against them. But, as she sank
from day to day, and grew weaker and weaker, she
grew more gentle ; and a better spirit seemed to enter
into her.

On this evening that we speak of, she had made up
her mind that she would try and tell her husband some
of the things that were passing in her mind.

"Tell John I want to see him," she said to her
mother. "I wish he would come and sit with me."

This was a summons for which John invariably left
every thing. He laid down his book as the word was

brought to him, and soon was treading noiselessly at her bedside.

"Well, Lillie dear," he said, "how are you?"

She put out her little wasted hand; "John dear," she said, "sit down; I have something that I want to say to you. I have been thinking, John, that this can't last much longer."

"What can't last, Lillie?" said John, trying to speak cheerfully.

"I mean, John, that I am going to leave you soon, for good and all; and I should not think you would be sorry either."

"Oh, come, come, my girl, it won't do to talk so!" said John, patting her hand. "You must not be blue."

"And so, John," said Lillie, going on without noticing this interruption, "I wanted just to tell you, before I got any weaker, that I know and feel just how patient and noble and good you have always been to me."

"O Lillie darling!" said John, "why shouldn't I be? Poor little girl, how much you have suffered!"

"Well, now, John, I know perfectly well that I have never been the wife that I ought to be to you. You know it too; so don't try to say anything about it. I was never the woman to have made you happy; and it was not fair in me to marry you. I have lived a dreadfully worldly, selfish life. And now, John, I am come to the end. You dear good man, your trials with me are almost over; but I want you to know that you really have succeeded. John, I do love you now with

all my heart, though I did not love you when I married
you. And, John, I do feel that God will take pity on
me, poor and good for nothing as I am, just because I
see how patient and kind you have always been to me
when I have been so very provoking. You see it has
made me think how good God must be,—because,
dear, we know that he is better than the best of us."

"O Lillie, Lillie!" said John, leaning over her,
and taking her in his arms, "do live, I want you to
live. Don't leave me now, now that you really love
me!"

"Oh, no, John! it is best as it is,—I think I should
not have strength to be *very* good, if I were to get
well; and you would still have your little cross to
carry. No, dear, it is all right. And, John, you will
have the best of me in our Lillie. She looks like me:
but, John, she has your good heart; and she will be
more to you than I could be. She is just as sweet and
unselfish as I *was* selfish. I don't think I am quite so
bad now; and I think, if I lived, I should try to be a
great deal better."

"O Lillie! I cannot bear to part with you! I never
have ceased to love you; and I never have loved any
other woman."

"I know that, John. Oh! how much truer and
better you are than I have been! But I like to think
that you love me,—I like to think that you will be
sorry when I am gone, bad as I am, or *was ;* for I insist
on it that I am a little better than I was. You remember that story of Undine you read me one day? It

seems as if most of my life I have been like Undine
before her soul came into her. But this last year I
have felt the coming in of a soul. It has troubled me;
it has come with a strange kind of pain. I have never
suffered so much. But it has done me good—it has
made me feel that I have an immortal soul, and that
you and I, John, shall meet in some better place hereafter.—And there you will be rewarded for all your
goodness to me."

As John sat there, and held the little frail hand, his
thoughts went back to the time when the wild impulse
of his heart had been to break away from this woman,
and never see her face again; and he gave thanks to
God, who had led him in a better way.

.   .   .   .

And so, at last, passed away the little story of
Lillie's life. But in the home which she has left now
grows another Lillie, fairer and sweeter than she,—the
tender confidant, the trusted friend of her father. And
often, when he lays his hand on her golden head, he
says, "Dear child, how like your mother you look!"

Of all that was painful in that experience, nothing
now remains. John thinks of her only as he thought
of her in the fair illusion of first love,—the dearest
and most sacred of all illusions.

The Lillie who guides his household, and is so motherly to the younger children; who shares every thought
of his heart; who enters into every feeling and sympa-

thy, — she is the pure reward of his faithfulness and constancy. She is a sacred and saintly Lillie, springing out of the sod where he laid her mother, forgetting all her faults for ever.

Cambridge: Press of John Wilson and Son.

ⓟ   (0452)

There's an epidemic with 27 million victims. And no visible symptoms.

It's an epidemic of people who can't read.

Believe it or not, 27 million Americans are functionally illiterate, about one adult in five.

The solution to this problem is you... when you join the fight against illiteracy. So call the Coalition for Literacy at toll-free **1-800-228-8813** and volunteer.

Volunteer Against Illiteracy. The only degree you need is a degree of caring.